Past Perfect

Danielle Steel has been hailed as one of the world's most popular authors, with nearly a billion copies of her novels sold. Her recent international bestsellers include *Accidental Heroes*, *The Cast* and *The Good Fight*. She is also the author of *His Bright Light*, the story of her son Nick Traina's life and death; *A Gift of Hope*, a memoir of her work with the homeless; and the children's books *Pretty Minnie in Paris* and *Pretty Minnie in Hollywood*. Danielle divides her time between Paris and her home in northern California.

Danielle Steel

PAST PERFECT

PAN BOOKS

First published 2017 by Delacorte Press, an imprint of Random House,
a division of Penguin Random House LLC, New York

First published in the UK 2017 by Macmillan

This paperback edition published 2018 by Pan Books
an imprint of Pan Macmillan
20 New Wharf Road, London N1 9RR
Associated companies throughout the world
www.panmacmillan.com

ISBN 978-1-5098-0037-7

1 3 5 7 9 8 6 4 2

A CIP catalogue record for this book is available from the British Library.

Typeset by Palimpsest Book Production Ltd, Falkirk, Stirlingshire
Printed and bound by CPI Group (UK) Ltd, Croydon, CR0 4YY

Visit **www.panmacmillan.com** to read more about all our books
and to buy them. You will also find features, author interviews and
news of any author events, and you can sign up for e-newsletters
so that you're always first to hear about our new releases.

To my much loved children,
Beatie, Trevor, Todd, Nick, Samantha,
Victoria, Vanessa, Maxx, and Zara.

May your past, present, and future
be a blessing and a gift to each of you.

And may the history you share be
a bond of love, strength, and tenderness
now and always, for all your days.

With all my heart and love
forever and always.

With all my love,
Mom/d.s.

Foreword

Dear Reader,

I have never liked "ghost stories," nor books about time travel, which seem too far-fetched to me, and not very productive. Someone cast back in time to fall in love with someone who lived hundreds of years ago—and is then faced with the dilemma of staying in another century (abandoning everyone they know in their "real" life), or leaving their love to go back to their present-day world alone—just doesn't do it for me, and frustrates me. So this is a very unusual book for me, and stays within the confines of what seems reasonable.

I have a particular fondness for old houses, and have lived in several of them. One of them, a lovely Victorian house more than a hundred years old, was said to have ghosts, which I denied, pooh-poohed, and tried to ignore for the years I lived there. But undeniably there were some odd sounds, sights, and experiences that no one could explain, and others felt the same "vibes," and were convinced there were ghosts in the house—which I staunchly continued to ignore until the end. But old houses have a history of their own, of the people who lived there, happy or sad, the events that happened to them, and the lives they lived while they were there. Living in historic old houses, I have often wondered about the real stories of the people who lived there before. I've restored two old houses, and always felt they had a soul. I often say that there is a sense of romance with old houses, you fall in love with them or you don't.

In *Past Perfect*, a young, lively, energetic family—a young couple and their three kids—moves to San Francisco from New York, moves into an old historical mansion, and brings with them their very modern point of view, their computers, their electronic games, their current trendy lifestyle. A mild earthquake the night they move in shakes them up a bit . . . and suddenly, for an instant, a group of elegant, charming-seeming people from another century appears for an instant, and disappears just as quickly. Their portraits and furnishings are still in the house. There are psychic phenomena that I don't understand, but some people swear to, and they aren't always easy to explain or deny. In this instance, a few days after the first sighting, the new owners of the house walk into the dining room, in jeans and T-shirts and sneakers and bare feet, and find themselves in the midst of the original family that owned the house, elegantly eating dinner in white tie. The two families are only visible to each other and no one else, and what begins that night is a powerful bond of respect, affection, and friendship, between two families who exist a century apart, and yet can see each other every day, in the house. The twentieth century was a particularly fascinating time of two world wars, the Crash of 1929, major social and industrial changes, a man landing on the moon, and all the enormous, incredible changes that transpired during those years.

The modern-day family lives a fascinating period of history with their new friends, while continuing their modern lives. They help each other, they teach each other, they share life experiences, they console each other, they love each other, and together they bring each other a richness of life derived from a bond of friendship that denies time and enhances their lives. It is a touching, poignant story of two families, who coincidentally live a hundred years apart under one roof, with a special gift that none of them ever expected to have. It adds immeasurably to their lives, and I hope you will love these two families as much as I did when I wrote the book. It's a very special book, about a special time, and people who have been blessed with a special gift that enriches their lives, and hopefully yours too, while reading about them. I hope you thoroughly enjoy it.

Love, Danielle

If you knew the future, and the past,
would you change your path, or assume that
your destiny was immutable and inevitable?
Can we alter the course of the future,
or the past, or only adapt to it?
Or should both be respected and untouched?

— d.s.

PAST
PERFECT

Chapter 1

Blake Gregory sat looking out his office window in New York, pondering the offer he had just been made to be the CEO of a new high-tech social media start-up in San Francisco. He'd had other offers before, in Boston and other cities, though none as enticing as this one, and he'd turned them down without hesitation. But this was different, it had several exciting twists. The company's founders were two young men with golden track records who had made vast fortunes with their earlier ventures. As a result they had plenty of money to invest in their new start-up. Their previous companies had been based on simple concepts, and so was this one, combining the principles of a search engine with social media, and the potential growth rate was astronomical.

Blake was in high-tech venture capital, with an established, extremely respected firm. But the idea they had outlined made sense to him, and even made him want to join their team, although he had done well where he was, and a new company was never certain to succeed. But if it worked, he could see it making billions. There were possible pitfalls involved, but he thought they could be overcome in the developmental stage. The offer had come out of the blue, based on some business contacts he had and his professional reputation as a smart, forward-thinking analyst of new ventures, highly adept at assessing risk and how to get around it to create a successful business. They were offering him twice what he was making at the firm where he worked in New York. His future was secure where he was now, and he had been there for ten years and liked his co-workers. Everything was unknown about the situation at the start-up in San Francisco, including how he'd like the people he'd be working for. He knew they were gutsy, brilliant, and ruthless, and they always made big money. It was so damn tempting, although he wasn't usually a risk taker. But the money was appealing, and so was the stock he'd own in the company when they went public, which was their goal.

It made him feel young again, thinking about doing something new and different. At forty-six, he had been on a safe, predictable path for a long time. Married, with three kids, he wasn't one to throw caution to the wind. He couldn't even imagine what his wife, Sybil, would say if he told her. They were both inveterate New Yorkers, loved the city, and had grown up there, as their kids had. Blake had never considered taking a job in another city, but he was now. If the start-up succeeded, he could make a fortune. It was going to be hard to turn down.

Sybil was thirty-nine years old, and had had a diversified career. She had been an art history major at Columbia, which was where she had met Blake, while he was at business school getting his MBA. She had been passionate about Frank Lloyd Wright, I. M. Pei, Frank Gehry, and all the avant-garde architects of modern times. She had gone back to Columbia to study architecture, after she married Blake and had kids, and then changed direction to pursue interior design, and had become a consultant to high-end furniture design firms, and she had created several pieces herself that had become iconic. She was a regular consultant to both MoMA and the Brooklyn Museum, advising them about their acquisitions of important pieces for their permanent collections, and curating shows for them. Everything she touched had a sleek, streamlined look to it, and in her nonexistent spare time, she was working on a book about the best of twentieth-century interior design, and her publisher was clamoring for it.

Blake was certain her book would be a success. She was a thorough, thoughtful writer, about the subjects she knew best. She wrote frequent articles for important interior design magazines and *The New York Times* design section, and was considered an expert in her field. Her personal favorite was mid-century modern, and anything designed earlier than 1950 was of less interest to her, but she wrote about all of it. Their two-story Tribeca loft apartment on North Moore, in an old textile warehouse, looked like the modern wing of a great museum. Every important designer was represented with pieces that could instantly be attributed to them by any expert. Sybil was, above all, very talented herself, and had a way of picking decisively what was new and chic. Blake didn't always understand it, but readily admitted he liked the effect.

Sybil had a respect for other periods and enjoyed exhibits at the Metropolitan Museum, and they both loved the archaic turn-of-the-century elegance of the Frick Collection, but what made Sybil's heart beat faster, what she was drawn to and created, was anything at the outer, forward edge of design. Their own apartment had a coolness to it, and a spare airy feeling. She had designed some of the furniture herself from a line she had created. Museums around the country asked her to curate exhibits for them. She almost never took on private decorating clients anymore, because she didn't want to be limited by other people's ideas and tastes. And the hub of all her creative activities was New York. Blake didn't think it would be fair to ask her to move to San Francisco for him. Normally he wouldn't have considered it, but the job he'd been offered was a once-in-a-lifetime opportunity. He wondered if he could do it for a couple of years, but if the business was a success, he'd want to stay longer.

His kids wouldn't welcome a move either. The offer in San Francisco had come the first week of school. Andrew had just started his senior year of high school, and would be applying to college that fall. Caroline was a junior, and firmly embedded in her life in New York. The prospect of moving at sixteen and seventeen would horrify them both. Only Charlie, their six-year-old, wouldn't care where they lived, as long as he was with them. He had just started first grade.

Sybil was in Philadelphia for the day, consulting with a museum about a show they wanted her to curate in two years. He didn't know if he'd tell her about the offer or even whether he should. Why upset her about a job he wasn't going to take? But they wanted him to go to San Francisco and see them that week to discuss it further, and he was sorely tempted to. They'd been incredibly persistent. It was Monday, and he had already figured out that he could get away on Wednesday afternoon, and had moved some meetings to do it.

He was distracted, thinking about it, when Sybil walked into their apartment that night, her long blond hair pulled back tightly in a bun, and wearing a very severe but chic black suit. She looked every inch a New Yorker, and always did. She was a beautiful woman, and their daughter had her tall, lean, classic appearance. Both boys resembled Blake more clearly, with dark hair, dark eyes, and all-American athletic bodies. They loved sports and were good athletes.

"How'd it go?" Blake asked, as she smiled at him, put down her bag, and took off her shoes. It was a hot Indian summer day, and she'd left the house at six A.M. to catch the train and be in Philadelphia in time for her meeting. Their housekeeper had picked Charlie up at school, Caroline and Andy took the subway home at different hours. One of the things Sybil liked about her eclectic work life was her flexible schedule, so she could usually pick Charlie up. Charlie had come as a surprise to both of them, but after the initial shock and adjustment, they'd agreed that he was one of the best things that had ever happened to them. He was their easiest, most loving child, and always happy whatever he was doing. Both his older siblings enjoyed spending time with him too.

Two of the children were in their rooms by the time Sybil got home from Philadelphia. Andy and Caroline were doing homework, and Charlie was watching a movie on the flat-screen TV in his parents' room. The children had had dinner, but Blake had waited for her. He followed her into the kitchen as she put out a salad and some cold chicken the housekeeper had left for them.

"I don't think I'm going to curate their show," she said as he poured her a glass of wine. "It's coming over from Denmark. They really don't need me to curate it, it looks incomplete to me, and they don't want me adding to it. It's been put together by a prestigious museum, so they want to keep it as it is. It's not for me." She turned down many of the opportunities she was offered. She was a purist about her work, and the periods and designers that interested her. "Besides, I need time to work on my book. I want to finish it in the next year." She'd been working on it for two years. It was going to be almost a textbook of the best of modern design. "How was your day?" She looked at him with a smile. They liked meeting up in the evenings to share what they'd each done.

"Fine. I'm going to San Francisco on Wednesday," he blurted out, realizing that he sounded insane. He looked startled himself, and had intended to introduce the subject more gracefully, but his nervousness about telling her had taken the upper hand.

"A new deal out there?" she asked and sipped her wine. He hesitated for a long moment, not sure what to say. And then he sighed and sat back in his chair. He never kept secrets from her. They were a team, and one that still worked well after eighteen years of marriage. There were few surprises in their life, and they both liked it that way. And they were still in love after almost two decades.

"I got an offer from a terrific start-up in San Francisco today," he said in a low voice.

"You're going to turn them down?" She knew the

answer to the question, but asked anyway. He always did. He was content where he was, or so she thought.

"This one's different. They're putting a lot of money into it, the two guys starting it have an impeccable reputation, and it's going to work and make everyone involved a fortune." He seemed certain. She looked at him as he said it, and set her fork down on her plate.

"But it's in San Francisco." She might as well have said it was on Mars or Pluto. California was not part of their universe.

"I know, but they're offering me twice what I'm making now and great stock options. If they win big with it, we'll be set for life." They both made a good living. They led a comfortable life, and had everything they wanted, and so did their kids. And neither of them had ever aspired to those leagues. "I'm not saying I'd make billions, but there is some very big money to be made on this deal, Syb. It's not easy to turn down."

"We can't move to San Francisco," she said simply. "I can't, you can't, and we can't do that to the kids. Andrew is graduating this year." Blake knew that all too well. He had thought of it all afternoon, with severe pangs of guilt for even considering the offer and not turning it down flat. He felt like the traitor in their midst.

"I'd like to just take a look so I can see what I'm declining," he said, knowing it was a poor excuse to go out there. And she knew it too.

"What if you don't want to turn it down?" she asked, looking worried.

"I'll have to, but I should at least listen to them." He knew that at forty-six, he wasn't going to get another offer like this one, and that if he didn't take it, he'd probably stay where he was for the rest of his career. There was nothing wrong with that, and his current job was respectable, but he wanted to be absolutely certain that declining it was the right thing to do, before he did.

"This sounds ominous," Sybil said, as she put their dishes in the sink.

"I'm not saying I'll take it, Syb. I just want to have a look. Maybe I could do it for a couple of years," he said, trying to find a solution to a problem she didn't want them to have.

"They won't let you do that. And we need to let Caro and Andy finish school here for the next two years." He knew that declining the start-up in San Francisco was probably a sacrifice he would have to make, but it was harder than he'd expected it to be.

"I'll just be out there Wednesday to Friday, and back on the weekend," he said quietly, but there was a look in his eye she'd never seen before and didn't like. He was thinking of himself and not of them.

"Why am I not reassured? You can't be serious about this, Blake." Her mouth was set in a thin line and she looked tense.

"It could set us up for the future. I'm never going to make that kind of money here."

"We don't need more than what we have," she said firmly. "We have a great apartment and a good life." She had never been greedy and was satisfied with what they both made.

"This isn't just about money. It's exciting to be part of something new. This could be groundbreaking. I'm sorry, Syb. I just want to check it out. Do you hate me for that?" He loved her and didn't want to screw up their marriage, but he knew it would gnaw at him forever if he didn't talk to the people in San Francisco now. He had promised to fly out before asking her.

"I couldn't hate you . . . except if you move us out of New York," she said and laughed. She wasn't angry at him, but she was afraid. "Just promise me you won't go crazy out there and accept the job before we talk."

"Of course not." He put an arm around her and they found Charlie asleep on their bed with the TV on when they walked into their bedroom. Blake carried him to his own room, Sybil changed him into his pajamas, and he didn't wake up once.

They said good night to Caroline and Andy, and after they turned off the lights, Sybil lay in bed, thinking about what Blake had said. She hoped this was just one of those moments when an idea looks enticing for a few minutes and then reality sets in, and you know it's not for you. She couldn't see any of them living in San Francisco, and didn't want to. And even if the job sounded exciting to him now, she was sure they'd all be miserable if they left New York for him. It was the last thing she wanted to do, even for the man she loved. They couldn't do it to their kids. And she didn't want a bicoastal marriage, where they flew to see each other on weekends. There was just no way it could work for them. Their life in New York was perfect the way it was. Blake agreed with her, but the opportunity he'd been offered in San Francisco was one of a kind.

*

Blake had left for the office before Sybil took Charlie to school, and by the time she got back to the apartment and sat down at her desk in her home office, she had decided not to worry about it. Blake had never been impulsive, he was a sensible person, and he loved New York too. He'd always been happy in his current job in venture capital, evaluating new deals. She was sure that once he got to San Francisco for the meeting, he'd figure out that the start-up wasn't for him, no matter how glamorous it seemed. Just like her, he was a New Yorker to the core, and he wouldn't want to disrupt their kids, or her. She decided it was better to let him go out to California and see for himself than to put her foot down and have a fit. He'd come to his senses on his own. She was sure of it.

They had a peaceful evening that night, and didn't talk

about it again. She didn't want to argue with him and he didn't bring the subject up. He went to the airport straight from the office on Wednesday. He called her before his flight to tell her he loved her and say goodbye, and he thanked her for being a good sport about him going to San Francisco to take a look.

"You might as well see it before you turn it down," she said calmly, and Blake sounded relieved. Sybil knew that no matter how much they offered him, they wouldn't be able to lure him away from New York. He was a creature of habit and liked his job.

"That's what I think too. Tell the kids I love them. I'll be back late Friday night." He would be catching the last plane out of San Francisco, and he knew that with the time difference she'd be asleep when he got home. His plane was due to land at JFK at two A.M. Even if it was late, he preferred it to spending another night away from her. They were going to the Hamptons that weekend, to a house they rented for a month in the summer and on occasional weekends. The weather had been so good they wanted to take advantage of it one last time, and the kids wanted to go too. They were looking forward to it, and so was Blake.

*

With the time difference in his favor, Blake met the two men founding the start-up for a late dinner at his hotel on

Wednesday night. They were on fire. Both were younger than he was by a dozen years, and had impressive track records and histories. He knew they were originally geeks and had become brilliant businessmen. Both were Harvard MBAs. They were ideas men who liked starting companies, selling them, and moving on. They wanted him to run the company while they developed the concept to its fullest until they sold it or it went public, whichever was most lucrative. They had all the money they needed to make it a success, and listening to their plans was as thrilling as he'd feared it would be, once he knew who was involved.

He couldn't sleep that night, and had a breakfast meeting the next day with the half dozen people who headed up various departments. They were all innovative men and women who'd had successful roles in other companies. The two founders wanted only stars involved, and considered that Blake could be one as CEO, and they liked that he had both feet on the ground. Their business plan was almost flawless, and the opportunity to make a vast amount of money was immense, especially for Blake, as CEO, with the stock options and participation they were offering him.

He sat in on meetings all day, and met with the two founders again before dinner to discuss his impressions, and they were pleased with what they heard. He added balance to the team, and he had a solid financial point of view. The meetings on Friday were even better. He liked the working environment as well. They were occupying a remodeled warehouse south of Market that had been made into offices, and they already had a fleet of young people working for them, full of dynamic ideas and energy. It was invigorating and exciting just being there, compared to what he did every day, although the concepts weren't entirely unfamiliar to him. Undeniably there was risk, but everyone involved seemed sensible and experienced. They were a surprisingly cohesive group, and Blake fit right in. They renewed their offer to him before he left, more convinced than ever that he was the right man for the job, and he was too. They had managed to dissipate all his reservations about it in two days. He sat staring into space, lost in thought, and wide awake for most of the flight back to New York. It was the best forty-eight hours he had spent at work in years. He felt like a new man.

Blake walked into their apartment in Tribeca at three A.M., and Sybil was sound asleep. He kissed the top of her head on the pillow and she didn't stir.

He looked tired and serious when he walked into the kitchen on Saturday morning. They were all packed for the weekend and ready to leave, and Sybil purposely didn't ask him what had happened in San Francisco until they were settled into the rented house in the Hamptons, and the kids had gone outside to play on the beach. They were sitting on the deck, watching them, when Sybil turned to him, as he searched for the right words to tell her what he knew she didn't want to hear.

"How did it go?" she asked him, seeming tense.

"I'd be insane to turn it down," he said, in a raw, husky voice. "I've never had an opportunity like it before. And I probably won't again." He told her precisely what kind of money he could make if he signed on with them, before they got going and eventually went public, or sold out to someone like Google, who could conceivably want to buy them out in time.

"Life is about more than money," she chided him. "Since when is that the big motivator for you? You can't give up our whole life for that." But she could see the longing in his eyes. He'd never looked like that about a job before. She knew it wasn't about money, but about doing something exciting and new. It was thrilling. This could be very big for him, and ultimately for them if it was a huge success. That wasn't negligible. Where the job was located didn't matter to him, for the first time in his career.

"It's different when you're talking about these kinds of amounts, Syb," he said softly. "Couldn't you base yourself in San Francisco for a few years? You could write there, and work on your book, and send your articles in from anywhere. And you could fly back to work with the museums and curate shows, and meet your clients in New York." He was trying to make suggestions that would work for her, but it was like trying to climb a glass wall. He got no traction from her.

"And spend my life on planes, with three kids at home," she commented, looking shocked by his question, and the fact that he would even consider it, for any of them. She could see he was evaluating the offer seriously. She could understand why, but it was going to disrupt their lives beyond belief. She couldn't do that to the children or herself. It wouldn't be fair.

The kids came back to the house then for something to eat, and they shelved the discussion until that night, and picked it up again when Andrew and Caroline went out to see friends, and Charlie was asleep in the room next to theirs.

"I know it's a lot to ask of you, but the kids would adjust," Blake insisted. "They'll make new friends, and Andy is leaving after this year anyway. The offer won't wait. If I don't take it, they'll make a proposal to someone else. They need someone now." He sounded desperate, and she felt sorry for him, but more so for herself and their kids. She could see how badly Blake wanted to do it, but it was in direct conflict with everyone else's needs.

"And they have earthquakes there," she reminded him, clutching at straws to deter him, and feeling selfish when she did.

"They haven't had a really big one in over a hundred

years," he said, laughing at her. But she was as stubborn as he was.

"Then they're overdue. Besides, there was a fairly big one in 1989."

"They're not going to have an earthquake just because we move out there," he said, pulling her into his arms, and he then forgot about the job in San Francisco for the rest of the night. And the next day they went back to the city, with nothing resolved between them. Neither of them was angry, but it was important to both of them.

They went back and forth arguing about it for several days, neither convincing the other, and she finally realized that he would never forgive her if he turned it down. It would remain a bitter pill stuck in his throat forever, more so than for her if she moved to San Francisco for him. She wasn't happy about it, but she also knew that he was right that at his age a chance like this wouldn't come again. And the money was a certain incentive for both of them in the end, since they and their children would truly be secure for life if it really took off. She could see the value of that too, after discussing it with Blake at length.

All he asked was that she give it two years, and he promised that if it was impacting them too severely, he'd quit and return to New York. Sybil loved him and didn't want to hurt his career, or their marriage, and at the end of two weeks, she looked at him, exhausted, and put her arms around him.

"I give in. I love you too much to make you give this up for us. We'll make it work somehow," she said, and knew she had done the right thing when she saw how grateful and ecstatic he was. He called San Francisco in the morning and told them the good news and resigned his position at the venture capital firm. They told the children that night after dinner.

They were horrified by what their parents said, but their mother was firm with them, saying that it was a sacrifice they would all have to make for the common good. It was important for their father's career and their own security in the long run. Caroline and Andrew were both old enough to understand it and Sybil gave them no choice, pointing out that it was a huge adjustment for her too. She had already called Andy's school that afternoon, and they had agreed to let him come back and graduate with his class, if he wanted to. He could walk with the friends he had been with all through high school, as long as he successfully completed senior year at his San Francisco school.

Blake had agreed to let them finish the fall semester in New York, and Sybil and the kids would all move to San Francisco in January. He would be leaving in the next two weeks, and this way he would have time to find them an apartment. Neither Blake nor Sybil wanted to buy, since they weren't sure yet if it would be a permanent move. Sybil had been clear that she wanted a bright, sunny, modern apartment, not a house. She had researched San Francisco schools and already contacted them. And they were leaving the apartment in Tribeca as is, in case they came back to New York in two years, and so she'd have a place to stay when she went to New York to work. She had two and a half months to get everything organized to leave. And Blake had that time to find a home for them, and settle in at work. Sybil was planning to stage the San Francisco apartment he found with rented furniture at first, and they could buy what they needed if they stayed. For now, they were considering it a temporary move for a couple of years, to see how it worked out. Knowing that they might return to New York took the sting out of it for Sybil and the kids, and she hoped that San Francisco would be short-term. But she threw herself into the move for Blake's sake, and tried to convince their children and herself that it wasn't the end of the world.

Andy was upset about it but tried to be reasonable, once he understood the financial potential for them. He was proud of his father, and relieved that he'd be graduating with his friends in June. Caroline was dramatic, and threatened not to come, but there was nowhere for her to stay in New York. She didn't have grandparents or uncles or aunts, and didn't want to go to boarding school, which her parents offered as an alternative because she was so adamantly against the move. So she had no choice but to accept the plan to go to San Francisco. And, predictably,

Charlie was the easiest of all, and said he thought it would be fun. He wanted to know all about his new school.

Two weeks after Blake left, Sybil had them enrolled in excellent San Francisco schools, based on their transcripts. Blake had visited the schools and said he was pleased, and the apartment search had already begun. But when he came home for Thanksgiving, he still hadn't found them a place to live. It had been harder than he thought to find an apartment to rent within reasonable distance of the schools, with all of Sybil's requirements: light, sunny, airy, modern, with high ceilings and excellent views. And the rents in San Francisco seemed ridiculously high to him, even compared to New York.

Blake was loving his new job, and looked ten years younger when he came home. Sybil knew it had been the right thing for him to do. But she was anxious for him to find an apartment for them and he promised to search even more vigorously when he went back after Thanksgiving.

"Can we live in a hotel?" Charlie asked after his father had gone back to San Francisco.

"I hope not," Sybil said with a stern expression. She didn't want to live in a hotel with three children, no matter how much Charlie liked the idea. "Daddy will find something before we get there," she promised. The realtor was negotiating for an apartment in the Millennium Tower on Mission Street on the fifty-eighth floor, with fabulous views, but it was in a somewhat dicey neighborhood, not ideal for children. It was in the financial district amid office buildings in an area that had been gentrified, but there was no park or playground for Charlie. The apartment was in a very fancy high-rise and had been up for sale for the past year, since the owner had moved to Hong Kong, and there had been construction problems in the building, which made the apartments harder to sell, but possibly easier to rent, and maybe at a more reasonable price. The realtor was hoping to get them a lease for a year or two. It was still a great building despite the construction issues. Blake was waiting to see the apartment, and several others, as soon as the realtor could organize it and get him in, while Sybil pressed him about it daily.

In the meantime, the children were enjoying their last month in New York before the holidays. Andy was seeing all his friends while he could, and going to basketball and hockey games. And Caroline still thought her parents were cruel, but managed to have fun with her friends anyway. They were going to spend Christmas in New York, and then fly to San Francisco on New Year's Day. Sybil just hoped they had a place to live by then, and so did Blake. Not finding one so far was beginning to unnerve them both. He had a day set aside to see apartments with the realtor on the first of December, and hoped he would have better luck than he'd had in November. He didn't see how it could be that hard to find a four-bedroom apartment, in a modern building with light and views, per his wife's instructions. They had five apartments to see that day. The one at the Millennium Tower hadn't come through yet, but Blake and Sybil were hopeful. Blake had been living at the Regency since he got there, which was a combination of co-op apartments and hotel suites, but he wanted to find a home for Sybil and the children, not a temporary solution.

The realtor picked him up on a foggy San Francisco morning and assured him that she felt in her bones that they would find what he was looking for that day. He hoped she was right. He was grateful to Sybil and his children for being willing to move there, and now he was determined to find a home they'd love.

The first apartment they looked at was in a 1930s building in Pacific Heights, the city's prime residential district, but the apartment was dark and depressing, although it was a floor-through with spectacular views. It didn't have the modern feeling Sybil wanted, and it faced north. As they drove on to the next location, Blake was beginning to wonder if he'd ever find the right apartment. He didn't have the heart to text Sybil and tell her he'd seen another bad one. There had to be a home for them in San Francisco somewhere. All he had to do now was find it, whatever it took.

Sybil had allowed him to pursue his dream. Now he owed it to her to find them a decent home in the city that his family had graciously agreed to come to. He had his eyes closed for a minute, thinking about her and missing her, when they stopped at an intersection, and he opened his eyes and found himself staring at a building that looked very much like the Frick museum in New York. He didn't recognize it and had never noticed it before, although they had driven through Pacific Heights several times.

"What's that?" he asked, intrigued. It had more the appearance of a small museum than a home. There was a wall of trees around it, with the house peering over them, an elaborate gate, and a courtyard just inside. The garden seemed overgrown.

"It's the Butterfield Mansion," the realtor answered as she drove past the stop sign, and Blake turned around to gaze at the house behind them. It was an impressive building, in a European style, but appeared abandoned despite its grandeur.

"Who lives there?" he asked, curious about it.

"No one, not in a long time. They were an important banking family at the turn of the century, when the house was built over a hundred years ago, before the 1906 earthquake. They lost their money in the Great Depression, and sold the house. It changed hands a number of times after that, and a bank foreclosed on it five or six years ago. It's been empty ever since. No one wants houses that size anymore. They're too expensive to run, and too much trouble to staff. Eventually some land developer will buy it and tear it down. I don't think the bank wants the bad publicity that will go with it when that happens. It would make a great hotel—it sits on quite a bit of land—but the area's not zoned for that. So it's just empty for now. It has something like twenty bedrooms, a million maids' rooms, and a ballroom. We have the listing, but I've never been inside. It's a piece of San Francisco history. It's too bad no one has bought it, with all the high-tech money around the city now. The bank has it listed for a ridiculously low price, just to get rid of it, but it's too big a headache for anyone to take on." Blake nodded. It was easy to see that would be the case, but it had such dignified elegance, even in its untended, unoccupied, slightly forlorn state. Blake could tell that no one had loved it in a long time.

"What happened to the family who lived there? The Butterworths?"

"Butterfields," she corrected. "I think they disappeared after they sold it. Or they died out. I vaguely remember that they moved to Europe. Something like that. They're not part of the San Francisco social scene anymore." It was sad to think about a family who had lived in so much elegance and splendor dying out. Blake was fascinated by the house and what she told him about it, but they drove on to see four more apartments he knew Sybil would hate, and he went back to his office south of Market, and to his hotel that night. He told Sybil on the phone that he had struck out again finding them an apartment.

"Something will turn up," she said, trying to sound optimistic. "What about the one in the Millennium Tower?" she asked, although she felt squeamish about living on such a high floor in what she insisted was earth-quake country, or even in case of a fire, with three children to walk down fifty-eight floors.

"The owner in Hong Kong hasn't responded to them yet. Maybe he doesn't want to rent."

"That's just as well," she said, referring to the high floor again. He almost told her about the huge empty mansion he had seen that morning, but they moved on to other subjects, and then he forgot. But he thought about it again in bed that night, and wondered what it looked like inside. Feeling ridiculous for doing so, he called the realtor in the morning and, just as a matter of interest, asked her the price. There was something so unusual and compelling and discreetly beautiful about the house. When she quoted him what it was listed for, he was startled.

"It would probably cost you a fortune to run it, but I think the bank would take even less than that. There's been talk about an auction, but they're afraid a commer-cial buyer would tear it down. The land alone is worth more than that." She had quoted a price that was less than any of the apartments they'd seen that were for sale, although he didn't want them. Real estate prices were high in San Francisco. Their loft in Tribeca was worth ten times the asking price of the Butterfield Mansion. It was a steal.

"What kind of shape is it in, inside?"

"I have no idea, but I can ask. Do you want to see it?" She sounded surprised. It was everything he had said he didn't want. He wanted brand-new, modern, an apartment, not a house, and had said he didn't want to buy. All of which was true, but the old abandoned house was gnawing at him.

"I don't suppose there's much point seeing it, except out of curiosity. My wife would kill me."

"You can lowball it if you like the house," the realtor said, lowering her voice and ignoring his comment about Sybil.

He almost didn't need to lowball it, the price was already so low. They could fix it up and sell it for considerably more when they left San Francisco. Thinking about it that way made it sound more like a business deal than a folly. "Maybe I will take a look at it, just for the hell of it," he said, intrigued.

"I'll call you back." She hung up and called him five minutes later, having gotten the keys from her manager and confirmed that the bank still had it on the market. She knew that it was a property they'd been anxious to get off their hands for some time. "I can show it to you at noon, if you want." He felt foolish but agreed to meet her there, and arrived at the front gate promptly by cab.

Walking through the house was like time travel back to the beginning of the twentieth century. The home was antiquated, but spectacularly beautiful and elegantly built inside, with carved moldings, a wood-paneled library, gorgeous parquet floors, and a ballroom that reminded him of Versailles. It looked like a museum, or a small hotel. It was in surprisingly good shape. There was no evidence of damage or leaks. And there was a long row of bells in the kitchen that the numerous servants had responded to in its days of grandeur a century ago. The reception rooms on the main floor were very large in scale, and all of the family bedrooms were on one floor, with small sitting rooms and dressing rooms and enormous bathrooms for each bedroom. There was a floor of guest rooms and additional sitting rooms, all with spectacular views and marble fireplaces, like the main bedrooms, and an entire level of maids' rooms on the top floor. An enormous family could have lived there, with an army of servants to attend them. Blake wandered up and down the grand staircase, going through the house again, and saw that the kitchen had been modernized at some point, although it still needed some updating.

"What an amazing house," he said in awe after he'd seen everything for a second time.

"Do you want to make an offer?" she asked bluntly. He

stood silently, staring up at the elaborate ceilings as he thought about it, and noticed that the chandeliers were all gone and would need to be replaced. Due to its size alone, the house would be a decorating challenge to furnish.

"I think I will," a voice he didn't recognize as his own said softly. "Even if we never live here, it would be an incredible investment. If you put a coat of paint on the inside, and take the boards off the windows, for the right price, it would be a remarkable house to have." He wasn't sure if he was trying to convince himself or the realtor, and he decided not to tell Sybil for the moment. There was no way he could explain it to her and do it justice, and it was everything she didn't want. But in a bold move, he cut the bank's price almost in half, like betting on a roulette wheel in Las Vegas, just to see what would happen. He was sure he wouldn't get it, but it was fun to try. Based on square footage and location alone, it was an incredible deal, if they accepted his offer.

The realtor had the forms to him in his office an hour later, and he signed them. It seemed almost like a lark he couldn't take seriously, given his absurdly low offer for a house no one wanted, and then he forgot about it and spent the rest of the day in meetings. He didn't get back to his desk again until six P.M., and found a message from the realtor. It just said to give her a call, and he did before he went back to his hotel, certain that he would hear that the bank had turned down his offer. He wasn't sure if he hoped they would, or not.

"The Butterfield Mansion is yours, Mr. Gregory," the realtor said in a solemn tone, and it took a moment for her words to sink in. "The house is yours," she repeated. "The bank accepted your offer. They want to close in two weeks, after your inspections," which had been his only contingency.

"Oh my God," he said, and sat down with a stunned expression, trying to think of what he was going to tell his wife. He had bought a twenty-thousand-square-foot 1902 mansion with a ballroom, on an acre of land. And fighting a wave of panic, when he thought of how Sybil would look when he told her, he started to laugh. He could still get out of it, based on the inspections, if he wanted to. But he didn't. He had no idea why, and it made absolutely no sense, but he had fallen in love with the house. He wondered if he was having some kind of midlife crisis. First, he had taken the job in San Francisco, and now he had bought a hundred-and-fifteen-year-old mansion. This was definitely not the rented modern apartment Sybil had in mind.

He walked back to his hotel, musing about what had possessed him. But whatever the reason, or the madness, now they had a house to live in. And the price he had paid for it was so low that it would hardly make a dent in their savings. At least Sybil couldn't be angry at him for that.

And once painted inside, the Butterfield Mansion was going to be a remarkable home for them, at least for the time being, even if they sold it later for a profit. Now all he had to do was convince Sybil of that. Buying it had been the easy part. Selling it to her was another matter entirely. But it might be fun to live in a house that large for a couple of years. "The Gregory Mansion," he said to himself out loud, and then he laughed.

Chapter 2

Blake thought about it all week, with some trepidation, and he knew that there was no way he could tell Sybil about the Butterfield Mansion on the phone. He just couldn't. He couldn't convey the beauty of it to her, even with photographs, from a distance, or the fact that in the long run it made sense financially. But most of all, he couldn't explain how spectacular it was, or once had been, without seeing her to tell her, and he felt he owed her that. He knew he had sorely tested the strength of their marriage by taking the job in San Francisco, and now he was pushing further, asking her to move their family into a home that was everything she didn't want, although he hoped she would fall in love with it when she saw it, as he had. Something about the house had beckoned to him, and he couldn't resist it. It seemed to be alive and have a soul. He had always been vulnerable to stray dogs and homeless children. When they'd gone to India several years before, he'd wanted to bring half the country home. But this was a house and not a person, and when he had walked through it, he had felt an inexplicable bond to it.

He had gone back with the realtor and taken hundreds of pictures on his phone, of every room and detail. And the photographs didn't do it justice. In the pictures it appeared darker than it was, and more than anything it looked enormous. He realized that he needed to see her to tell her about it, and he took the red-eye to New York on Friday night, without telling Sybil he was coming. He wanted to surprise her. She stared at him in amazement when he slipped into bed beside her at six o'clock on Saturday morning. She smiled as she sat up in astonishment, and he was already half asleep on his pillow as he put an arm around her.

"What are you doing here?" she said, startled.

"I missed you," he said, and pulled her down beside him, as she smiled, happy that he was home. The weekend together was an unexpected gift. She'd been planning to write an article for *The New York Times* about a design exhibit at the Metropolitan Museum, and her deadline for the piece was Monday, so she was busy too. All three children had plans, and Blake and Sybil would be alone for most of the weekend. She snuggled up next to him in bed, and they both fell asleep for a few more hours. The flight from San Francisco had been short, with good tailwinds, and he had slept only an hour or two on the plane. But he felt rested as he lay in bed and stretched lazily next to her when they both woke up.

"This is a nice surprise," she said happily, as they got

out of bed and she went to make breakfast for them. Andy and Caroline had both eaten already, and Caro had poured cornflakes into a bowl for Charlie and warmed a blueberry muffin to go with it, and he was sitting in front of the TV watching cartoons. And he had an iPad where Sybil downloaded movies for him, so he had plenty of entertainment. He let out a whoop when he saw his father, and then Sybil and Blake sat down to breakfast while Charlie went back to the TV.

"I have an article to write for *The New York Times,* but I'll do it Sunday night after you leave. I thought you had work to do this weekend," Sybil said as she smiled at Blake and set scrambled eggs and bacon down in front of him with the sourdough toast that he loved. It felt good to be home, although he was dreading his confession about the house.

"I did have work," he answered her, "but I wanted to see you." And as soon as he said it, Sybil saw something in his eyes that told her this was more than just a random visit. She knew him too well for that, and a little shiver of fear ran down her spine. What else could he surprise her with now? Had he met a woman in San Francisco and had come to tell her? He had never done anything like that, but after the surprises of the last several weeks, anything was possible.

"Did something happen in San Francisco this week?" she asked, trying to sound more confident than she felt, as she watched him carefully. There was a look on his face she couldn't decipher, and he glanced away and seemed busy with his eggs when he answered.

"No, just a lot of meetings. I'm still trying to get up to speed."

"Problems with your colleagues?"

"Of course not. Why would you ask that?"

"I'm just wondering why you're here, and didn't tell me why you were coming."

"Am I interfering with your plans?" He sounded hurt momentarily, and he wondered if she was getting too used to not having him around. Maybe *she* had met someone, and wasn't planning to move out of New York. They were both a little skittish after all their changes of plans recently, and unusual decisions.

"Of course not. This is your home, silly, and I'm thrilled to see you," she said, but she realized now that he was nervous and acting guilty. And she wanted to know why as soon as possible. "I just get the feeling that there's some reason why you came home, other than the pleasure of my company." She looked straight at him as she said it, and he didn't answer for a minute. He knew he couldn't put off admitting it to her for much longer, and he didn't want to. He had come home to confess, and now he had to.

"I do have something to tell you," he said hesitantly, "and I wanted to do it in person." She braced herself for bad news, and he pulled his cellphone out of his pocket and laid it on the table, so he could show her the photographs after he told her.

"Are you in love with someone in San Francisco?" she asked him in a strangled voice, and Blake was horrified at the suggestion.

"Are you crazy? Of course not. I love you." He leaned over and kissed her. "But I did something this week that I didn't expect to. It sounds a little nuts, but trust me, it isn't. In the long run, it will make perfect sense." It was the same thing he had told her about the job, and she was beginning to wonder what was happening to him. He had never surprised her like this before, and it was an odd show of independence that made her uneasy, but at least he had said it wasn't another woman. She sat waiting expectantly, and Blake took a breath and leapt in. "I bought a house this week. It just happened. It's hard to explain. I don't know what came over me. I saw it and fell in love with it, and I hope you and the kids will too. It's a fantastic house." He looked serious and wasn't smiling, and she suddenly remembered a house they'd once seen in Paris during a vacation there. It was a 1920s Chinese pagoda that had been on the market forever in a good neighborhood, and he had decided it would be fun to own a pagoda in Paris. But he normally wasn't impulsive, and had come to his senses immediately and never bid on it. Reason had always won out with him, except lately.

"What kind of a house, and why didn't you tell me?"

They had always operated as an equal partnership, which was one of the things she loved about their marriage. Now he was going off half-cocked in all directions, without consulting her.

"I didn't think they'd accept my offer. I just did it as kind of a wild gamble, and it was hard to explain it to you over the phone. I made a ridiculously low bid on it, and they took it, which I never expected. I paid so little for it, and if we spruce it up a bit and throw a coat of paint on it, we could make a hell of a lot of money on it when we leave." Sybil was frowning. This did not sound like good news to her, particularly if it needed "sprucing up" and a "coat of paint," and he was trying to convince her it was a great investment. It sounded like a hard sell to her.

"What's wrong with it? Why is it so cheap, and how much was it, anyway?" She wondered if he had lost all perspective about money, working with two young billionaires, but when he told her what he had offered for the house, even she was amazed that he could buy anything for so little, and knew it had to be in terrible shape. And the last thing she needed in San Francisco was a major decorating project. She wanted their two years there to be carefree and easy. As far as she was concerned, they weren't going to stay longer, the apartment in Tribeca was still their home, and their apartment in San Francisco would be only temporary, which was why she wanted to rent there and not buy, and even rent furniture, or fill in the gaps at IKEA. She was not setting up a permanent home in San Francisco, and now he had bought a house there.

"There's nothing wrong with it," he insisted. "It's just unusual, and it's a piece of San Francisco history," he told her gently, with explanations that sounded weak, even to him. He was hoping he could sell her on it and convince her it was a good idea. "It looks like the Frick," he added, as he reached for his cellphone and pulled up the pictures to show her as she stared at him.

"The Frick? You mean that size or that style?" She was horrified at the mention of it, even if it was one of her favorite museums.

"Both," he said honestly, as he held up one of the best photographs he'd taken of the exterior. It seemed very grand in the photo and Sybil stared at it with her mouth open.

"Are you crazy? It looks like the public library. How big is it?" She got right to the point and he flinched as he answered.

"Twenty thousand square feet, on an acre of land in Pacific Heights, the best residential neighborhood in the city. There's a park across the street, with a playground for Charlie. Sybil, the place is gorgeous. Trust me, it's the most beautiful house I've ever seen."

"Since when do you fall in love with houses? You didn't even want to see this apartment when I found it. And you practically slipped into a coma every time I told you what I wanted to do to it, after we bought it. How old is this house? Does it just look old or is it really?" But she had already guessed the answer from the picture he had shown her, and knew more about historical architecture than he did.

"It was built in 1902," he said humbly, "but look at it this way, it survived the 1906 earthquake without damage, so you don't need to worry about earthquakes." He tried to think of every selling point he could to win her over. And so far, it wasn't working.

"You won't need an earthquake with a house that old. The place is probably ready to fall down around our ears without one."

"It's beautifully built, and exquisite inside, with lovely old moldings, marble fireplaces, high ceilings, a wood-paneled library, a ballroom, and spectacular views." He showed her the rest of the pictures then, and she looked grim as she flipped through them.

"Blake, have you lost your mind? Are you having some kind of crisis, or psychotic break? First the job in San Francisco and moving us all out there, and now this. What are we going to do, living in a twenty-thousand-square-foot hundred-and-fifteen-year-old mansion? How are we even going to clean it? Or live there? It's a crazy idea."

"Some crazy ideas are good ones," he said with a boyishly guilty look, and she understood now why he hadn't told her before he bought it. She would never have let him bid on it, and he knew it. "Sometimes you just have to throw all your preconceived notions out the window and go for it," he said fervently, wanting to sweep her along on the wave that had carried him since he'd taken the job in San Francisco.

"Maybe, but not with a wife and three kids, a life in New York, an apartment we love here, and my work. Blake, we're not kids."

"Don't you want to do something different and exciting?" he asked her, and she thought about it. The honest answer was that she didn't. He seemed to have lost his mind. She hadn't.

"Moving to San Francisco is already different enough for me." Too different, but she had gone along with it anyway. And asking her to live in a mansion, take care of it, and "throw a coat of paint on it" was asking a lot of her. "Did you get inspections on it?"

"Of course. They've all checked out so far, and they'll be finished next week. The plumbing and electricity aren't new, but they're in decent shape, and the structure is sound, I promise you. It's a magnificent home, Sybil."

"Yes, for the sultan of Brunei maybe. What do we need with twenty thousand square feet?"

"We can keep the maids' rooms closed or use them for storage, and even the guest floor if you want to. We can just use the reception rooms on the main floor, and the one with the family bedrooms, and the kitchen." He had figured it all out, and in spite of herself, Sybil smiled and shook her head.

"I'm not sure I can trust you alone in San Francisco. God knows what you're going to do next, without telling me first." It upset her that he seemed to be making all the decisions on his own these days, knowing that they were not choices she wanted or would approve of, and he did it anyway.

"I couldn't help myself. I knew the minute I saw the house that it was special, and we should buy it. I know it's not what we wanted, but I think you'll fall in love with it too when you see it." And if she didn't? she wanted to ask him. What choice did she have now? She could make a huge stink and insist he renege on the purchase, or she could go along with it. Her role now seemed to be supporting him in dubious decisions that ran counter to reason, her desires, and their plans. And just how far was he going to push her, if she continued to give in to him? That worried her too.

"I want you to promise me, Blake Gregory, that you are not going to make one more single important move or decision without consulting me. You can't just buy a house without talking to me about it first. I don't care how cheap it is. Is that a deal?" He nodded in full agreement with her.

"I promise. And I did discuss the job in San Francisco with you, but this house just threw itself at me."

"As long as it's not a woman," she growled at him, and looked at the photographs on his phone again. There was no question, it was a beautiful home, or had been, but it looked enormous, impossible to maintain, and in need of a lot of loving touches and a mountain of furniture to make it livable. It was of a bygone era that no longer even existed or made sense in the modern world. She wouldn't dream of living at the Frick either, although she loved it. "Do you really think it will work for us and the kids?" She couldn't see how or imagine what it would cost them to furnish, and she commented on that too.

"Charlie can roller-skate in the ballroom. He'll love it, and think of the parties the kids can give. And the bank told me that there is a storage unit with a lot of the original furniture that one of the previous owners didn't use, but kept in case it ever became a museum, and out of respect for the original owners. I don't know what the stuff looks like, but we can go through it and see if we want to use it."

"I need to come out and see it," Sybil said, looking distracted. She had to see what he had gotten them into. She was trying to be a good sport about it.

"I want you to," Blake encouraged her, relieved that he had come to talk to her in person and now she knew. "You have to see it." He looked excited and proud as he said it, and she wasn't sure whether to kill him or kiss him.

"I'll go back with you. I'll write my article on the plane." She didn't want to wait a minute longer, and if she needed to have painting done on the rooms they'd live in, she needed to do it right away. They were moving to San Francisco in three weeks, and she had to get organized. This was going to take a lot more than rented furniture or staging to get it up and running, which was precisely what she hadn't wanted. But now he'd gotten them into this, and she wanted to see if they could make the best of it, or if he was totally insane. The latter seemed more likely.

"Are you furious with me for buying the house, Syb?" he asked her, looking worried, and she laughed at him.

"I'll let you know after I see it. Until then, you're on probation." It sounded fair to him. He knew he had really pushed her, with the job, the move, and now the Butterfield Mansion. "You'd better behave yourself in the meantime."

"I promise," he said, smiling at her, grateful that she was an extraordinary woman. He knew he was a lucky man, and she had always felt lucky too, although she had no idea what they were going to do with a century-old mansion, no matter how beautiful he said it was.

They spent the weekend together, doing things around the house, talking, and in and out of bed when they could get away with it, when the kids were out. She got their housekeeper to come in on Sunday to stay with the children so she could go to San Francisco with Blake. They boarded a 6 P.M. flight, which was due to arrive at 9:15 P.M. local time, midnight in New York. She had scheduled an appointment the next morning to see the house with the realtor. Blake had meetings and didn't have time to go with her, but he felt confident that she would fall in love with the house too. She had asked him a million questions during the weekend, and they had told the children about their new home. Charlie liked the idea of roller-skating in the ballroom, Andy said it looked like a Federal Reserve Bank, and Caroline wanted to see a picture of her bedroom and thought the house was cool. They weren't totally sold on it, but Sybil could tell they would get there, if she and Blake pushed them a little to convince them, and believed in the house themselves as the right home for them, which she didn't yet, but Blake did.

"Are there ghosts?" Charlie had asked, looking panicked when he saw the photographs, and Sybil smiled at him.

"Of course not, silly. There are no such things. Don't get started on that." Caroline had made ghostly noises to tease him, and Sybil had reprimanded her immediately, so she stopped, but at six he was easy to tease. "If there are ghosts, I hope they know how to use a mop and a vacuum cleaner," she said, and Charlie laughed.

Sybil studied the photographs again once they were on the flight to San Francisco, after she wrote her article on her computer. She had brought all her notes and research with her and finished it while Blake watched a movie. She was still wondering how Blake had gotten her into yet another challenging adventure, but he was relieved that she wasn't mad at him, although she was still skeptical and uneasy about his buying the Butterfield Mansion, no matter how good an investment he said it was. She'd put the last touches on her article for *The New York Times* by the time they landed, and Blake was sound asleep. She looked over at him and smiled, thinking that it was lucky they loved each other. If they didn't, she might have strangled him for buying a twenty-thousand-square-foot mansion. But what the hell, life with him was evolving, she just wasn't sure into what.

When Sybil got to the Butterfield Mansion by cab the next morning she stood at the gate and stared at it for a long moment, trying to absorb the fact that this was now her home. She couldn't relate to it, or even understand it, as the realtor opened the gate and she walked into the courtyard, looking up at the elegant windows and the dignified architecture. She had to admit, it was one of the most beautiful houses she'd ever seen. Walking through it took her breath away. There was room after room of century-old grandeur, remarkable workmanship, exquisite moldings and carvings, lovely floors that had withstood the test of time, the wood-paneled library, the graceful splendor of the ballroom—although she had no idea what they'd do with it, other than letting the children play there or give parties for their new friends, or set up a basketball hoop and use it as a gym, which seemed like a sacrilege. But she couldn't imagine living in a house that size.

And in defiance of all reason, the house had begun to feel like theirs by the time she had gone floor to floor, opened every closet and explored every nook and cranny, and figured out which rooms to put the children in. They were going to sleep on the same floor with their children, which she liked. And she earmarked a room on the floor above, with a sweeping view, as her office. She began making lists of what they needed, electronics, Wi-Fi, Internet connections for all of them. She noticed that most of the antique curtains were still in surprisingly good condition, since the windows were boarded up and sunlight hadn't touched them, and she decided to continue using them. Surprisingly, other than the practical basics, and all the usual kitchen equipment they could get at IKEA, the house didn't need any work, just paint and a lot of furniture.

The following afternoon, she and Blake went to the storage company the bank referred them to, to see the furniture and art objects past owners had acquired with the house and preserved but never used. There was some very handsome furniture of the period, much of which they liked, and some art.

An executive of the bank who seemed fascinated by the house's history had told them that a woman named Lili Saint Martin in Paris was the last member of the family to own the house. She had inherited it from her mother, Bettina Butterfield de Lambertin, and sold it immediately upon her mother's death in 1980.

The couple who had originally built the house in 1902 for themselves and their four children were Bertrand and Gwyneth Butterfield, and Gwyneth had sold it in 1930 after her husband's death during the Depression. Their oldest daughter, Bettina, had bought it back in 1950 and lived there for thirty years, until she died at eighty-four and left it to her daughter, Lili, who sold it. Lili Saint Martin had grown up in France, after leaving the house as a baby with her mother. She had been married in France and had a son, but she had no particular sentiment for the house. Since then, it had gone through a number of hands. No one had kept the house for long, and it had been unoccupied now for a dozen years, and looked it, abandoned and unloved, though not damaged. It sounded to Sybil, when she heard it, as though the history of the house had originally been a happy one, and the house and the families who owned it had subsequently fallen on hard times.

Bettina Butterfield had lived in it the longest, and she had apparently been very attached to the house. The woman at the bank mentioned that Bettina had written a history of the house and family, just for private purposes, and a copy of her book and many family photographs were in a box at the bank and would be turned over to Blake and Sybil. The female banker confirmed that there were no Butterfields left in the area, no one who cared about the house anymore, and the once-important family had moved away or died out. It made Sybil sad to hear about, and made her love the house more. It deserved a happier fate than to stand empty, forgotten, and unloved. She was suddenly glad Blake had bought it. She felt inexplicably protective of the house and the family that had lived there.

It was Lili who had left all the furnishings in the home, to be sold with the property, and subsequent owners had put it in storage and left it there, as a legacy no one seemed to want, although the furnishings had been both purchased and made for the house originally. But Sybil thought the new owners must have thought them too old-fashioned, perhaps couldn't sell them, or felt guilty selling them or throwing them away, so they all went to storage and stayed there.

It was dusty work when Blake and Sybil pulled everything out and examined it all. It hadn't been touched in nearly forty years, and Blake discovered that all the chandeliers were there, and he and Sybil agreed to have them reinstalled. Everything had been carefully packed, and nothing had been damaged since Lili Saint Martin had abandoned it. There were handsome pieces, and some antiquated ones, and many Sybil thought they could use. She planned to re-cover some of the upholstered pieces with new fabrics. There was a beautiful antique dining table that looked English, with twenty-four matching chairs. There were several very large-scale Victorian couches, which Sybil planned to re-cover in better colors. There were side tables, credenzas, and a great many pieces they both thought would work well in the house and be useful, and they could always replace them later if they found things they liked better. But for now, what had been stored would spare them the need to rush out and buy furniture, and some of it was really elegant, and just right for the mansion. The original owners had exceptional taste. There was a lovely bedroom set for Blake and Sybil's bedroom, all done in pale pink satin, and despite her usual preference for all things modern in her home, Sybil loved it.

And even the pieces that seemed old-fashioned were perfectly chosen. Blake and Sybil were very pleased with their exploration at the storage facility, and decided to use most of it. It would suit the house better than IKEA. Sybil scheduled an electrician to hang the chandeliers and sconces. She located a good upholsterer, and had the pieces delivered to them to keep until she found fabrics for them. They went to IKEA after Blake finished at the office to get what they needed for the kitchen. And Blake got the name of a painter from someone he worked with, and hired them to paint the two main floors before the family arrived on New Year's Day, and paint the third-floor rooms, where Sybil would have her office. Blake thought he might set up a home office too, if he needed to work on weekends.

They had decided to turn the servants' dining hall in the basement into a playroom for the children with a pool table, comfortable couches, and a large flat-screen TV to watch movies.

By Wednesday night, Sybil and Blake had made enormous headway, organizing their new home. The inspections were complete by then, and were all satisfactory. The house would officially be theirs in a week, and the bank was allowing them to start painting before that so they could finish before they moved in. And as they had promised, the bank had turned over a large box to them, with the original plans and blueprints of the house, a leather-bound book which was Bettina Butterfield de Lambertin's family history, a family tree, and a wealth of photographs of events at the house and members of the family. Sybil noticed that there were dates marked on the back of most of them, and occasionally the names of who was in the photograph, and she carefully put the book about the family into her bag to read on the plane home to New York. She was hungry to know more about them, and she left everything in the box, except the book, in her new office, to go through after they moved in. Family histories always fascinated her, and she wanted to read about the family that had built the mansion and lived there. It made living in the house, and owning it, more meaning-ful.

By the time Sybil left San Francisco on Thursday, things seemed to be in good order. She had hired a gardener to clean up the grounds and trim the hedges. And she had forgiven Blake for his insanity, buying the enormous man-sion. Now that she had seen it herself, she understood what had happened. There was something magical and deeply moving about the mansion. You could see how greatly loved it had once been, and how carefully thought out the building of it must have been, a hundred and fif-teen years before. And some of it still made sense today. Sybil had fallen in love with the house too, and was excited to show it to the children. She took more photographs, particularly of the children's sunny, spacious bedrooms, since they wanted to see them. And she had described to them the playroom they were going to set up in the base-ment. She had broken the bad news to Charlie on the phone that he'd have to roller-skate outside, because the ballroom was too pretty to skate in, and she didn't want him wrecking the antique floors. She and Blake both felt proprietary about the house. And now that she had seen it, it was bringing them closer together, rather than tearing them apart, as Blake had feared at first.

She answered all their children's questions when she got back to New York, and went to look for the right fab-rics for the upholstered pieces, and she found many she liked that she thought would be perfect in the house. She had to laugh at herself—after a whole career focused on modern design, she was now steeped in all things Victorian, but it was fun to do the research. She was so busy, she hadn't time to read Bettina Butterfield's book yet, but she was going to as soon as she could. She had wrapped it in plastic to protect the century-old leather cover in her bag.

She helped the children select what they wanted to ship to San Francisco, which in Caroline's case meant her entire wardrobe, but given the size of the house they were moving into, Sybil didn't argue with her. There was room for it all. And Charlie wanted to take most of his toys. Both boys wanted their favorite videogames and PlayStations, and Andy was taking his new Xbox. Sybil packed for her and Blake, while also trying to get ready for Christmas. Blake came home a few days before the holiday. He was spending their last ten days in New York with them, to help them get ready, and would fly back to San Francisco with them on New Year's Day.

There were tearful farewells at school, mostly for Caroline. Andy was planning to come back in a few months to visit friends, and had invited some to visit him in San Francisco during vacations, and by the week after Christmas they were all ready. They had a peaceful Christmas Eve at home, with all their usual traditions, gifts on Christmas Eve, and a turkey dinner, and a lazy day on Christmas

Day, in their pajamas, enjoying one another and their gifts, all of which they were planning to take with them to their new home. And Blake and Sybil gave an informal buffet dinner to say goodbye to their friends, even though Sybil was planning to come back often for work.

Caroline and Andy went out with their New York friends for a last time on New Year's Eve, and Blake and Sybil stayed home and toasted each other at midnight. It had been a busy month, and January would be even more so, getting settled in San Francisco, with the children starting new schools. Blake was loving his new job and associates, and Sybil was grateful to have a lull in her work schedule, so she could turn her full attention to the move.

"Here's to our new home," Blake said, and kissed her as the ball fell in Times Square on their TV.

"Thank you for finding it," Sybil said sincerely. Blake had been lucky. She was falling in love with the house more day by day, although she had been stunned and horrified when he first told her. "And to no earthquakes as long as we live there," she said half-seriously, and he laughed at her.

"There won't be. I promise," he said confidently, and she hoped he was right, since there hadn't been a really big one in a very long time, and hopefully there wouldn't be for the next two years, or for however long they lived there. She had stopped worrying about it in her excitement about the house. All she could think of now was how beautiful it was going to be. From their comfortable and predictable life in New York and their apartment in Tribeca, they were moving to San Francisco to live in an enormous mansion. It was going to be an adventure, and all five Gregorys could hardly wait.

Chapter 3

Caroline texted her friends until the plane took off at JFK, and Charlie looked faintly nostalgic as the plane circled over New York and headed west, and then he turned to his mother with his big brown eyes and dark hair just like Blake's.

"You're sure there are no ghosts there?"

"Positive. I promise." She smiled at him, and handed him his iPad so he could play a game. They all watched movies on the plane and had lunch, and Sybil knew that the children were still faintly apprehensive about seeing their new home for the first time. They were intrigued by how big it was; Sybil said they'd get used to it, and told them how much fun it would be. They could have as many friends over as they wanted in a home that size, and play outdoors on the lawn.

Blake had reported that the painters finished their work on time on the two floors they'd been assigned to work on. The kitchen still needed some help, but was functional. IKEA had installed new cabinets and appliances. And they already had all the linens they needed.

She had gotten the upholsterers started on the pieces from storage. The chandeliers and sconces were now in their original locations, and the rest of the furniture that had been stored was placed where Sybil believed it went originally, by guesswork and logical conclusion, and had instructed the movers accordingly. Blake had used the original photographs to place the chandeliers in the right rooms and they had filled in what the children needed for their bedrooms from IKEA. All their Internet and Wi-Fi connections had been set up, so they could use their computers as soon as they arrived. The only things they didn't have yet were the flat-screen TV and pool table for the basement, but they were due to arrive in a few weeks.

They had worked wonders in a short time, but mostly because there was so much already there, particularly from storage. And the house was theirs now. It felt as though it was meant to be.

They went straight to the house from the airport when they arrived at one o'clock local time on New Year's Day, and the realtor had very kindly offered to leave food at the house for them. Alicia and José, the Mexican couple Sybil had hired long-distance, with Blake conducting interviews, were off on New Year's Day, but would be back the next day. They were enthusiastic and energetic, had good references, and said they liked kids. They were going to clean, and José would work outside too. Blake said they didn't seem daunted by the size of the house. Several other couples they'd interviewed had turned the job down unless they hired more staff, which Blake and Sybil didn't want to do. They thought two hardworking people would be enough, since they didn't plan to use the entire house. Alicia had said she would babysit Charlie when Sybil needed her to, and all of José's references had said that he was tireless and willing, with a great attitude. They were both in their early forties and had done domestic work for many years, since moving to California from Mexico in their teens. They were American citizens now.

Blake rented a van at the airport to accommodate all their equipment and bags. Everything else had already been sent. He had left his own car at the house, in the old garage, which had a chauffeur's apartment they could use for storage. Blake had shipped his car from New York when he first moved out. And they were going to buy Sybil an SUV to drive the kids around, since she had left her old station wagon in New York for work. Both Caroline and Andy were maneuvering for cars of their own, but Blake was adamant about their waiting until they went to college, and Sybil agreed, which made her car a hot bartering item on weekends.

They chattered noisily on the ride from the airport, but when they drove up to the gate and saw the house, there was silence in the van. It looked bigger and more impressive than it had in photographs, and all three of the children stared as they drove into the courtyard when the gates opened by remote control. For a long moment, no one got out.

"Welcome home," Sybil said gently, and she and Blake exchanged a smile. One by one they looked around, as Blake went to unlock the house and turn off the alarm. He left the front door open, and went back to the van to help them with their things, and carry Sybil's bags.

"Go exploring if you want," Blake invited them, as they entered the house shyly at first, carrying their tote bags and backpacks with what they'd needed for the plane. Sybil led them around the main floor. It looked nice now, and homier with some of the original furniture in it. It was a little sparsely furnished, with many items still at the upholsterers, but it was bright and airy with the fresh coat of paint. Sybil had selected a warm off-white color that went well with the house. All three children stared at the enormous hall with portraits hung along the walls, which Sybil and Blake had brought out of storage, and gave the entrance an ancestral air. The portraits in the hall were of various Butterfields. They looked like historical portraits in a British home. They peered into the living room and dining room, and the library, where she had put a huge partners desk they'd also found in storage. It was a beautiful English antique that was perfect in the room.

"Are there secret passages?" Charlie asked, turning to his mother with excitement in his eyes.

"I don't know. I haven't had time to study the plans in

detail yet. I'll check," she promised, after they peeked into the kitchen and straggled up the stairs to the second floor to find their bedrooms. They had checked out each room on the main floor from the doorway, but had not gone into the reception rooms like the drawing room and the library. It was a little overwhelming. The chandeliers made the rooms seem more formal, and the long table in the dining room looked endless as Sybil glanced at it from the door, but it was meant for the room. She wondered if the Butterfields had given grand dinner parties, with all twenty-four chairs filled with elegant men and women in evening clothes, and then she ran up the stairs after her children and directed them to their respective rooms. All of them were pleased, particularly Charlie, who was directly across from his parents, and knew he could find his mother easily if he had a bad dream. All he had to do was walk out of his bedroom across the hall into hers.

Andy had a private suite, with a little living room of his own, and Caroline had a dressing room that Sybil had had painted pink, and an enormous pink marble bathroom with a gigantic bathtub. It was just as "cool" as Caro had hoped.

Then they all congregated in their parents' room, and checked that out. Andy and Caroline and their parents had beautiful views of the bay.

"So what do you think?" Sybil asked Caroline and Charlie, while Blake and Andy brought up their bags. The things that had been shipped were already in their rooms. Blake had organized it all before he left.

"It's BIG," Charlie pronounced as he looked around, and his mother and sister laughed.

"Yes, it is," Sybil agreed. "Does your room look okay?" She'd sent out his favorite pale blue bedspread, the chair he loved to sit in, and a lot of toys, along with his PlayStation. Charlie nodded in answer, and went back to looking around again, while Caroline explored her mother's dressing room. Half an hour later, they all met in the kitchen to see what there was to eat. There was just enough for lunch and breakfast in the morning, and they were going to order pizza for dinner. Sybil was going to send Alicia to the store for them the next day. The kids had a few more days free before school started, and they were going to look around the city with Sybil, to get to know their new home. Blake was going back to work. He'd been off for ten days.

Sybil made sandwiches for all of them, they helped themselves to sodas, and she poured a glass of milk for Charlie and handed it to him. None of them were comfortable in the house yet, but they were fascinated by everything they saw. After they ate, Andy and Caroline explored the upper floors, which were unfurnished and unoccupied and still in the process of being painted, and they left Charlie in his room. He was still not absolutely certain that there were no ghosts, but the others continued to reassure him that there were none. So he focused on wanting to find the secret passages instead, and Blake said he doubted that there were any.

They went to bed early after the trip and the excitement of moving in. Charlie was asleep before his head hit the pillow. Andy watched a movie, Caroline texted all her friends and sent Instagrams of her suite and her bathtub, and Blake and Sybil retired to their room, pleased that their arrival had gone well.

"Well, that seemed to go okay," Sybil commented to her husband as she lay on the bed and smiled at him.

"They'll get used to it in no time, especially once they get busy at school," he reassured her and lay down next to her. He was tired and knew he had a heavy day of meetings the next day. He was happy that his family was in San Francisco with him now, and Sybil was pleased too. They fell asleep in each other's arms that night, and she could hear him in the shower when she woke up in the morning. They had the only proper shower in the house. The others all had tubs, with handheld showers added, which Andy had complained about and Caro loved. Blake had told Andy he could use theirs.

Sybil noticed, as she waited for Blake to emerge from the bathroom, that he had managed to open the window that had been stuck the night before. The painters had painted it shut, and neither of them had been able to open it before they went to bed. She had planned to ask José to do it, but now she didn't have to. It was a sunny day, but the air was cool outside and felt fresh in the room. When Blake emerged from his dressing room, ready for the office, she thanked him for unsticking the window.

"I didn't. Maybe it just worked itself open after we played with it last night," he said blithely and headed downstairs. She forgot about it when she followed him to make breakfast, while he read the paper that had been delivered to their door. He preferred reading *The New York Times* and *The Wall Street Journal* online at the office, but had ordered the local paper for her.

They talked about his meetings that day, and he left a little while later. She kissed him goodbye in the great hall, and they both smiled at the Butterfield portraits they had hung there: Bertrand and Gwyneth, the couple who had built the house, a daunting old dowager in an elaborate gown with a fierce expression, wearing a tiara, and an older man in a kilt. Sybil wondered if those two were Bertrand's or Gwyneth's parents. And there were portraits of two pretty young girls in white dresses, a young man in a military uniform with a wistful expression, and a little boy who looked full of mischief and a little bit like Charlie. It made her think that she really wanted to get to Bettina's book and find out who they all were. It surprised her that none of their descendants had wanted the portraits and had left them with the house. They were respectable works by different artists, and added dignity to the front hall. The Gregory children had looked at them when they walked in, but didn't inquire who they were. They were too excited by the rest of the house.

Sybil walked toward the grand staircase to go upstairs, after Blake left for work, and noticed that two of the tables in the front hall had been moved from where she and Blake had wanted to place them when they came from storage, and she wondered if he had moved them. The tables had been switched to opposite sides of the room, but she had to admit they looked better in their new locations as she stopped to examine them for a minute, and then hurried upstairs to get dressed. She and the children had a busy day ahead too.

The children turned up in her room half an hour later, and they went downstairs so she could make their breakfast. They were still eating when Alicia and José arrived, and she introduced them to the children. They were warm and kind, and Charlie liked them immediately. A short time later, Sybil took the children out in the rented van. She was going to keep it until they bought her SUV.

She showed them all the sights, the Golden Gate Bridge, and Alcatraz sitting in the bay. They followed a cable car downtown on California Street to the Embarcadero, and drove past Fisherman's Wharf, up to Coit Tower and then around Union Square, and back up to Nob Hill, and then walked through Chinatown, looked at all the souvenir stores and markets, before they had lunch at Ghirardelli Square.

They had noticed a skating rink set up in Union Square, still there after the holidays, and she promised to take Caroline and Charlie skating that weekend. Andy wanted to go to a Warriors basketball game with Blake. After lunch, she drove Caroline and Andy past their new school, which wasn't far from their house. She explained to Charlie again that he'd be picked up by a school bus every day, at a nearby stop, since his school was in Marin County across the Golden Gate Bridge.

They seemed satisfied with their new city, and kept occupied in their rooms when they got home, while Sybil spent some time with José and Alicia, and told them what she wanted done first. They had been working there for several weeks, under Blake's direction. Out of curiosity, she asked them if they had switched the tables in the front hall and they said they hadn't, so she knew it must have been Blake, which was fine. She didn't want anyone else changing the décor on their own.

Sybil had dinner on the table when Blake got home from work. It was already beginning to feel like home. The children told him everything they'd done, and he was impressed. And they were planning to drive around Marin County the next day, and drive past Charlie's school too. He was a little nervous about it, since he'd never seen it and had no friends there, and Sybil thought a drive by might help.

They all played Monopoly after dinner, and everyone was in good spirits when they went up to their rooms. The move was going much more smoothly than Sybil had expected, and she tried to organize her own dressing room that night. She still had shoes everywhere when she finally gave up and decided to finish the next day. She had lain down next to Blake on the bed and was dozing when he shook the bed from side to side. She turned to look at him with a puzzled expression when he woke her up with the sudden movement.

"What are you doing?" She'd already been half asleep.

"Nothing." He seemed perplexed, and just as he said it, a violent jolt shifted back and forth and nearly threw them out of bed. The chandelier in their bedroom began swinging and they both realized what had happened, and was still happening.

"Oh shit! You lied to me!" she shouted at Blake, as she ran to get Charlie, who was wide awake and terrified in his room. It was an earthquake, and Sybil had no idea what to do. She pulled him toward her own room, as Andy and Caroline came running down the hall from their rooms, looking scared, just as the shaking stopped. It had lasted less than a minute, but felt like forever. And Sybil had noticed a horrible groaning sound that seemed to come from the ground outside while it was going on. She had never been so frightened in her life. The chandeliers were still swinging, and Sybil stared at Blake in terror. "Do you think that's just the prelude to a bigger one?" she asked, still shaking from head to foot, as Charlie clung to her, and the other two children stood in her bedroom, panicked.

"No, I don't," Blake said calmly. "I think that was it. I don't think it was even a very big one. There may be a few small aftershocks later," he said, trying to soothe everyone.

"You said there wouldn't be any earthquakes." Sybil glared at him accusingly.

"It was just a small one, Syb," he said insistently. "Welcome to San Francisco, kids," he said to his children, trying to make light of it. "It's fine." Nothing had fallen or gotten damaged. It had just scared the hell out of them. They had never experienced an earthquake before.

"Do you think we should go downstairs and make sure nothing fell and broke?" Sybil asked, worried. They had candelabra with crystal drops, a lot of lamps, and a number of small delicate objects that could have fallen in the rooms downstairs. And dishes in the kitchen that could have slipped off the shelves if the cupboards had opened.

"You can if you want to," Blake answered. "I'm sure it's fine." None of the others were anxious to go anywhere, in case it wasn't over, or the aftershocks would be too strong. "Why don't we watch something on TV?" Blake suggested to the children and switched on the remote. All three piled into their parents' bed, where they saw on CNN that it had been a 5.1 earthquake on the Richter scale in San Francisco, with the epicenter 150 miles away, where it had registered 6.4. It wasn't huge, but it had been a noticeable quake.

"I'm going downstairs to check," Sybil said in a soft voice, and Blake nodded, and indicated that he'd stay with the kids.

Sybil turned the lights on in the second-floor hall, and headed down the stairs to the main floor. She wanted to check the living room and the kitchen to see if anything had fallen and broken, and she had just passed the dining room when a woman in a grand gown walked past her. She looked like a dowager, and she looked right at Sybil and spoke to her clearly as she leaned on her cane.

"I thought the chandelier was going to fall right on my head. We have to ask Phillips to check it tomorrow." And then she narrowed her eyes at Sybil, as a man in a kilt approached her. "And what are you doing downstairs practically naked?" She looked sternly disapproving at Sybil and headed toward the stairs with the man in the kilt, who was reassuring her that it had only been a small quake. As Sybil stared at them, a little boy ran past her, with a terribly pale young woman holding his hand, as a man and a woman left the dining room less hastily and smiled at Sybil, and a tall, handsome young man in white tie and tails asked her if she was all right. There was a young woman with him in an evening dress, and Sybil felt as though she had lost her mind as she tried to answer them and couldn't speak. And as she turned to look at them on the grand staircase, where they'd been headed, she saw them disappear, and suddenly she was alone in the main hall. She looked at the family portraits she and Blake had hung, and she knew exactly who they were. And while she tried to absorb it, a stern-looking man also in white tie and tails stared at her from the dining room doorway and closed the door. She had no idea who he was, and she didn't know the names of the others, but they were clearly the Butterfields who had lived there a century before. She was shaking as she ran to the kitchen, saw nothing broken, decided not to check the living room, and raced upstairs. As she entered her bedroom, she was breathless and deathly pale.

"Are you all right?" Blake asked her, and she shook her head to indicate that she wasn't, and then remembered the children in their bed, whom she had momentarily forgotten about completely in the terror and confusion of what she'd just seen. "I'm fine," she managed to croak out, as Caroline stared at her more closely.

"You're pale, Mom. Do you feel sick?"

"The earthquake just took me by surprise—I'm fine," she insisted, lying down next to her daughter on her pillow and waiting for them to leave. They had all calmed down an hour later, when their father switched off the TV.

"The excitement is over, back to your rooms," he said firmly, and went to tuck Charlie in, while Sybil lay on their bed, trying to understand what she'd seen. She knew who, but couldn't figure out how or why.

"What happened to you?" Blake asked her when he came back from putting their youngest son to bed. "You looked like you'd seen a ghost."

"I did," she whispered so Charlie couldn't hear her, still pale. "Eight of them . . . nine including a man I didn't recognize in the dining room. They were all leaving the dining room, talking about the earthquake, and headed up the stairs . . . and the old dowager accused me of standing there naked in my nightgown . . . and when they reached the top of the stairs, they all disappeared. *All* of them! They were the people in the portraits, even the little boy." Her voice was shaking as she described them to him.

Blake grinned at her as she lay there looking terrified. "What did you drink while you were downstairs?" Sybil sat bolt upright in bed and glared at him in frightened fury.

"Don't give me that! You lied about the earthquake, you said there wouldn't be one, and now we just had one on our second day. And a whole family of ghosts just walked past me in our new house. No wonder the bank practically gave it away. They must have been scaring the hell out of people for the last forty years!"

"Sybil, please. You're upset about the earthquake. It jarred your mind. Besides, the bank would've had to tell us if anyone had seen ghosts here. It's the law." Legally, in California, the bank had to disclose it if a house was thought to have ghosts, but maybe they didn't know.

"I am going to jar your head if you don't listen to me. I just saw the whole Butterfield clan leave the dining room and walk up the stairs and disappear. Two of them *talked* to me. The young man in uniform in the portrait downstairs. He was in white tie and tails. He asked if I was all right. And the old dowager scolded me, and I saw the old man in the kilt, he was talking to her. And they all saw me, I could tell. I saw them, plain as day." She was badly shaken and Blake was skeptical.

"Do you want a drink now?" he offered, trying not to make fun of her, but he thought the shock of the earthquake, and the fear, had played tricks with her mind. She was obviously more afraid of earthquakes than he'd realized.

"I do not want a drink. I want to know what the hell is going on here. If our children start to see them around the house, they'll be out of here in five minutes, and this house is toast. Especially Charlie."

"I don't know anything about psychic phenomena, but if you didn't imagine it, maybe earthquakes shake ghosts out into the open. I'm sure they'll disappear again if that's the case. They weren't in the front hall to greet us when we got here, after all." He couldn't take her seriously. It sounded absurd to Blake. He was a practical person, but Sybil was too.

"No, but they could have been. Maybe they're all here in the house, just waiting to scare us away." She looked panicked.

"Were they scary?" he asked her sensibly, trying to keep a straight face.

"No, just the old lady, and the man in the dining room afterward. The others were perfectly nice."

"Why don't we just give them a chance to vanish again?" he said soothingly, making her feel like an escaped mental patient.

"What if they don't? Blake, I am not going to live with a family of ghosts. They scared the hell out of me."

"Why? They're all dead."

"Are you crazy? What if they try to chase us away? Isn't that what ghosts supposedly do if you've taken possession of a house they haunt?"

"Why don't we just calm down and see what happens. We can't move out just because we had a small earthquake and you think you saw a ghost." Blake didn't want to feed the insanity. It was unlike Sybil to be hysterical, but clearly she was.

"You don't believe me." She glared at him, even angrier at his condescending tone.

"I believe that you think you saw them, but I don't know what you really saw. Maybe you just saw the portraits downstairs. Maybe they were moving from the quake." He was looking for a reasonable answer to what she'd seen, or thought she did. But he did not for a minute believe she'd seen a family of ghosts.

"The portraits were *not* moving—the people were. And it was the same people as in the portraits, *all* of them. And they *talked* to me, Blake!" She was insistent and knew what she'd seen and heard. "And walked up the stairs!"

"Sybil, try to relax and be sensible. I'll bet we never see them again. And there probably won't be another earthquake for years." She refused to answer him and lay down on the bed. He clearly didn't believe her, and she didn't know what to do next. There was no one she could tell. But she knew now that there were ghosts in the house. And whatever Blake said, the Butterfields were still there. "Did they try to frighten you away?" he asked her cynically.

"No," she admitted. "But just seeing them nearly gave me a heart attack." She was so enraged at Blake for everything that had happened, and for not believing her, that she didn't speak to him again that night. She was up early the next morning, cooking breakfast, when she saw him again.

"How do you feel today?" he asked her quietly after the children finished breakfast and went back upstairs. They had talked about the earthquake all through breakfast, and how scary it had been. But that had been nothing compared to what Sybil had seen after that, when she went downstairs.

"Are you asking me if I'm sane again?" she said coldly.

"Of course not. You were frightened out of your wits last night, after that shake. I don't blame you for being upset." He sounded condescending, and she was just as angry at him as she'd been the night before.

"I know you don't believe me, but I saw all of them, the whole family, and some other man."

"Who knows, maybe that's the way those things work. Maybe they appear every hundred years on some anniversary, or only during earthquakes. They're certainly not hanging around on a daily basis. We never saw them here before."

"We've only lived here for two days. Maybe they don't want us here, and they think we're disturbing them. This was their home."

"And now it's ours. We can't let a family of ghosts frighten us away," he said, still refusing to enter a state of panic with her.

"Oh, no? I've heard horror stories about things like that. They could push one of us down the stairs, or scare us into falling. The old lady is pretty damn scary, and there was some weird old guy with her, the one in the kilt. And who unstuck the window in our bedroom that had been painted shut the night before? You and I didn't, and there's no one else. In the morning, it was unstuck and the window was open. And who moved the tables in the front hall? Someone switched them and Alicia and José said they didn't." And Blake had said he hadn't either when she asked him, so she assumed the moving men had. "Maybe they're here watching us right now." The idea gave her a shiver. "I'm not going to have my children living in a house full of poltergeists, if that's what they are."

"Maybe they're benign spirits who wish us well," he said, thinking that his wife was going nuts. "Let's just try to keep a grip on reality, shall we? If you see them again, we can call in an exorcist or something, I'm sure there's some way to get rid of them. They're dead, after all."

"Precisely. And if they're still hanging around here a hundred years later, you can be damn sure they're not planning to leave anytime soon."

"Maybe they're friendly," he said, but he could see that he wasn't going to convince her. The experience of the night before had been too vivid for her.

"I don't care if they are friendly. This is our house, and I'm not going to live here with them. This is a little too *Twilight Zone* for me."

"Try not to think about it today. Enjoy the kids, before they start school." They were going to drive by Charlie's school in Marin County, and take a look at Sausalito on the other side of the bridge. Charlie wanted a tour of Alcatraz, but she had found out you had to book it months in advance. Instead, they were going to see the sea lions at Pier 39. "Have a good day," Blake said cautiously, blew her a kiss, and left for the office, where everyone would be talking about the earthquake and where they'd been when it happened.

The children commented on it again on the drive to Marin, and Sybil was relieved that none of them had seen any of the Butterfields on the second floor. There was no mention of them.

When they got there, Charlie liked the look of his school. They drove through Sausalito, then went back to the city and visited the sea lions, who were barking, and occasionally snapping at each other, and lying in the sun. They had lunch at Pier 39, and then the children all wanted to go home. They still had things they wanted to unpack, and Andy had promised to play a videogame with his little brother. Caroline wanted to call her friends in New York. Once they were busy in their rooms, Sybil took a quiet walk through the house to see if she noticed anything unusual, but all seemed normal. Nothing was out of place and there was no sign of the Butterfields. But despite her husband's cynicism, she refused to believe she had imagined it.

When she got back to her room, she grabbed Bettina

Butterfield's book out of her travel bag and put it on her night table, and then she opened her computer and started surfing the Net, not sure what she was looking for. There were several sites that referred to ghosts, and even a chat room for people who had seen them, but she was looking for something more scientific. She finally discovered a website for the Psychic Institute in Berkeley, and jotted down their phone number. She closed her bedroom door and called them immediately, and when they answered, she asked to speak to someone for advice. The receptionist told her that all their counselors were busy, and asked if she'd like to make an appointment. On the spur of the moment, she made one for the next day, when all the kids would be in school. She wondered if they'd think she was crazy too, but she wanted to know if there was any basis for what she had experienced. Was it a common occurrence or totally unheard of, and what could she do about it before a family of dead people took over her home? She didn't tell Blake that she'd called them and made an appointment. He would have been convinced she was crazy. She was relieved when that night there was no repetition of the activity of the night before. The house was peaceful, and Blake was comforted to find that Sybil was no longer on a crusade about ghosts in the house when he got home. She didn't mention them at all.

The next day, when Sybil got everyone off to school, and had waved Charlie off on the school bus, she got in the van and headed across the Bay Bridge to Berkeley. She found the institute easily with the help of the GPS, and when she got there, it looked like a normal office or a small medical building. There was a very ordinary receptionist, and when Sybil said she had an appointment with Michael Stanton, the girl at the desk asked her to wait. Two minutes later, he came to greet her, and took her to his office. He was wearing jeans, a plaid shirt, and hiking boots, and had a beard, but his hair was short. He was about Sybil's age, and he looked like a schoolteacher of some kind, or a college professor. And in his office, she saw that he had a number of degrees, including a master's in psychology from UC Berkeley. He explained to her that he had been studying psychic phenomena for twenty years, and had written several books on the subject, to reassure her that this was a serious vocation for him.

"It's surprisingly scientific, even though it's not always easy to explain to people who haven't experienced it," he said pleasantly, and then he turned to her with a warm look and asked what he could do to help her.

"I know this sounds ridiculous, or it would to most people, and my husband is acting like I'm psychotic. We just moved into a new house three days ago. It was built in 1902 by the Butterfield family. They moved out around 1930—I think they lost their money—and a member of the family bought it back many years later and lived there until 1980. It's had a number of owners since then. My husband and I bought it a month ago. We just moved out from New York. There have been a couple of minor incidents, nothing terrifying, but the other night during the earthquake, I saw them. All of them. The people who built the house, their children, and three other people." Sybil looked agitated as she explained it to him, remembering how frightened she had been, both by the earthquake and the people in the hall afterward. "I saw them perfectly clearly. They walked out of the dining room, right past me, up the staircase and vanished. Two of them talked to me, and I heard them talk to one another, just as though they were right there with me." Michael Stanton didn't look surprised by what she said.

"How do you know it was them?" he asked quietly.

"We have their portraits up in the front hall. We bought the house from the bank, in a foreclosure, and there was quite a lot of furniture and some art in storage. We're using it, and I liked the idea of hanging the paintings of them, like a portrait gallery in a European château or an ancestral home. It seemed respectful of them."

"Did anyone else see them the other night?" he inquired, and she shook her head.

"I was alone downstairs and they disappeared before I went back up to the second floor. I went down to see if anything had broken or fallen during the earthquake." He nodded and jotted down some notes on a pad on his desk.

In some ways, he reminded her of a shrink, but he didn't act as though she was crazy, as Blake had.

"What were they wearing?" he asked, and Sybil thought about it.

"They were dressed in clothes similar to the portraits, though not exactly, but they were wearing clothes of the time when the house was built. Evening gowns, white tie and tails, a kilt." He nodded again. "Does this sound nuts to you?" she asked him, and he smiled at her.

"Not at all. I hear it all the time. Something about the earthquake the other night may have replicated an incident in their lifetimes, and shaken them loose, literally. Given when the house was built, I assume they must have lived there during the 1906 earthquake. And your moving in may have jarred them too. If the house has been unoccupied for a long time, you may have startled them. Hanging their portraits may have made them feel welcome. And they may be curious about you. Ghosts are sometimes very curious about people in their space."

"It's our space now," Sybil said firmly, and Michael smiled.

"They may not think so. It's not unusual for people from the spirit life to become quite attached to the homes they lived in during their lifetime. They may have happy memories there. It's possible that they never left the house and have remained there for all this time. But it's very unusual for an entire family to stay together in a home. It's more common for one or two spirits to linger, but not a large group like the one you describe. They must be very comfortable there. Did they feel menacing to you? Did you have the sense that they were trying to frighten you?" Sybil thought about it and shook her head.

"The old lady was pretty daunting, but it was more the way she looked at me and the way she was dressed. I think she had an accent too."

"What kind of an accent?"

"British . . . Scottish maybe, and there was a man with her wearing a kilt. He didn't talk to me. There's a book about the family and their history in the house, but I haven't had time to read it yet."

"Maybe you should."

She nodded in agreement. "One of their daughters wrote it—the one who bought the house back and stayed until her death many years later. Her daughter had no interest in the house and sold it when her mother died."

"There could be several reasons why they let you see them the other night. Two, most typically. Either they are trying to reach you and make contact with you, for some unknown reason. Perhaps even because they like you, or had some earlier relationship with you. Or they don't want you on their turf and are determined to scare you, but it doesn't sound like that to me. When spirits from another dimension want to frighten people, they're not shy about it and can really wreak havoc. They don't sound hostile or ominous to me."

"They weren't," she agreed. "It's just the idea of them that is unsettling. I'm not even sure that I believe in ghosts. Or I never did before this. But they were extremely real, and stood right next to me. They appeared to be perfectly normal living people, like you and me, and then they disappeared. They just faded away like mist at the top of the stairs."

"They normally do that extremely well." He smiled at her. "You see them one minute, appearing quite alive, and then you don't."

"The couple who built the house looked entirely alive and smiled at me, and so did the young man. I think he must be their son. There is a portrait of him in uniform."

"He might have died during the war, so they had him painted in uniform to honor him," Michael explained. "I have a feeling that they were just comfortable with you, and recognized you as a benign person, so they let you see them. As I said, what's unusual here is that the entire family still appears to be together, in their home. You don't hear about that very often. An individual, or a couple occasionally, but not the whole family, including several generations, intact as they were when they occupied the home. They must be a very strong presence to be there over a hundred years later. They may have always remained there, or perhaps they returned more recently, or they may come and go. Their daughter living there for many years would have made remaining there easier for them, and if the house has been unoccupied for many years, that opens the doors for them too. Spirits don't usually like a busy home, or one where there is too much activity."

"I don't want them frightening my children," Sybil said sternly.

"Of course. Would you mind if I came to visit you? One can often sense what kind of spirit activity is there, and how powerful a force it is. And if they have been there for all this time, they won't go away easily. You and your family may have to learn to coexist with them."

"I'm not willing to do that," Sybil said stubbornly. "I have a six-year-old son who would be traumatized if he ever sees them."

"You might be surprised. Children are often very receptive to spirits. Their minds are more open than ours."

"He's afraid of ghosts," Sybil insisted. And so was she, now that she had come face to face with them. It was Blake who didn't believe in them, and thought they were a figment of her imagination. "And a few pieces of furniture have been moved, after I placed them where I wanted them."

"The phenomenon of moved furniture is fairly typical, particularly if you're using what was theirs." He was unimpressed by it. "They may want it all back in its original location, if you've placed it differently. Somehow you may have disturbed them, which brought them back en masse, or they are comfortable in your home."

"I don't want them to get comfortable. I want them to go away. And if you think it would help to visit the house, by all means come and see it."

"Would tomorrow work for you?" She nodded. She wanted to find out as much as she could. She was preparing a show for the Brooklyn Museum, but was under no time pressure yet. And she wanted to know more about the Butterfields and make sure they didn't reappear. They may have been comfortable there, but they were not welcome in her home. She wondered if she should take their portraits down. She asked Michael about it, but he said it wouldn't change anything, if they were determined to stay in the home, particularly now that they had appeared. She told him it was important to her to get rid of the ghosts in her house, before they drove her and her family away.

"I'll see you tomorrow then," Michael said pleasantly, as he stood up and ushered her out.

Sybil thought about what he'd said all the way back to the city. In some ways it wasn't reassuring, although she was happy to know that she was sane. But the fact that whole families who had remained in a home in spirit for a hundred years almost never wanted to leave was not encouraging. At least she was happy he didn't think they were trying to terrorize them or drive them away. But she had no intention of coexisting with them. She had already decided not to tell Blake what she had learned that day. She wanted to hear what Michael would say when he visited the house, and what kind of vibrations he picked up, hostile or friendly, and if he could tell her anything more.

As she walked into the front hall, she looked at the portraits more closely than she had before. They were exactly like the people she had seen in the hallway the night of the earthquake. And she could have sworn that the grand dowager was gazing right at her in the portrait with a disapproving stare, as she held her fan and a lorgnette. Sybil could still hear her voice that night. She noticed a black pug dog in the painting then too, sitting on the floor next to the woman. The old man in the kilt appeared to observe her with interest as she walked past, trying not to let them unnerve her. This was her house now, she thought with determination, and no longer theirs. And as she walked upstairs to check on her children after their first day of school, Sybil didn't see the little boy sitting under a table, wearing knee breeches and a cap, holding a bag of marbles, as he smiled, watching her.

Chapter 4

Michael Stanton from the Berkeley Psychic Institute came to visit Sybil the next morning at ten A.M. The house was quiet. Alicia and José were cleaning their bedrooms, the children were at school, and Blake was at work.

Sybil told him as soon as he walked in that she had only had time to read a few chapters of Bettina's book the night before, but it was fascinating, and everything appeared to be there. All she knew about them so far was that Bertrand and Gwyneth Butterfield had built the house in 1902, which she knew anyway. Their oldest son was named Josiah, and he'd been eight years old when they moved in. His sister Bettina was two years younger than he. Their son Magnus was three when they arrived, and he had been killed three years later, in a tragic accident, run over by a runaway carriage at the age of six. A daughter, Lucy, had been born in 1909, four years after Magnus's death, and she had always suffered from frail health—she had a weak chest, as her older sister put it. Sybil also knew now, from the book, that the daunting dowager in the elegant gown was Gwyneth's mother, Augusta Campbell, née

MacPherson, who lived with them, and she was indeed Scottish. Gwyneth Campbell Butterfield had been born in Scotland as well. The older gentleman in the kilt with the mane of white hair was Augusta's much older brother, Angus MacPherson. And Bettina had shared that he played the bagpipes atrociously, at every opportunity, and for some reason had come to live with his sister, his niece, and her husband and children in America, and was like an eccentric grandfather to them more than a great-uncle.

Sybil had gotten no further than that, but she shared the information with Michael Stanton, as he walked slowly from one portrait to the next, observing them closely. And for the first time, Sybil noticed that there was a set of bagpipes leaning against Angus MacPherson's chair in his portrait. Bettina had added that her grandmother had had a black pug named Violet, which Sybil had noticed in the dowager's portrait before. The tiara she wore in the painting was the same one Sybil had seen her wear the night of the earthquake. It was slightly concealed by her elaborate Victorian hairdo, and she was wearing several long strands of very large pearls.

Sybil didn't say anything to Michael Stanton while he looked at the portraits, other than to explain who each of them was, which she knew now from Bettina's book. She told him she had a box of photographs of them too. And then she walked him around the main floor. He stood for a long time in the dining room with his eyes closed, and when he opened them, he followed her up the grand stair-case to the bedrooms on the second floor. They toured the entire house before she took him into the sitting room off her bedroom and they sat down. He looked tired, as though he had poured all his strength and energy into what he was trying to discern.

"What do you think?" Sybil finally asked him, and he nodded thoughtfully as he looked at her.

"The spirits are incredibly strong here," he said. "I don't think I've ever been in a house quite like this. It's almost as though they're still alive here, or think they are. I can hear Angus playing the bagpipes, and the old lady talking, the children laughing, and their parents are totally benevolent spirits. The little boy who had the carriage accident is very strong here too. His spirit must have returned here to be with his family, which isn't surprising since he was so young. He's full of mischief, and I get the sense that he wants to meet your little boy. And that the others want to meet you. I think the man you saw watching you from the dining room is not ominous. He's some kind of manser-vant, who must have spent his entire career working for them here, so his spirit never left. He's a less significant member of the group."

"Are they going to stay here?" Sybil asked him uncom-fortably.

"I don't think there's any question of it," he told her honestly. "The question is, are you? They're not going anywhere. They live here, and always have. I'm not sure what part of the house they have settled in. I don't feel them strongly in the bedrooms or the upper floors. They seem to be mostly downstairs, on the main floor. Their aura is strongest in the dining room, and I think you might see them again there. They might be willing to simply leave the upper floors to you, and share the reception rooms with you. Bertrand Butterfield seems to be a very determined benevolent presence, and his wife is an extremely gentle, kind spirit, unlike her indomitable mother, who is harmless but a force to be reckoned with. And her brother, Angus, must already have been quite old when he got here. I get a sense from him that he's slightly confused."

His observations were fascinating, but it was not what Sybil wanted to hear, and how was she going to explain to Blake and her children that they would be sharing their home with the Butterfields for as long as they lived there? For a minute she hoped it was just hocus-pocus, but something very powerful told her it wasn't, and that Michael Stanton's reading of the situation, and the personalities they were dealing with, was accurate, even in the spirit world.

"I think that Bettina, their second child and oldest daughter, is the only one in the family who attained a great age," Michael said, and Sybil knew from the bank that she had died at eighty-four. "Except for Augusta and

Angus, of course," he added, "but their spirits were already old when they arrived in the house. I think Bertrand died somewhere around sixty, during the Great Depression, when they lost their money, and Gwyneth not long after, although she was a few years younger than he. I don't get the feeling that she died here. She must have passed away after the home was sold. And Bettina's daughter, whom you mentioned sold the house after her mother's death, doesn't seem to be here at all, except as a baby. I don't think she ever lived here as a child or an adult, and she seems to have no emotional tie to the house. She comes to me as foreign, French probably, and her adult life must have been there. She doesn't feel American, nor linked to the house, to me."

"Bettina said in the chapter I read last night that she moved to France shortly after Lili was born. Lili was the child of Bettina's first husband, who died in the Great War. Bettina moved to France with Lili after the war, married a Frenchman, and remained in Paris until she was widowed for the second time. She returned to San Francisco then to reclaim her parents' home and bought it back from its owners at the time, and lived the final thirty years of her life in the house. But her daughter, Lili, remained in France." Michael's psychic sense about them was amazingly accurate. "You know who all the players are now, Mrs. Gregory," he continued. "What are you going to do?"

"Do you think I will see them again?" Sybil asked, looking worried.

"I think you will. Their spirits are too present not to. They think this is still their home. They may not even understand what you're doing here."

"I'm not sure I do either," she said ruefully. "I feel like we've moved into someone else's home. It will never feel like ours, if they're attached to it this strongly."

"They're spirits, and no longer live people. You should be able to find a way to coexist. It depends on how present they wish to be, and how powerfully they make themselves felt. Spirits can either be very determined or very discreet, depending on how they react to you, and how firm you and your husband want to be about it."

"I don't want to have to fight for our turf."

"Maybe you won't have to. They're not aggressive people, most of them seem very gentle, and the children are very sweet."

"Do you think Bertrand and Gwyneth want to drive us away?" she asked him.

"I don't get that sense at all. Their energy seems very welcoming and warm. Augusta may give you a hard time"—he smiled as he said it—"but that's just who she is as a spirit, and who she was then as well. And Angus is entirely harmless, he's just an eccentric old man. I think he never married and had no children of his own."

"I'll have to talk to my husband and find out what he

thinks, if he even believes me," Sybil said thoughtfully, and she wasn't at all sure he would.

"He may have to see them himself to take it seriously," Michael suggested.

"If they show themselves to him."

"I think they will. And Magnus is aching to play with your youngest son." That worried Sybil too.

"I hope he doesn't frighten him. Charlie is terrified of ghosts, as I said before."

"Magnus won't appear as a ghost to him. They're just two little boys."

"A hundred years apart," Sybil said, still trying to sort it all out in her head. It was a lot to digest. But at least Michael had validated what she knew she'd seen, and told her a great deal more. Along with Bettina's family history, she had all the information she needed now, but she still wanted to finish the book to learn more about them. She and Blake had bought much more than a house, they had acquired a century of history, and the family that had lived there too.

"I hope you'll tell me how it all works out," he said kindly.

"I will," she said solemnly, grateful for his visit and the light he had shed on the situation they were in, which only she believed so far.

"They're a very endearing group of people, if you ever get to know them," Michael said. "My visit may have stirred them up a bit. Psychic contact from me today may bring them forward again. They can feel me, even if they don't know who I am. It may draw them to you. They can sense you too, and your interest in them. You have a very open spirit," he told Sybil, and wished her luck before he left. He told her that she was very fortunate to have drawn the Butterfields toward her own light, which he said was very attractive to spirits, who sensed other pure spirits around them. She wasn't sure that was a good thing, and she didn't know if she was ready to meet them again. She wanted to talk to Blake first.

She was quiet when the children came home from school that afternoon. She was lying on her bed, reading Bettina's book, and went to ask them how school had gone. Andy and Caroline seemed to like their new high school, and Charlie was happy at his school and said the teacher was nice, though not as nice as his teacher in New York, but he didn't know her as well yet. He went to play outside in the garden after that, and Sybil went back to her book to learn more about the Butterfields and their history.

Blake came home from the office looking tired, and said he'd had difficult meetings that afternoon with their bank, and he was happy to see Sybil at the end of his day. It had been lonely for him before they arrived in San Francisco, and he loved having his family around him again.

"What did you do today?" he asked with interest as she got dinner ready and gave him a vague, distracted answer.

"Nothing much." She was making roast beef, which was a favorite of his. He went upstairs to change from his suit into jeans, and they all came into the kitchen when she sent Charlie to get them for dinner. She wanted Blake to carve the beef, and she'd set the kitchen table with pretty place mats and flowers. But before she could ask Blake to slice the meat for them, they heard noises in the dining room that sounded like a party, voices talking and laughing, and they looked at each other, wondering who was there. All the Gregorys were in the kitchen, and there was no one else in the house.

"Did someone leave a TV on?" Blake asked, looking confused as the children shook their heads, and there was no television in the formal dining room anyway. Not knowing what else to do, Sybil opened the door into the dining room from the kitchen with a feeling of trepidation, sensing what was about to happen. One by one, she, Blake, and the kids walked into the dining room, as all the Butterfields seated at the dining room table, elegantly dressed, stopped talking and stared at them. Sybil knew what it meant and who they were, but it was too late to warn any of her family, even Blake.

"Good Lord! Who are they and what are they wearing?" Augusta said loudly, glaring at them through her lorgnette, and Angus turned to observe them with a look of surprise. He couldn't take his eyes off Sybil, who was wearing jeans and a T-shirt and ballet slippers. "Are those costumes of some kind?" Augusta asked. She was wearing a gray velvet gown with lace at the neck.

Bertrand had risen to greet them, and looked at Blake with a welcoming smile, as though they had been expected and were properly dressed. His manners were impeccable, his eyes warm, and all of the Butterfield men were in white tie and tails, as they wore to dinner every night, except Magnus, who looked immaculate in a sailor suit. Charlie, his counterpart, was wearing the corduroy pants, sweatshirt, and running shoes he had worn at school. Andy was in khakis and a sweater, and Caroline had on a miniskirt, which Augusta noted with horror. She rapped her brother's hand with her fan when he stared at her, and he laughed. He had never seen anything like it, but thought it excellent attire for a pretty girl. Gwyneth and Sybil exchanged a shy smile. Gwyneth was wearing a beautiful lavender silk gown and a diamond choker, and Sybil thought she was even more beautiful than her portrait. She had flawless porcelain skin, pale blond hair upswept in a loose chignon, and huge blue eyes similar to her mother's and Bettina's. Gwyneth turned to the butler, whom Sybil recognized, standing at attention behind the Butterfields, and Gwyneth spoke to him in the same Scottish accent as her mother, but in a gentler tone.

"Phillips, please set five places for our guests," she said

softly, and he nodded and disappeared to carry out her orders. Blake stared around the room, as did the children, trying to understand what had happened. But the Butterfields weren't frightening, they felt like friends. Blake glanced at Sybil, and she nodded to reassure him. Blake and Sybil's children weren't frightened either. They were fascinated by the Butterfields.

A moment later, Phillips reappeared and set places at the table for all five Gregorys where Gwyneth indicated as Bert chatted good-humoredly with them. The fact that they weren't dressed for dinner didn't seem to bother anyone except Augusta, who spoke under her breath to Uncle Angus. He found the women in the group delightful, whatever they were wearing. The families introduced themselves to each other, and Blake was seated between Bert and Bettina, who was a beautiful young woman. Sybil sat between Bertrand and Josiah, their oldest son. Andy was between Gwyneth and Lucy, whom he thought was the most exquisite girl he'd ever seen. She had her mother's perfect creamy skin and blond hair, and was wearing a demure white evening dress. She appeared to be about twenty, which Sybil knew from the book was the age she had been at the time of her death. Magnus looked to be six, the age he was when he died, three years after they'd bought the house. Caroline was between Lucy and her brother Charlie, who sat next to Magnus on his other side, who looked totally delighted. The two little boys hit it off immediately and were enchanted to discover they were both six.

Augusta continued to gaze at their guests through her lorgnette, with her lips pursed in disapproval and the little black pug at her feet. Angus's English bulldog was sound asleep near the fire, snoring loudly. Charlie noticed him and laughed. Magnus said the dog's name was Rupert. And his grandmother's pug was Violet.

Everyone at the table looked happy except Augusta, who rarely did anyway. She was their collective conscience and always complained about the children's manners or what they were wearing.

"I have no idea who these people are," she said in a loud whisper to her brother, as he continued to stare at Sybil and Caroline with a look of delight. He thought them an excellent addition to the meal.

"What a wonderful surprise," Bertrand said warmly to their guests around the table, which was beautifully set with silver and gleaming crystal. Everyone began to talk at once as dinner was served, and the food was delicious. Blake commented on the excellent wine. Sybil was dying to talk to Gwyneth, but they were too far apart, and she enjoyed chatting with Bert and Josiah about San Francisco and the house. She explained that they had just moved in, and had arrived from New York.

"We built the house fifteen years ago," Bert explained, which Sybil instantly calculated meant that the year was

1917 for them, exactly a hundred years before the date that night for the Gregorys. The Gregorys had somehow walked back a century when they entered the formal dining room from the kitchen. Bert and Blake talked business for part of the evening, the older children of both families were having fun with one another, and Charlie and Magnus were plotting happily about things they wanted to do together. Magnus suggested they meet to climb the trees in the garden, which sounded like fun to Charlie too. Magnus confessed to his new friend in a whisper that he wasn't allowed to, but did it frequently.

It struck Sybil as she watched them that if the year was 1917 for the Butterfields, as it appeared to be from their conversation, Magnus had been a ghost by then for twelve years, since he had died in 1905 when he was six. His age appeared to have remained fixed there, at the age he was when he died. It was an extraordinary phenomenon that Sybil wouldn't have understood if she hadn't met with Michael Stanton that day. She was less baffled and confused than the others after everything he had explained. But one thing was for sure, the Butterfields seemed to have no desire to frighten them away. They made the Gregorys feel warmly welcomed, like honored guests. And nothing about them suggested that they were ghosts—they appeared to be entirely real, normal people, although their style of dress, conversation, and manners dated back to 1917. But both families seemed to have much in common, shared interests, and enjoyed each other's company immensely, even laughing at each other's jokes.

The meal ended too soon, and Bert said quietly to Sybil and Blake that something extraordinary had happened, and he hoped they would join him and his family again very soon, the following night if they were free. No one mentioned the divergence of dates, or the fact that their two worlds had converged in an astonishingly real way that night.

"I hope they come properly dressed next time," Augusta added and harrumphed loudly, as Phillips appeared with a decanter of brandy on a silver tray, and another one of port, and Bert invited the Gregorys to join them in the living room. Blake and Sybil stood up with the others, and the entire group followed Bert and Gwyneth into the large living room, as Sybil admired Gwyneth's dress, and they chatted. But as soon as they entered the living room, the Gregorys found themselves suddenly alone. The Butterfields had disappeared, and when they glanced back into the dining room, the fire was no longer lit, the room was dark, and all signs of the meal had disappeared.

"What just happened, Dad?" Andy asked his father, and Blake looked puzzled as he stared at Sybil, and didn't know what to say to his son. And Caroline was visibly confused as well.

"I think something very strange and very wonderful

happened tonight," Blake said slowly. "We met the family who built the house and used to live here."

"And still do," Sybil said softly.

"Can we see them again?" Charlie asked, looking anxious. "Magnus said he'd come to my room to play tomorrow." And he had promised to show Magnus his videogames, and how to play them.

"Then maybe he will," Sybil said gently, as the Gregorys walked into the kitchen, still confused. Their roast beef was in the oven, vastly overcooked by then, and Blake looked at Sybil as their children left the kitchen and went upstairs to their rooms to do their homework. It had been a wonderful evening, and they all hoped they'd see their new friends again. No one was upset by having met them, or afraid of them. It had been a positive experience for all.

"What just happened here?" Blake asked her, shocked and mystified.

"They still live here," Sybil said calmly, and she sat down at the kitchen table with Blake to tell him what Michael Stanton had said.

"They're such nice people," he said afterward. "How is this possible? They thought it was 1917 tonight, and it's a hundred years later for us."

"Maybe it's some kind of gift that life is giving us," Sybil said thoughtfully. "We see history through their eyes and they see the distant future in us."

"Are you frightened?" he asked her. What had just

happened had shaken him, despite how enjoyable it was. And he'd really liked Bert, they saw eye to eye on many subjects they had discussed.

"I'm not afraid anymore," she said quietly. "I was at first." And then they laughed about Augusta and Angus, and talked about the children, and Gwyneth and Bert. A little while later, Blake and Sybil went upstairs, after she'd thrown out the burned roast beef and put away their unused plates. There was no way to explain it, or tell anyone else, but all of them agreed, when they said good night to their children, that it had been a magical evening, and they hoped it would happen again. Sybil was almost certain it would. This was only the beginning of a friendship between two families that had been determined by the fates, and would ultimately bless both. She could feel it deep in her soul.

Chapter 5

Sybil devoted the next morning, after Blake and the children left, to finishing Bettina's book. The Butterfields' history was all there. Josiah had died a hero's death in the First World War. They had lost their entire fortune in the Crash of '29, and Bertrand's bank had closed, which bruised his spirit badly, along with everything else. Their daughter Lucy died that year as well, before her father's death, which had added to his sense of devastating loss and grief. He had lost three of his four children by then, which shattered Gwyneth too.

Bert had fought valiantly to maintain their home, but their greatly reduced circumstances and Lucy's death had been too much for him. He had died in his sleep of a heart attack a year later, in 1930, at the age of sixty, just as Michael had guessed. And Gwyneth had lost too much by then, and too many people she had loved. She had sunk into a deep depression, and Bettina had returned from Europe to comfort her and help her sell the house. They had sold many of their valuables, some art, and Gwyneth's and her mother's jewelry. Their whole life had changed.

After the house sold, she had gone back to Europe with Bettina, and lived with her and Bettina's second husband, Louis de Lambertin, who was a kind man, and Bettina's daughter, Lili, who was twelve years old then. Gwyneth died two years later in 1932, during a hard winter, of pneumonia, like Lucy three years before. She had lost her will to live when Bert died and she sold the house. It was a sad end to their story, but she had no desire to live without him and never adjusted to her life in France, with no home of her own and only her daughter's charity to support her.

Bettina and Louis had no children of their own, and he had adopted his stepdaughter, who grew up more French than American, and had no memory of the States, only of France. Lili's late father's family had no interest in her, nor contact with her, and had never desired any. Louis and his family had embraced Lili as their own. Bettina spoke French fluently, and spoke it with Lili.

The book said that Lili had been a nurse during the Second World War, and when it was over, she married a doctor she had worked with, Raphael Saint Martin. They had a son, Samuel, a year later in 1946. Lili would have been twenty-eight by then, Sybil calculated, as she read the details she had only skimmed before.

Bettina's husband Louis died of causes she didn't mention, in 1950, when she was fifty-four. He had been eighteen years older than she was, so it was a reasonable age to die at the time. He divided his considerable fortune between his widow and adopted daughter, and two months after his death, Bettina had returned to San Francisco and bought her parents' home from the family that had purchased it from Gwyneth when Bert died twenty years before. In her book she said that she had been happy there until her final days, when she wrote the book, in 1980. She wrote that for thirty years, she had been content in the home where she'd grown up, and the obituary that had come with the material from the bank indicated that Bettina Butterfield de Lambertin had died peacefully in her sleep six months later, at eighty-four. There was a photograph of her with the obituary, and Sybil noticed that she looked like an older version of Gwyneth.

In the book, Bettina said that once she moved back in 1950, Lili had come to visit her in San Francisco every few years at first, but she had been busy with her husband, Raphael, and son, Samuel, who was only four when Bettina moved back to San Francisco. She said she had seen Samuel only a few times as a young child after she left France. She mentioned that Lili had health problems and later on could no longer make the journey to the States. At the end of her life, Bettina hadn't seen Samuel since he was a child, nor Lili in several years. Sybil wondered if Lili had even been able to come for her mother's funeral. The bank seemed to know that Lili had died ten years after her mother.

Sybil felt a wistful sorrow for all of them as she closed Bettina's book. They had been so closely tied to each other, and so many things had happened to them over the years. Some of them were events that one couldn't avoid in life, and others tragic accidents that must have marked them forever, like Magnus dying at six, and Josiah and Bettina's first husband getting killed in the war. It reminded Sybil that the night she and her family had dinner with them had been January 1917 for the Butterfields, exactly a hundred years before the year the Gregorys were living in. In the Butterfields' world, America had not yet entered the war, and Josiah was still alive.

She wondered, what if she or Blake could warn them of what would happen next, and change the course of their destinies? Could one do that a century later? They were meeting in a neutral space in time. And did Josiah have a choice then? What if he didn't go to war? His family would have been proud of him when he went. And he would have been considered a coward and a disgrace if he had shirked his responsibility and stayed home. There seemed to be no way to alter the course fate had designed for them, but it was so painful knowing what would come and the losses that would occur. And a hundred years later, no matter what Sybil tried to warn them of, they would all be dead anyway. As far as Sybil knew, the only one who could be alive now was Samuel Saint Martin, Lili's son, and any children he might have. The Butterfields by name had all died out, and their bloodline had continued somewhere in France.

Sybil was still thinking about it when she decided to try to dine with the Butterfields again that night. Blake and the children came home to find their evening clothes laid out on their beds, where Sybil had left them that afternoon, and when she walked into Charlie's room to find something for him to wear to dinner, like a blazer and gray slacks, she saw Magnus there, playing marbles with her son. She gave a start, and then all three of them laughed. She was happy to meet Magnus again, despite his dirty face and grimy hands. He looked like he'd been playing in the garden all afternoon.

"What are you two up to?" she asked, smiling at both boys and sitting down on Charlie's bed, as though Magnus were any ordinary friend.

"He's teaching me to play marbles," Charlie said happily, delighted with the promised visit. Magnus had said the night before at dinner that he would come to play with him the next day, and Sybil was pleased to see that he had. There was a bond between the two families now that even time could not displace. "I'm going to show him my videogames after this." Sybil couldn't help wondering how that would work. How would Magnus adapt to games that were a hundred years ahead of his time? It was an interesting turn of events.

Alicia wandered into the room with milk and cookies

for Charlie, while Sybil watched them, and she asked her for a glass of milk and cookies for herself as well. Alicia looked surprised and returned with them a few minutes later. As soon as she left the room, Sybil handed them to Magnus, and he guzzled the milk and ate the cookies like any normal playmate of Charlie's. There was nothing ghostly about him. But Alicia had been totally unaware of him and didn't see him, which Sybil found interesting too.

Charlie asked him about the secret passages in the house, but Magnus said he didn't know where they were, if there were any.

She took out Charlie's blazer, gray slacks, and a shirt and navy tie and laid them on the bed, as the boys looked at her quizzically.

"What's that for?" Charlie asked her. It wasn't Christmas or Thanksgiving. "Why do I have to get dressed up?"

"I thought we'd try to have dinner with Magnus's family tonight," she said easily, and Magnus grinned happily.

"My grandma's in a really bad mood, though," he warned them. "Uncle Angus's dog, Rupert, ate her embroidery this morning, and she said she was going to boil him for dinner. I don't think she really will, though. She usually likes him, but she was really mad about her embroidery. She was making napkins for my mother, and he ate them all. And she said Uncle Angus playing the bagpipes gave her a sick headache." He used the terms of his time to refer to common ailments, and it reminded Sybil of Victorian novels she had loved to read when she was young. "He plays really bad," he said about his great-uncle, and all three of them laughed. "My mother says he gives her a headache too."

Sybil left them to their games then, as Charlie started to introduce Magnus to his PlayStation, and Magnus was fascinated by the intricacy of it. The two boys were squealing with excitement and shouting when she moved on to Caroline's room, and ran into Alicia in the hall.

"Is he all right?" She looked concerned about the violent noises emanating from his room. She didn't know the children yet, but it didn't sound right to her.

"He's fine. He just gets a little overexcited when he plays with his PlayStation. He just got a new one for Christmas." She wondered if she should tell her that he had an imaginary friend, in case she heard him talking to Magnus, but she decided not to mention it yet.

She laid Caroline's only long dress out on her bed; they had bought the dress when her best friend's mother remarried in New York six months before. Sybil wanted her family to look respectable for the Butterfields that night, to make up for how unsuitably dressed they'd been the night before. She didn't want them to think they were savages, and she hoped they'd reappear since they had invited the Gregorys to join them again that night. She hoped they'd meant it. She thought about renting tails for

Blake and Andy, so they could be dressed as the Butter-field men were, but instead she took their dinner jackets out and laid them on their beds, with their cummerbunds, suspenders, dress shirts, and black satin bow ties. Andy had just gotten his first tuxedo for a deb ball he'd gone to before Christmas, for the sister of one of his friends. Sybil was sure their dinner jackets would be enough to satisfy even Augusta.

And then she dove into her own closet and came out with a black velvet dress with a big white satin ruffle and a low back. She'd had it for a year and she loved it. She had been saving it for a special occasion, and this was it. She felt a little crazy getting everything ready, and Blake looked at her in confusion when he saw his dinner jacket on the bed when he got home from the office.

"Are we going to something black tie tonight? You didn't tell me."

"I thought we'd dress for dinner with them tonight, so they know we're respectable."

"Them?"

"The Butterfields," she said cautiously, wondering how Blake would react to wearing black tie for no special reason, and her acting as though dressing up for a family of ghosts was normal. But maybe it was for them now. She wasn't quite sure how to react to it herself.

"Oh," Blake said, and then sat down on their bed, next to his tuxedo. He didn't object, he just looked confused.

"Are we going to do this every night now?" He couldn't imagine wearing a tuxedo on a daily basis, and didn't want to, even though the previous evening with them had been fascinating and enjoyable.

"I don't know. This is new for me too. Magnus came to play with Charlie today. They had a good time together. He said his grandmother was in a bad mood because Uncle Angus's dog ate her embroidery." Blake didn't know whether to laugh or cry as he listened.

"I think I need a drink. Have we gone crazy? Are we in *The Twilight Zone* here? This is beginning to feel like a weird movie." And yet when he'd been with the Butterfields it felt totally comfortable, and even pleasant. He had liked talking to Bert on a variety of subjects. Their ideas and their opinions were not so different, although times had changed radically since Bert had been a banker a hundred years before. But good economic principles still held up over time. "What if we get all dressed up and they don't show up?"

"Then we'll look great having pizza in the kitchen," she said, smiling at him. "But I think they will. They invited us to dinner tonight. And we were all dressed like such a mess last night."

"They didn't seem to mind," he said, seeming relaxed about it. "Except the grandmother, of course. But she probably won't approve of us tonight either." And then he shook his head again. "Listen to us. They're real to us, Syb. Has everyone forgotten they're ghosts?"

"Very real ghosts," she reminded him. "And we happen to be living together. I was thinking about it today, when I finished Bettina's book about the family history. There's so much we know that they don't, about what's going to happen to them. It doesn't seem fair. Why can't we warn them?"

"Because you can't change destiny, life isn't fair, and they're already dead, for whatever reason, no matter what we tell them."

Sybil nodded and knew it was true. "They probably have more to teach us than we can teach them, even though they don't know our future. But we can use them as examples. It's so strange being trapped in a time warp, yet when we're with them, it feels so right," Sybil said as she headed for the bath to get ready for dinner.

"I hope they show up," he called after her, as he took his dinner jacket to his dressing room, and then realized that the space had once been Bert's. He wondered where Bert dressed now. He had looked impeccable the night before.

They were both in their evening clothes when they rounded up their children, who had grudgingly gotten dressed up for the evening to indulge their mother. Magnus had left Charlie an hour before, dazzled by playing with the PlayStation. Charlie told his mother that

Magnus had been good at it, for a beginner. And they all headed to the dining room at seven-thirty, guessing it was the time for dinner. The room seemed quiet at first, as they approached it, and Blake suspected no one was there, but as they reached the door, they saw that the Butterfields were getting seated. Bert and Gwyneth smiled broadly when they saw the Gregorys and waved them into the room. Augusta examined each of them closely when they walked in, and Sybil and Blake and their children greeted her formally. Angus teased them about how respectable they looked.

"Bought some decent clothes, I see. Lovely dress," he said to Sybil, nearly fawning over her when he saw the low back and admired her slim figure, and his sister gave him a wicked look and told him to sit down.

All the young people were delighted to see one another, and the Gregorys took the same places as the night before. Phillips bowed politely to Sybil and held her seat for her. She felt like a queen as she sat down and Bert complimented her on her dress, as Augusta made a comment about their being informally dressed for dinner. At the time, white tie and tails were the appropriate dinner dress, and black tie was considered informal, but they passed muster with everyone else.

The talk that night turned to the war in Europe, and whether or not President Wilson would allow the United States to get involved. The war had been raging in Europe for three years by then, and America had stayed out of it so far, much to everyone's relief, and particularly Gwyneth's.

"You must be worried about Andy too," she said kindly. Sybil didn't know what to say. It was a hundred years later, and there was no risk to him. Only to Josiah.

"He's applying to college for the fall," Sybil said and changed the subject. He had three more weeks to apply, and then they'd have to wait till March for the results. He had applied to Princeton, Harvard, Yale, and Dartmouth. He was thinking of applying to Stanford too, but didn't think he'd get in. Two of his friends and he had become interested in the University of Edinburgh, which was an unusual choice. Andy liked everything about it except the weather, and going to school in Europe appealed to him. Andy mentioned it at dinner and Uncle Angus heartily encouraged him.

"Wonderful school. I went there myself. Much livelier than Oxford or Cambridge. You should apply. Use my name if you like." Andy smiled at that, and couldn't imagine they'd remember him unless he had built the school, but decided to look at it online again that night. He was considering Oxford, but the University of Edinburgh sounded like more fun.

"Thank you, sir. I'll read up on it again tonight," Andy promised.

"Good lad," Angus said, and complained that his sister

hadn't allowed his dog in the dining room, since Rupert was in disgrace for the napkins he'd destroyed.

Caroline flirted with Josiah, and Andy was extremely attentive to Lucy, who had worn a gauzy pink dress that made her look like an angel with her fair skin and pale blond curls. Blake watched his two older children carefully. However agreeable this was, he didn't want them losing track of reality and falling in love with ghosts. He was going to mention it to Sybil later that night.

The adults enjoyed a lively conversation, and Gwyneth and Sybil got to chat for a few minutes. Gwyneth was fascinated that Sybil had studied both architecture and design, curated museum shows, and wrote articles for newspapers. Blake had been bragging about her dedication during dinner, and Gwyneth was wide-eyed with admiration and in awe of Sybil's talents. She was artistic herself, but had no real outlet for it.

"It must be so wonderful to work," Gwyneth whispered, and her mother stepped in immediately, having overheard her.

"Don't be ridiculous, Gwyneth. What would you want to do? Take in washing? Be a governess? Leave work to the men, and do something more useful with your time." Augusta added that Gwyneth used to do lovely watercolors but had stopped when she had the children. And Gwyneth added modestly that they weren't very good.

"I don't have time," she said to her mother.

"Nonsense, they're old enough now. You should take it up again." But Gwyneth was much more excited to hear about what Sybil did. She thought it remarkably brave of her, and she was impressed by the way Sybil expressed her opinions without offending anyone, and remained feminine at the same time. She thought her very modern. The two women had formed an almost instant rapport, and Gwyneth thanked her for allowing Magnus to come and play that afternoon. "He had a wonderful time," she told her new friend, and Sybil said he was welcome whenever he wanted to visit them.

They all lingered over coffee and dessert that night, not wanting the meal to end. Gwyneth told Sybil that at formal dinners the women normally went into the drawing room at the end of the meal and left the men to their cigars. But with close friends, they no longer did. It was a practice Sybil had heard about but never seen, except in old films.

Bert said they might go to their home in Woodside soon for a few days to ride their horses. They kept them there, and he was thinking of getting a new motorcar, a Cadillac, and asked Blake's advice about it, who admitted he knew very little about cars but would love to see it when Bert got it, and then realized he never would, because it was long gone.

"I'd love to learn to drive," Bettina whispered to Andy, and he smiled at her.

"You should. My sister does," he said matter-of-factly, not thinking of how rare it would be for Bettina in 1917, and considered quite racy for her as a woman.

"At sixteen?" She looked shocked. "Did you teach her?" she asked hopefully, and he didn't want to explain about driver's ed in school, so he said yes. Bettina didn't go to school—she was twenty-one—but when she was younger, she had been tutored at home in languages, history, literature, and the feminine arts, such as drawing and needlework and writing poetry. Her father had said proudly at dinner that she wrote very well, and might write a book one day. She wanted to write a family history, she said, even if she didn't publish it. It jolted Sybil to realize she had just read it.

"If she does, she'll wind up an old maid," her grandmother predicted. "Women do not need to write books. Men don't like it." She was very definite about it, although there were women authors of their day.

Eventually the time came when Phillips appeared with the tray of after-dinner drinks, and they followed him into the living room, as Blake explained to Bert the concept of the company he was running. Gwyneth and Sybil talked about their children, and the young people followed, talking and laughing, with Augusta and Angus bringing up the rear. And just as they had the night before, when they reached the living room, which Sybil had filled with flowers for them, the Butterfields disappeared and the

Gregorys stood looking at one another, alone in the room. They had done it again. No one was surprised this time, and they walked slowly upstairs, talking about their new friends.

"This is really strange, Mom," Andy said, turning to his mother on the stairs with a troubled expression. Sybil didn't attempt to deny it.

"I know it is. Things like this happen apparently, but they're hard to explain." No one disagreed with her, but they had all enjoyed the evening, even more than the first one. And being appropriately dressed had made them feel more at ease.

When Blake and Sybil got to their room, he took off his dinner jacket and stared at her, as though seeing someone new. She looked exceptionally beautiful, and he hadn't seen her in an evening gown in ages. It was very romantic.

"You look spectacular tonight," he said, as he took her in his arms and kissed her. And Sybil smiled as he held her.

"You look very handsome too." She had always loved seeing him in evening clothes, and thought he was very dashing.

"Maybe they have the right idea, dressing for dinner every night," Blake said, as he unzipped her dress and she stepped out of it. He admired her body in the soft light in the room, with the moonlight coming through the window. He wanted to say how strange it was to be dining with ghosts, but the odd thing was that it didn't feel wrong, just different. It felt right to both of them, and they were both happy in their new home and new city. But all he could think about now was his wife, whatever century they were in. It really didn't matter to him, he loved her whatever year it was.

Chapter 6

The day after the Gregorys' second dinner with the Butterfields turned out to be hectic. Sybil had to do errands with
Caroline to buy things she needed for school, Blake
needed her to do some things for him, *The New York Times*
had called her and wanted an article on short notice, and
there were details to organize for the Brooklyn show. A
museum in Chicago called her about a show they were
considering and wanted her to curate in November. Alicia,
the housekeeper, was sick, and Sybil had to go to the
supermarket, since there was nothing to eat in the house,
in case the Butterfields didn't appear that night.

She encouraged them all to dress for dinner again, but
Blake couldn't find his second tuxedo shirt, and Andy had
misplaced his studs and cuff links the night before. And
she realized that the dress she wanted to wear was in New
York. It also occurred to her that if she had to wear an
evening dress for dinner every night, she was going to run
short. She didn't have that many, and had few occasions
to wear them.

"Do we really have to do this again?" Blake complained,

as he put on the same shirt as the night before, after she pressed it for him. "I brought work home from the office."

"I have work to do too," she said, after lending a set of Blake's cuff links to Andy. "This is fun. And I don't want to hurt their feelings and not show up. That would be rude."

"Sybil, they're ghosts, for chrissake. They're not going anywhere, and they can't expect us to do this every night. They'll get tired of us too." Blake felt strongly that they needed a real life too, with living people. He had met several men he liked at work and wanted to have over for dinner.

She rushed them downstairs, and they arrived right on time. There were no sounds from the dining room, and when they reached the doorway, the room was dark, there was no fire in the grate, the table wasn't set, and the Butterfields were not there. All of the Gregorys were unhappy as they walked into the kitchen, and Sybil scared up something to eat, grateful that she'd made it to the supermarket that day.

"I'm sorry. I don't know what happened." Magnus hadn't come to play that afternoon either, and Charlie looked glum.

They didn't come the next day either, and the morning after that, Sybil called Michael Stanton.

"They disappeared," she said sadly, and described the evenings they'd spent together, and the two nights they hadn't shown up. "Do you suppose they've moved out?"

He laughed at the idea. "Not likely. They've been in the house for over a hundred years. Spirits do that, they fade away and get weak for a while, and then they come back stronger than ever. They need to recharge. Don't worry. They'll be back."

The Butterfields were gone for another week, and all of the Gregorys started to miss them. The children talked about them at dinner, and Blake said it might be for the best, although he missed Bert too. Sybil wrote her next article, but thought about them at night. And she went through the box of old photographs. They felt like old friends now. The Gregorys had gone back to eating dinner in jeans and old sweaters, moccasins, flip-flops, and bare feet. It wasn't elegant, but their meals in the kitchen were casual and brief, and they talked about what they did daily. They also had dinner with a couple from Blake's office. Sybil wasn't crazy about them, but it was a good thing to do. Andy and Caro were busy with their home-work, and she and Blake were both catching up with work after dinner. Only Charlie was bored without Magnus to play with. He looked unhappy, and even Alicia noticed it with some concern.

"I think he has imaginary friend. I hear him talking to him when there's no one in the room with him," she said, concerned. "He no play anymore with him, though," she reported to Sybil, and she smiled.

"Sometimes he takes a little time off." And she realized

then that that was what the Butterfields had done. They were on a time out.

They'd been gone for nine days when Sybil heard voices in Charlie's room one afternoon after school, and wondered if he'd brought someone home. She opened the door and poked her head in, and he and Magnus were playing videogames and shrieking with delight. She laughed when she saw them and waved at Magnus. They were back, and she hoped they'd see the whole family for dinner that night.

She checked on the boys again a little later, and they were gone. She glanced out the window and didn't see them outside, so she assumed they were somewhere on the grounds. There were a lot of places to play in the garden and around the house. She wasn't worried about them, and she went to her office upstairs to work on her computer. It was six o'clock when she came back downstairs to her bedroom. Blake was home by then, and she had just asked him how his day was when they both heard heavy pounding in Blake's dressing room. Blake went to see what it was, and Sybil followed him, and they both realized the sounds came from behind the wall. He opened his closets and the sound grew stronger, and then they could hear the boys calling for help from the other side of the closet wall.

"Charlie? Where are you?" his father shouted at him, as Sybil listened and could hear Magnus shouting too. They were calling out and pounding alternately, and she could hear that her son was panicked. "Where are you?" Blake said loudly next to the heavy wood paneling so they could hear him.

"I don't know. It's dark." They could barely hear him. "We're in the secret passage," he yelled again after a minute, afraid they'd get in trouble, but even more afraid now not to get out.

"Great," he said with a look over his shoulder at Sybil. "How did you get in there?" he called back.

"There was a door in a closet on the third floor. There's a staircase, but there's no handle on this side, and there's no way out from downstairs. We tried."

"Okay. I'll get you out in a minute." Blake grabbed a flashlight he kept in a drawer and headed for the back stairs, and shouted at Sybil over his shoulder, "Keep talking to them." He dashed up the stairs to the third floor, where the guest bedrooms were, and checked every closet. There was none with a door at the back of it, and Blake was starting to worry. He was thinking about calling the fire department when he checked one closet for a second time, and saw the thin outline of a door. It wouldn't release when he pressed it, there was no knob, and it looked painted shut. He turned to go back downstairs to call the fire department, and found Bert standing right behind him with a frown. He had appeared from nowhere, and startled Blake.

"Now what are those two up to?" Bert said with a rueful look at Blake, who was happy to see him, after their hiatus, and particularly now with the boys trapped behind the wall.

"They found some secret passage behind the wall in one of the closets. Charlie says they got in from up here." Bert beckoned to him to follow, and led him to another closet that was used for storage. At the very back, they found a door. Bert tried it and it was jammed. They needed something to pry it open, and the two men looked at each other, trying to decide what to do next.

"I never told my boys about this because I knew they'd wind up stuck in it one day," Bert said to Blake. "It's not on the plans. It serves no useful purpose, except for a fast escape. Our builder thought it would be fun to add it, to use if we were ever under an attack of some kind."

"I think I saw a crowbar downstairs. I'll run down and get it," Blake offered and Bert stopped him.

"Never mind, I can take care of it," he said, laughing. "I'll put my full weight against it when I get them back up here, and when we get them out, we can both box their ears." And as soon as he said it, he was gone. He had gone right through the wall, while standing there, talking to Blake, and he shouted back from the other side, "I hear them. I'll be back in a minute."

"They're on the floor below," Blake told him. "Sybil's talking to them."

"It's filthy in here," Bert said in a tone of disgust, and then stopped talking. A minute later, Sybil could hear Bert talking to the boys on the other side of the wall, and he shouted to her so she could hear him. "I've got them. Blake is waiting upstairs. You'll have Charlie back in a minute," he reassured her, and she could hear their voices fading as Bert walked them back up the stairs, and then he called out to Blake in the closet where he was waiting for them to emerge. "Stand back," Bert warned him, and Blake took a big step out of the closet. An instant later Bert burst through the stuck door. He didn't do his walk-through-walls trick, since he had to get Charlie out too. A moment later the four of them were standing amid the splintered wood of the door, with two of the filthiest boys Blake had ever seen, and they both looked scared stiff. Bert was almost as dirty as they were, and didn't look pleased.

"What were you two thinking?" he asked them. "What if we hadn't found you, or didn't hear you? You could have been stuck in there for weeks. And I'm sure there are bats in there," he said with an ominous look, and both boys started to cry. The two men repressed a smile, now that they had them safely in hand.

"Mr. Butterfield is right," Blake told Charlie. "There could have been a well or a trap door. You could get killed." Then he realized that only his son could. Magnus was already dead, but he was every bit as frightened as any other six-year-old boy. Blake made a mental note to have the entrance to the passage sealed off so they couldn't do it again.

"You both need a bath," Bert said to the two blackened faces. "Magnus, I want you to apologize to Charlie's father for doing something dangerous with your friend. You'll have dinner in your room tonight." Bert sounded stern but loving, and Magnus hung his head when he apologized to Blake. By then, Sybil had come upstairs and gasped when she saw how grimy they were. And Bert looked just as bad.

"How long were you in there?" she asked, relieved to see them, after she thanked Bert for rescuing them.

"A long time," Charlie answered, and both boys cast furtive looks at each other. It had been fun until it got scary and they couldn't get out.

The five of them headed back downstairs, and Alicia saw them when they reached the second floor, or she saw Blake and Sybil with Charlie. She couldn't see Magnus with Bert, but the Gregorys acted as though they were talking to more than just one another, and she stared at Charlie.

"What you do up there?" she asked Charlie.

"They found a secret passage," Blake said, since he could see Magnus clearly and was referring to both boys.

"You lucky you no find ghosts in there," she said, wagging a finger at Charlie, and went back to the kitchen, and they all laughed after she left. Sybil led Charlie straight to the bathroom to put him in the bath, and Bert chatted with Blake for a minute, then apologized again, as Magnus waited for him meekly.

"That was a very effective trick you managed," Blake complimented Bert with a grin, and he laughed.

"I don't do it often, only in emergencies. It's very tiring and requires a lot of concentration," he said seriously.

"Could Magnus have gotten out that way?" Blake was fascinated, and Bert shook his head.

"He's not old enough, I think. He's never been able to do it, fortunately. That's all we need, a six-year-old who can walk through walls." Blake was silent for a minute, thinking about it.

"We missed you," Blake said. "It's nice to see you. We were afraid you weren't coming back," he admitted.

"We were in Woodside. We never stay down there for long." Blake wondered when they had sold that house, and who lived there now. It had been their country home a long time ago, and Bert had said it was where they kept their horses. He and Gwyneth were excellent riders and so were their children. He mentioned that Gwyneth rode sidesaddle and Augusta had been a terrific rider in her day, although she no longer rode. "Dinner tomorrow night?" he asked, and Blake nodded with a look of relief. He was so pleased that they'd returned, even if the boys got into mischief together.

"We'd love it," Blake accepted with pleasure, and Bert

waved as he escorted Magnus down the grand staircase, holding him by one ear. Halfway down the stairs, they both disappeared.

Blake wandered into the bathroom where Sybil was scrubbing Charlie in the enormous tub, and he was telling her how scared they had been.

"I don't want you doing anything like that again," his father scolded him, "or we won't let you play with Magnus anymore."

"I promise," he said, looking clean and subdued, as Sybil lifted him out of the tub and toweled him off.

"Bert said they were in Woodside all week," he told Sybil, and she nodded. There had been a few mentions of it in Bettina's book, but Bettina had said they had sold the property after the crash and brought the horses back to a stable in Marin County, which was more convenient for them to ride whenever they wanted. She hadn't said much about the house in Woodside, and didn't seem to remember it well, or care much about it.

They had dinner in their kitchen that night, and Charlie told the others about his big adventure. He said he had been with Magnus, and Andy and Caro were happy to hear they were back.

"They invited us to dinner tomorrow night," Blake told them, and everyone was pleased. Blake mentioned to Sybil that he had to give a business dinner in a few weeks with some of his new partners. He wanted to ask Bert about it, to make sure that the plan met with their approval too, and didn't interfere with them. He didn't intend to give a business dinner with Augusta staring at his associates through her lorgnette, although he assumed that his guests wouldn't see her, but he and Sybil would. Alicia not being able to see them suggested that no one outside the family would be able to. It appeared to be a privilege reserved only for them.

Bert laughed when he asked him the following night when they dined together for the first time in ten days.

"Of course you can give a dinner! It's *your* house!"

"Well, not really. You lived here first, and you still do," Blake said respectfully with a grin.

"But we can accommodate you whenever you want. We don't want to interfere with your life," Bert said kindly. "Just let us know and we'll go to Woodside for the night. The air will do us good." It was really as though they were alive. They acted like it, and they looked it to Blake and Sybil and their children. It was the oddest sensation being with them, just like ordinary people, but knowing that they weren't really there. Blake was learning that they were only visible to family and people they were close to and felt at ease with, and only within the house or the grounds. They weren't visible even to the Gregorys beyond that. They existed in a very specific, limited dimension, and yet it defied space and time. It was a phenomenon Blake couldn't explain but accepted. "Just let me know when. I'll keep my mother-in-law busy." He smiled at Blake. "What sort of guests?" He was curious about them and the other parts of Blake's life.

"They're my associates. What's referred to as 'geeks' nowadays. Men who are experts in technology. It's a form of communicating using complex formulas. I'm the finance guy. I don't always understand what they do myself."

"I'm sure it's beyond me too," Bert said. Angus had overheard them discussing a party, and leapt in immediately.

"Happy to play the bagpipes for you, dear boy. It always adds some life to a party," he said jovially, as Magnus made a horrible face and pretended to plug his ears, and the others laughed. And then Angus turned to Andy and asked if he had applied to the University of Edinburgh, and Andy was serious in response.

"I did. I really like it. I sent in my application about a week ago, right before the deadline. We'll see how it goes." He had no idea if he'd get in. And his two friends had applied too.

"Wonderful place," Angus told him. "I've never been so happy in my life as I was there. No women at the school in my day, of course, but they started accepting them twenty-five years ago, in 1892. You'll have fun." Andy was stunned when he heard the year and did the math, as

Angus continued to reminisce. "I was engaged twice while I was there, to local girls," he chuckled.

"How many times have you been engaged, Uncle Angus?" his great-nephew Josiah asked him, and Angus thought about it for a minute before he answered.

"Oh, dozens, easily . . . maybe forty or fifty. I used to get engaged at least once a year. Things have slowed down a little lately," he said with a look of regret as the others laughed, even his sister.

"You were a menace," Augusta scolded him. "You nearly killed our poor mother with all your cavorting around and misbehaving and chasing after women. And most of the time, you *weren't* engaged," she reminded him, and Angus looked nostalgic as she said it, which made them laugh more.

"Those were the good days." And he still had a wicked gleam in his eye whenever he looked at Sybil or her daughter. Sybil had worn a strapless red satin evening gown that night. It was old but pretty, and molded her figure. Caroline had worn a short black cocktail dress that showed off her legs.

"Are you a dancer?" Augusta had asked Caroline innocently when they walked in, and Caro said she wasn't but had gone to ballet class when she was little.

"I thought that might be a tutu," she said, referring to her dress, and Caroline blushed while the others giggled. The comment was typical of their grandmother, who didn't approve of new fashions, or anything that showed an ankle or a bit of leg.

*

After that, they had dinner together several nights in a row, and they were growing familiar with each other. The teasing and jokes were more familial, and Andy had started treating Bettina like a sister, although he still had a noticeable crush on Lucy, whose real age would have been much younger in 1917, but her spirit seemed to have settled on the age she had died. But whatever her age, Andy was sensible about it and knew a romance with her wasn't possible or realistic. He loved her fragile beauty and worried about her health, and brought her books he thought she'd like, particularly poetry, which was her favorite form of literature.

She was so delicate and so frail she seemed like a porcelain doll to him, and on days when she didn't feel strong enough to go out in the garden, he came home from school and read poetry to her. She loved the work of Elizabeth Barrett Browning, and sometimes Josiah teased him about it. The two young men got along well too. Josiah wasn't dating anyone at the moment, and Andy hadn't met any girls he liked at school yet, just boys he played sports with, so they hung out together sometimes when Andy came home from school.

Josiah was beginning to treat Caroline like a sister too.

Although heartrendingly pretty, she was only sixteen and he was twenty-three. His mother had delicately pointed out that she was too young for him. And at sixteen she wouldn't even be "out" yet, in society, for two more years, so she wasn't fair game. He reluctantly agreed and said "Maybe in two years." His mother hoped he'd be married by then, since he was old enough, and worked at his father's bank. But no well-born young woman of their acquaintance had snagged his heart yet. Caroline was much more exciting and more daring than the girls he knew. But Josiah understood that she came from another century and, like Andy, he was sensible. He had been engaged two years before, but it hadn't worked out.

*

Sybil helped Blake organize his business dinner. They invited eight couples and hired a caterer to serve Thai food. They had told their guests to come dressed casually, which Sybil thought would mean slacks and a pretty silk shirt, or short fun wool dresses, or miniskirts and boots for the women, since the techie crowd was very young, and she was shocked when all the men showed up in T-shirts and jeans or jogging pants with running shoes, and the women in jeans and sandals with sweatshirts and no makeup. It was a far cry from their elegant dinners in the same room with the Butterfields. But the evening was interesting. The right people had come, and Blake was pleased, and said there were at least four young high-tech billionaires in the room, in addition to the two founders of his firm. He hoped he'd be one of them one day, although Sybil always told him she was happy as they were. She didn't know what she'd do with a plane and a boat, a house in Atherton or Belvedere, and houses in the Hamptons and the Caribbean. They lived in a mansion and had a perfect life, with great children, and they loved each other. That was enough for her. But Blake was more ambitious than that.

*

Several times during the evening, their guests asked if they'd seen any ghosts yet. The historical appearance of the house looked as though it would lend itself to that. Blake and Sybil answered immediately that they hadn't, and changed the subject before anyone could pursue it. They didn't want anyone guessing or making a joke of it. And they felt deeply protective of their new friendship with the Butterfields.

The food served by the caterer Sybil had hired was excellent. Blake had selected some very fine Napa Valley wines to go with it, and everyone was pleased. They were in awe of the Gregorys' home. Several people asked about the house's history and how they'd found it. It was so elegant and impeccably put together that people assumed they'd paid a fortune for it, which they hadn't.

As Blake and Sybil looked down the long dining table at each other, they both found they missed the Butterfields. Their dinners with them were more elegant and more fun. And as brilliant as the "geeks" from Blake's business were, many of them were socially awkward and not the best conversationalists unless they were talking business, money, or high-tech. And Sybil didn't find the women very interesting either. They talked about their planes, their workout programs, or their kids.

It made them both laugh afterward when they admitted to each other that they had more fun with the family of ghosts they lived with. But Blake was satisfied that the evening had been a success. He thanked Sybil for doing it so nicely, and as they got undressed and discussed the evening, it seemed amazing to both of them that their best friends in San Francisco were a family that had been ghosts for nearly a century.

Chapter 7

In February, Sybil had to go back to New York to do some prep work at the Brooklyn Museum for the modern design show she would be curating for them in the fall. She wanted to start selecting pieces and contacting other museums for iconic items she needed on loan. She already had a huge research file of what she wanted in the show. In some ways it was good to be back in the cultural mecca of New York. San Francisco was an easy city and a less pressured life, but the cultural resources there were much more limited since it was smaller. It energized and inspired her to be back in New York, but it surprised her to find that the apartment in Tribeca seemed tiny to her now, and no longer felt as much like home. She missed their enormous new house after a few days. She planned to be away for a week.

She called Blake and the children every night, and they hadn't seen the Butterfields since she left. She had talked to Gwyneth about the trip at dinner, and Gwyneth had been wistful, saying how much she wished she could work, but it wasn't even an option for her. She said that none of the women she knew worked, and Bert would never let her.

Gwyneth was four years older than Sybil, but in many ways seemed more innocent and more protected. Bert handled all the practical details of their life and shielded her from everything unpleasant, which was his role, while Gwyneth ran his home flawlessly, as she had for twenty-four years, and took care of their children. They had faced Magnus's death together twelve years before, and given each other the courage they needed to go on. They were a strong couple, and their roles were well defined as to what a man did and how a woman complemented him. It was all more confusing in Blake and Sybil's time. She had to be powerful and sturdy in the world, and yet make adjustments for him, and not lose her own sense of womanhood. Gwyneth didn't see the nuances and was impressed by the freedom Sybil had to work, make decisions, travel, and do as she chose. She liked Sybil enormously, and envied her to some degree.

"I wish I could have a job," she had said longingly.

"What would you do?" Sybil asked her, curious about how she'd respond.

"I'm not sure. I'd go to university and study art history. I think I'd like your job. It sounds so interesting and varied. Or I'd like to teach art."

"I used to think about teaching too." Sybil smiled. "Jobs are so crazy these days. There are so many elements combined. And you can design your own. With computers, you can work from home or anywhere in the world."

"I don't really understand them," Gwyneth admitted, looking embarrassed.

"I don't either." Sybil smiled at her. "And I'm not very good with them. It's like a box with a small typewriter in it," she explained. "You write whatever you need to on the keyboard, you can even send photographs or designs, or music on it. It shows up on the little screen, and then you hit a button, and it goes to anyone you send it to, who has one of those little computer boxes. It always seems like magic to me, and it's incredibly fast. It gets to the other person seconds later. It makes it very easy to work from far away. You can even draw on it with a special program."

"What an incredible invention. I thought it was remarkable when Bert got us a telephone, although I don't use it very often. Or I didn't. I don't use it at all now." And they both knew why.

"I can show you my computer when I get back, if you like." Gwyneth's face had lit up at the suggestion. And when she was away, Sybil downloaded several art programs for her.

It snowed while Sybil was in New York, and it was beautiful for a night, and after that it was a mess, with slush everywhere. She was relieved when she got on the plane to go back to San Francisco, and she was happy to see Blake and the children when she got home. She had missed them, but had gotten all her work done.

"How was New York?" Blake asked, as he kissed her when he got home from work. He had missed her too.

"Noisy, dirty, messy, exciting, lonely, fun."

"That about sums it up," he laughed.

"And it didn't feel like home anymore." She sounded surprised. "The apartment was depressing without you and the kids. I couldn't wait to get back." He looked pleased. He'd been afraid that she'd fall in love with the city all over again. "And I missed the house. I've gotten spoiled," she admitted with a grin. It was all good news to him. He was enjoying his job and in no hurry to go back to New York.

"I ran into Bert in the garden this morning, and he invited us to dinner tonight, if you're not too tired."

"I'd love it." She smiled at him, and she couldn't wait to see Gwyneth and start their computer lessons. She was anxious to show her the programs she'd downloaded for her. She'd been playing with them herself, and had done some drawings that looked like pen and ink. There was a painting application too.

Both families were delighted to see each other when they met for dinner that night. The young people were particularly pleased, and Sybil got a few minutes alone with Gwyneth before they sat down.

"Come up to my office tomorrow afternoon," she told

her. "We're all set." Gwyneth didn't want Bert to know and said he'd be upset, but she wanted to learn to use Sybil's computer. It sounded like a magical invention to her. And after dinner, Gwyneth looked excited when she and Sybil said good night. Blake asked her about it when they went upstairs.

"What was that about between you and Gwyneth? You two look like you're up to mischief." He knew Sybil well, but she didn't want him to tell Bert. The two families had a tacit agreement not to interfere with each other's lives and respect the dimensions they were in. Blake had been adamant about it. To Sybil, that meant not telling them what was going to happen in their lives in the future. It didn't mean not teaching Gwyneth computer skills, just like Charlie teaching Magnus to play videogames, which Bert didn't want him doing either, but the boys had a ball with it, and Sybil was sure Gwyneth would with their lessons too.

"Just girl stuff," Sybil said vaguely, and asked Blake to help her unzip her dress, and he rapidly lost interest in whatever secret the two women shared.

*

Gwyneth came to Sybil's office the next day, on the floor above their bedrooms. She walked in shyly and sat down at Sybil's desk, where Sybil showed her how to turn on the computer and how to operate it, and then explained the art applications, as Gwyneth stared at the screen in disbelief.

"How can you do that with a machine?" She tried it herself and was in awe of the pen and ink app, and was amazed at the brushstrokes she could achieve with the painting application. And they both had fun trying it out. They played with it for two hours and Sybil printed the results out for her, as Gwyneth noticed Sybil's cellphone on the desk.

"What do you do with that?" It didn't look like anything she'd ever seen.

"That?" Sybil looked surprised. "That's my phone." Gwyneth looked amazed as she picked it up.

"It's a telephone?"

Sybil showed her how it worked and Gwyneth laughed in astonishment. It had been an exciting day for her, and they decided to put her artwork in a file in Sybil's office. She asked if she could come back the next day.

"You can come back every day if you want." She had an old laptop she could dedicate to her, and Gwyneth looked thrilled as she hugged Sybil and thanked her, and she left a minute later. Sybil waved from her office doorway as Gwyneth headed for the stairs and disappeared. It had been a wonderful afternoon for both of them.

They didn't have dinner together that night, but Gwyneth came back the next day, ready to practice the painting application again. She was already addicted to the computer and the miracle Sybil had introduced her to. A whole new world had opened up for her, a hundred years ahead of her time.

*

Gwyneth continued to come back every afternoon after that. She diligently worked with the art applications while Sybil did her work. And Gwyneth was fascinated watching Sybil do her emails. Sybil taught her how to email and showed her how to Skype, although no one could see her except Sybil. Skype was not made for ghosts. They sent an email to Blake, and Gwyneth laughed at Blake's response. He thought he was emailing Sybil when it was really Gwyneth writing to him, and both women laughed. Gwyneth was learning her lessons well. Her artwork was beautiful, and Sybil was sorry she couldn't show it to anyone. It was their dark secret. And Gwyneth was proud of what she'd learned.

Sybil showed her Facebook one afternoon just for fun, and Google, and eBay. The possibilities were endless. But what Gwyneth loved most was creating art on the computer. And she was impressed by how seriously Sybil worked and the volume of emails she dealt with.

"You need a secretary," Gwyneth said practically one afternoon, and Sybil nodded. She'd had an assistant in New York, but didn't want one here.

"I do it all myself. I don't want to train someone to do

what I do, but sometimes I get overloaded, especially when I have an article due, or a museum show to organize and curate, with things coming in from all over the world."

They were talking about it when Alicia came upstairs to offer Sybil a cup of tea and heard her talking to Gwyneth, although Alicia could see and hear only Sybil.

"I'm sorry, are you on the phone?" she whispered.

"No, I'm finished, and I'm fine, I don't need anything, but thank you," Sybil said, and the housekeeper went back downstairs. She had noticed that the whole family talked to themselves a lot. They were a little eccentric. The children did it, and Mrs. Gregory. She'd never known people who talked to themselves before, and after she was gone, Gwyneth and Sybil burst into gales of laughter. "She thinks we're all crazy," Sybil explained. "Who knows, maybe we are."

"No, you're not," Gwyneth said gently. "You're a remarkable woman, Sybil. You've given a whole new meaning to my life with the computer." The earnestness with which she said it touched Sybil deeply, as though she'd given her a priceless gift. It cemented their friendship as nothing else had. They continued to meet every afternoon in Sybil's office. They talked about life, and their husbands and children. Their fears and their dreams. Gwyneth was desperately worried about America getting pulled into the war and Josiah getting drafted. And the subject came up at dinner constantly too.

Bert was increasingly concerned with how badly the war was going in Europe. He didn't see how President Wilson was going to keep the country out of it, and by March it was even worse. Bert was predicting that America would enter the war in the immediate future. Blake didn't offer what he knew, nor did Sybil; that Josiah would be enlisting in the army soon, and the country would be at war.

It finally happened on April 6. President Wilson asked Congress for a declaration of war on April 2, and four days later, war was declared, and the families shared a somber dinner in the dining room that night. Two days later, Josiah told his family he had enlisted, and Sybil felt her heart sink, knowing what would come next. Gwyneth saw it on Sybil's face and whispered to her at dinner.

"Is there something you're not telling us?" And after a long, long pause, Sybil nodded.

"He mustn't go," Sybil said urgently, and Gwyneth understood.

"But how can we stop him? All the boys his age will be going now." He'd been one of the first to enlist, and Bert was very proud of his son. "Bert thinks he should," Gwyneth added.

"Is there nothing you can do to stop him?" Sybil looked so sad.

"He'll be labeled a coward if he doesn't go," Gwyneth said, and Sybil realized again that she was powerless to change it. Gwyneth stopped coming for her computer lessons, too worried about her son for frivolous distractions.

Two weeks later, they had a farewell dinner for him. The Gregorys were there, and when Sybil said goodbye to him and hugged him, she told Josiah he must be very, very careful, and not take any undue risks. "Don't be a hero, just come home!" The men smiled at each other over her warnings, and Blake mentioned it when they went up to bed. Sybil was deeply moved by saying goodbye to Josiah, and had prayed that her warning was enough to change something just a little.

"He'll be fine," Blake assured her, as though Josiah were still alive, forgetting the truth about them, that none of them were "fine" anymore, even though they seemed to be. They had all died long ago and were now ghosts.

"No, he won't," Sybil said to Blake with a pointed look, and he understood, and seemed shocked when she reminded him. "Unless something happens to change the course of history, he won't be back. Or, he will, but the way Magnus is, as a spirit." It was confusing at times remembering who was meant to still be alive and who was dead among them.

"He was killed in the war?" Blake had forgotten. Sybil nodded and Blake looked sad too, wishing he could say something to Bert to alter it. But what could he say? It was already done, a century before.

"I keep wishing we could change things. It's not fair

that we know what we do, and they don't and have no warning," she said sadly. Her computer lessons with Gwyneth had brought them even closer.

"But that's the way life is, isn't it? None of us are ever warned. And even when we are, we don't believe it," Blake said wisely. "They probably wouldn't do anything different even if they knew."

"But what if they did? What if we could make a difference?"

"By now, a hundred years later, something would have killed them. We don't have a right to interfere with their destinies. Perhaps in small subtle ways. But would you have him called a coward when the country went to war? It would break his father's heart. Would you want that for Andy?" he asked her honestly.

"Yes, I would," she said emphatically. "I would want my son alive, whatever it took."

"Bert was very proud of him tonight," Blake commented, remembering the look of pride on Bert's face.

"If someone knew something that could help me change the course of history to save my son, I would want to know it," she said fiercely.

"I'm not sure people would listen. Perhaps it will work out differently than you think." She shook her head, knowing the truth, and there were tears in her eyes when she went to bed that night, thinking of Josiah and the grief that lay ahead for all of them. She wondered how long it would take him to come back to them, after he died. She was in a world of phenomena she didn't know or understand, and neither did Blake. "Magnus seems to be all right, in spite of what happened to him," Blake tried to reassure her.

"He's not all right, Blake. He's dead," she said, and blew her nose.

"They're all dead," he reminded her, and she laughed through her tears.

"I guess that's true." She smiled. "They just don't look or act dead, and they don't seem to know it."

"No, they certainly don't," he agreed. They seemed as alive as any friends they'd ever had, and the two families had come to love each other and gave each other strength. Blake vowed to himself to be there for Bert in the months ahead. It was all he could do. Despite what they knew, they were unable to interfere, and he wondered if maybe that was how it was meant to be, as cruel as that seemed to them.

*

Josiah left the next day. He was being sent by train to New Jersey for basic training, and then would embark for Europe. They wouldn't see him again before he left for the front, by troop ship from New York. He wouldn't be allowed to tell them when he was going, but Bert thought they would train him for combat for about a month, or a little longer, which would land him in Europe in early June. The war was chewing up all the young men in Europe, and they were hoping that fresh troops from the States would turn it around.

There was no dinner with the Butterfields the night he left, and they didn't come to the dining room for two days. Gwyneth was trying to be brave, but she looked ragged when they dined together again, and even Augusta was subdued, missing her grandson, and there suddenly seemed to be a huge hole at the table where Josiah had been.

Bert and Blake talked business that night, as Blake explained to him how the progress at the start-up was going. There were a few problems, but he wasn't worried about them. Blake felt that the two founding partners were too fearless about taking risks, but he hoped they knew what they were doing. They'd been successful before. It seemed insignificant now compared to Josiah going to war, but at least talking to Bert about work was distracting. Sybil and Gwyneth were conversing quietly. Sybil had just said something to Gwyneth about coming back to her office in the afternoons, when she happened to look down the table toward Augusta and saw her turning purple, while Angus stared at her in a panic. There was no sound coming from her, and she was obviously choking. Her airway was blocked by something she had eaten, probably a piece of meat. They'd had leg of lamb for dinner that night. Sybil watched her for an instant and then ran down the length of the table to where Augusta was sitting. The old woman looked terrified, she was getting no air and could make no sound. Sybil knew she would be unconscious shortly.

"I'm going to help you," Sybil said as calmly as she could, hoping she could do the Heimlich maneuver on a woman her size. Augusta had a voluminous body, and Sybil pulled her up from her chair, stood as closely behind her as she could get, put her arms around her, formed one hand into a tight fist and curled the other around it, and plunged them into Augusta's abdomen sharply, as everyone at the table stared in shocked horror at what was going on and what Sybil was doing. Sybil, Blake, and their children had taken Red Cross classes many times, and Sybil was certified in advanced first aid and CPR. She made the classic movement twice, trying to force the object to pop out as the air in her lungs would propel it upward. Augusta was fighting her, but on the second try it worked, and the piece of lamb that had been stuck in her throat flew out of her mouth, shot across the table, and landed in front of Magnus. Augusta spluttered and coughed then, but her airway had cleared. She looked mortified and turned to Sybil, still standing behind her, and waved her away.

"How dare you put your hands on me, you wicked girl!" she berated her. "You tried to strangle me, while I was choking." She looked outraged. "You nearly broke my ribs!"

"No, truly, I didn't try to strangle you, Mrs. Campbell. It's called the Heimlich maneuver, to keep people from dying from choking. It saves a lot of lives. My children know how to do it too."

"Heimlich. Foreign, naturally. And German, that's even worse than French. The Germans are probably using it in France to kill British soldiers." Gratitude was clearly not part of Augusta's makeup, and she was obviously fine now, so Sybil apologized for manhandling her and went back to her seat, relieved that it had worked.

"Mother, Sybil was trying to help you," Gwyneth said, attempting to defend her friend. "You were choking." And Phillips had already removed the offending piece of meat that had nearly killed her. She glared at Sybil several times from the opposite end of the table, but as they left the dining room that night, she walked over to Sybil and spoke to her gruffly.

"I'm sure you meant well, but don't ever do that again. I'd rather choke than have you break all my ribs."

"I'm sorry if I hurt you," Sybil said meekly, but she knew that she had embarrassed her and hurt her pride more than anything. And it had been no easy task getting her arms around the corpulent woman.

"You didn't. But you can't trust those Germans. Leave it to them to come up with such a barbaric remedy for choking. Quite dreadful, I assure you." She left the room on her brother's arm then, and disappeared even faster than usual. As Sybil walked up the stairs that night, she thought about how tragic it was that she could save an old woman from dying who was already dead, but she couldn't save a twenty-three-year-old boy they all loved from going to war and being killed there. It truly wasn't fair, and Augusta Campbell might have recovered from choking another way, but Sybil couldn't take the chance. But she was sure that somewhere, though she would never have admitted it, Gwyneth's mother was grateful. Blake teased Sybil about it later when she climbed into bed.

"Tried to kill the old lady at dinner tonight, did you?" She laughed in answer, remembering Augusta's look of indignation once Sybil had saved her. "Don't forget, my darling, that no good deed goes unpunished, even with ghosts." He laughed at her again, while Sybil tried not to think of Josiah. She'd been worrying about him all night, and already missed him. She hoped they would see him again soon. In the meantime, at least she'd saved Augusta's life, whether she appreciated it or not. The children needed a grandmother, after all, and she was the only one they had, even if she was a ghost, and a cantankerous one at that.

Chapter 8

The whole family was subdued after Josiah left in April. The newspaper reports about the war suddenly had deeper meaning. Sybil found herself reading about the First World War online, so she would know more about it. The casualty reports and the nature of the casualties were grim. Mustard gas and poison gases of various kinds were released on the soldiers. The conditions in the trenches were ghastly. Sybil couldn't bear the thought of Josiah going through that once he went to Europe, and neither could Gwyneth. Sybil had to remind herself again and again that in real time, Josiah had been dead for a hundred years. But in Gwyneth and Bert's world, it hadn't happened yet, and Sybil dreaded when it would, and what it would do to them.

The first Battle of the Somme had ravaged the Allied troops the year before in 1916, and the fighting was still continuing. It hadn't ended yet. And what Sybil read had happened in 1917 was even worse. She tried to keep positive around Gwyneth, but she knew that it was all her friend could think of, and Sybil was grateful they both had Magnus and Charlie to cheer them up, and their daughters to keep them busy. Caroline missed Josiah too, and a few weeks after he left, she met a new boy at school, which Sybil thought might be a good thing. He was a senior and captain of the basketball team, a tall, handsome boy who was crazy about her and she liked him. She knew that Caroline would be shaken by what happened to Josiah. And it was better for her to dive into the real world for now, like a normal high school girl.

Caroline mentioned her new beau one night to Bettina at dinner, who warned her not to get involved with anyone, because he would be going to war soon. And Caro gently reminded her that he would be going to college like Andy, not to war.

Angus told Andy that he had best forget the University of Edinburgh, if he got in. It would be too hard to get to Europe, it was a dangerous time to be there, and he might get torpedoed on the way over. Andy politely didn't comment, since most of the time Angus forgot that they lived in two different centuries. He kept telling Andy that he'd be going to war soon, and if he wasn't drafted before he graduated in June, he'd have to enlist then, if he was even able to finish. Andy would nod and play with Rupert, who spent mealtimes either snoring loudly at his master's feet or waiting for something to fall from the table. Magnus and Charlie fed him scraps whenever they could, and Rupert would bark at them when they didn't and give them away, while the boys feigned innocence and insisted they hadn't given him anything.

Andy provided the families with good news for a change. He got into the University of Edinburgh, and so did his two friends, and he was thrilled. They celebrated him at dinner, despite Angus's warnings that he'd be drafted instead. Both families were delighted for him. But it was bittersweet for Sybil. She hated the thought of her firstborn leaving in the fall, but it was inevitable. She didn't dare complain to Gwyneth, who was worrying about Josiah night and day.

Magnus and Charlie had been less adventuresome since their escapade with the secret passage, and Charlie reported to his mother that Magnus had gotten really good at videogames. He was almost as adept as Charlie, and had a real knack for it, just as his mother had learned to use Sybil's computer with impressive skill. It was a dimension that neither of them could have dreamed of. Bert scolded Gwyneth when she hung around Sybil while she was working. She still talked longingly about having a job, which both her mother and husband told her wasn't appropriate for her.

"I don't see why not," Gwyneth answered petulantly. "If Sybil can work, why can't I?" She sounded more like one of her daughters than herself.

"Ladies do not work," Augusta had told her in no uncertain terms. "The next thing you know, you'll want to be wearing one of Caroline's indecently short skirts. That's for *them,*" she said, glancing at the Gregorys. "Not for *us.*" She liked them, and had accepted "the new family" as she called them, in their midst, but the same rules did not apply. And she had warned Sybil several times that if she ever choked at dinner again, she was *not* to leap on her with that German attack method to try to save her. She claimed that Sybil had nearly killed her, and said she was sure it was being used by the enemy in the war.

"She was trying to help you, Mother," Gwyneth reminded her, but Augusta was not convinced.

During the weeks after Josiah left, Sybil noticed that Bettina was unusually quiet, and hardly ever spoke. Her brother was two years older, and they were very close. Bettina was twenty-one and didn't have a beau. When Sybil had asked Gwyneth about it one afternoon in her office, while Gwyneth painted on her computer, she sighed and said it was a long story. Bettina was a beautiful girl, and from the moment war had been declared, she had severely withdrawn, and barely spoke to any of them. She had taken to going on long walks alone, and writing letters for hours in the garden. She seemed desperately unhappy.

"She fell in love with a boy two years ago, when we went to Lake Tahoe. He was a nice boy her age. He seemed very bright, and he was very taken with her, but he was entirely unsuitable. She had just come out the year before, and we presented her to a number of young men she refused. After a month at Lake Tahoe, she had her heart set on this boy. Bert was very upset about it, and he talked to the boy's father and told him that his advances weren't welcome. He completely understood, and I don't think they liked the idea either," Gwyneth said unhappily.

"What made him unsuitable?" Sybil was curious about it.

"It was quite impossible. Tradesman. The family is Italian, and they had a fish restaurant somewhere. The parents barely spoke English," she said in her soft Scottish burr. It was the first time that Sybil had heard her sound snobbish, but she was very definite about it. There were rules and standards that they lived by, and they expected their daughter to do the same, and the son of an Italian immigrant restaurant owner was unthinkable for one of their daughters, even if the business was successful. "My mother would have had a fit if she'd known," Gwyneth added. "His parents found the match as undesirable as we did, they had a girl picked out for him in Italy, which he was resisting. He had very modern ideas, and had no interest in working at the restaurant. He wanted to go to university. He was a bit of a revolutionary, and I think they blamed Bettina for his refusing the marriage they'd planned for him. After Bert spoke to the boy's father, he forbid Bettina to see him again."

"And did she anyway?" Sybil was intrigued. There was

nothing about him that she could remember in the book Bettina had written many years later. She hadn't mentioned the incident at all.

"I don't think so," Gwyneth said quietly, "but she was very angry at us for about a year. Bettina can hold a grudge for a long time." It was a side of her Sybil had never seen. She had always seemed very docile and adaptable, and very proper. "She hasn't been interested in anyone else since. And we don't want her to be a spinster. It will be even more difficult now with a war on. All the young men will go away. She should be married by now. Bert and I were married when I was eighteen. She's already a bit late." It was interesting to hear Gwyneth's views on the subject. She firmly believed in all the old rules, and so did Bert, no matter how open-minded they were with their new friends. But that was different, they all agreed.

"She seems very unhappy these days," Sybil commented, and her mother had seen it too.

"I think she's upset about Josiah. We all are. And they're very close."

A few days later, Sybil was up early and saw Bettina downstairs just before she slipped out the door of the house in a light blue dress and a navy blue coat, with a small elegant hat and a heavy veil concealing her face. She looked suddenly very grown up, and Sybil had an eerie sense that something important was happening that her family didn't know about. She picked up Bettina's book later that morning and combed it for answers. In the chapter on Josiah leaving to go to war, she saw a few lines and guessed what they meant and what she might be doing. Sybil had no way of warning Bettina's parents, and it was too late to follow her. Bettina didn't appear at dinner that night, and a note was hand-delivered to Bert halfway through the meal, which Phillips handed to him at the table. Bert apologized, read it with a grave expression, and handed it to Gwyneth, who looked at him with tears in her eyes as soon as she'd read it too.

"Is everything all right?" Sybil asked her, and touched her hand, fearing it was about Josiah, and Gwyneth dabbed at her eyes as she answered.

"I never thought she'd do something like this. She's so incredibly foolish. It's Bettina," she said, as tears ran down her cheeks. "She must have seen that boy again. The Italian."

"Is the letter from him?" Sybil asked her, remembering Bettina's book. It said that her parents had prevented her from marrying the boy she was in love with. They had waited two years and got married when war was declared, before he shipped out.

"It's from Bettina." Gwyneth spoke in a whisper. "She married him this afternoon at city hall. He's shipping out tomorrow, to New York, and then to Europe. She said she'll be back after he leaves. How could she do this?"

Gwyneth choked on a sob. "We tried to reason with her, and now look what she's done. They're married." Augusta was watching them intently, and Bert had just explained it to Blake. Bert looked livid, and Blake felt sorry for him. He was more stoic than his wife, but looked near to tears too. Bettina had upset them severely.

Sybil didn't have the heart to tell her that fate was going to take the upper hand here, just as it would with Josiah. Gwyneth excused herself shortly after, and left the table in tears. She couldn't bear it any longer, and wanted to lie down. Bert continued to be a gracious host until they left one another at the end of the evening, and Sybil and Blake talked about it that night and worried about them. Having their daughter marry someone unsuitable was a tragedy to them.

Bettina was back the next day, red-eyed and heart-broken after seeing her new husband off at the train in Oakland. She had taken a ferryboat back to the city and still looked windblown at dinner. Her grandmother was furious at her, having heard the whole story by then. Bettina was belligerent, and Bert was unusually silent at dinner, after a stern discussion with his daughter when she got home about how dishonorably she had behaved, sneaking off like a thief and marrying a boy she knew they disapproved of. "And will you work at the fish restaurant with him?"

"He doesn't work at the restaurant, Father. He's studying to be a lawyer. He'll finish his studies after the war." Bert was still not pleased and cast somber glances at her all through dinner. He had threatened to have the marriage annulled, and she had sworn she'd run away if he did, and live with her in-laws. He believed her, so he agreed to let the marriage stand, under the circumstances. She had spent the night with her husband at a hotel, after their wedding at city hall. She was desperately in love. And her father said he just hoped there would be no issue from it, and that she'd regain her senses when he returned and she saw how different their lives were. Bettina was the most stubborn of his children. Bert was not in a good mood at dinner, until he and Blake talked for a while and he calmed down. The two men agreed that no one could drive you as crazy as your children. Gwyneth still looked upset and shaken, and Bert was cool and disapproving with Bettina for many weeks.

Bettina's elopement was the main topic of conversation in the family for the entire month, all through May. They reported it to Josiah, and he wrote to his sister and told her she'd been very foolish and upset their parents deeply, and however nice the young man was—and he'd met him in Tahoe too—she would be miserable in the life he'd been born to, which was so different from hers.

Even Magnus and Charlie talked about it when they played in the garden, and Magnus told him his big sister was in trouble for marrying a fish merchant or something like that.

"Sounds smelly to me," Charlie commented, and Magnus agreed. "Why would she want to marry a man like that?"

"Just stupid, I guess," Magnus responded, and then they forgot about it. But the families' dinners together were tense for weeks, as they all worried about Josiah, after he wrote them that he was shipping out. He couldn't tell them where he was being sent, but obviously to the front somewhere, where he would receive more combat training. Tony Salvatore, Bettina's husband, left shortly after, and she was still in disgrace with her parents. Bert hadn't forgiven her yet, although her mother had. Gwyneth couldn't stay angry at any of her children for long, no matter how grievous the offense. Bettina's marriage to a man they disapproved of was the worst thing any of them had ever done.

Bettina had gone to visit Tony's parents at the restaurant, to do the proper thing after their rapid, stealthy marriage, and she was disappointed that they were upset and angry too. As far as they were concerned, he had a fiancée in Italy he had jilted. It had been arranged through their cousins, and the young Italian woman was supposedly a hardworking girl who would have been helpful to them, and it was obvious that Bettina was much too fancy to ever work in the restaurant. They were cold and unfriendly and barely spoke to her, and she had left in tears. They had made it clear to her that they had no intention of supporting her or helping her in their son's absence if that was why she had come to visit them, which it wasn't. They told her to stay with her own family and not come asking them for money, and if there was a baby on the way, they said they didn't want to know about it. They informed her that she and Tony were on their own, and that his family had enough mouths to feed. The smell of fish at the restaurant had been awful, and she felt sick when she got home and didn't even come to dinner. She told her mother where she'd been and how nasty Tony's parents had been. It was a harsh lesson to her for doing something so impulsive. Neither side was willing to approve the marriage or support it.

*

In June, Andy went to New York to graduate with his class, and the whole Gregory family went with him. Blake flew back to San Francisco after the ceremony to work, but the rest of the family spent a week in their apartment. The kids saw their friends, while Sybil spent several days working at the Brooklyn Museum.

A week after graduation, they returned to San Francisco. Dinners with the Butterfields were quiet and tense, as the reports of the war continued to get worse in the Butterfields' time frame. Andy spent time with Lucy to cheer her up, but she was worried about Josiah too. They all were.

In July, Bettina realized that she was three months pregnant, which upset her parents even more. The baby was due in early January, and she hadn't heard from Tony since he'd shipped out, so she couldn't write to tell him. She was so violently sick that she vomited all the time, and stopped coming to dinner. She couldn't bear the smell of food, and Gwyneth said she was living on toast and weak tea. She was so ill that Gwyneth felt sorry for her, and Bert was even more upset that a child would result from her foolish, headstrong behavior. She didn't contact Tony's family to tell them, since they had been so unfriendly toward her the first time, and had made it very clear that they wanted nothing to do with them or a baby. It was a heavy dose of reality for her. She had no idea what she'd do with a child. The whole thing seemed a great deal less romantic to her now, although she had been so in love with Tony after they met in Tahoe, and on the day they got married. No one had warned her she could get this sick if she got pregnant. She didn't know enough to take precautions on the one night they'd spent together, and he had been so anxious to go to bed with her that he had done nothing about it either. And now she was paying for her foolishness. Lucy was ill that summer too, and Andy spent hours keeping her company. He was going to miss her when he left for university.

In early August, disaster struck, and they received the telegram telling them that Josiah had been killed in France by a mine, when his unit had offered auxiliary support to British troops. Sybil found a black wreath on the door when she got home from taking Charlie to swim club, and her heart nearly stopped when she saw it and guessed what it meant. The house was in deep mourning for weeks afterward, and Blake and Sybil postponed their vacation in the Hamptons, in order to stay in San Francisco and support Bert and Gwyneth in their grief.

"Is this crazy?" Blake asked Sybil when they made the decision not to go east. "He's been dead for a century, and we met him as a ghost. Should we be canceling our kids' vacation for him?"

"They're our friends, Blake," Sybil said quietly. "I'd feel terrible leaving them."

"He'll be back anyway," her husband reminded her.

"But they don't know that yet, and we don't know how long that takes." She had called Michael, and he had said it could be months, or even years. "And we can't tell them he was dead anyway. In their lives, this just happened." In the end, Blake agreed with her, and wanted to do what he could for Bert, who was devastated by his daughter's poor judgment and the death of his son, four months after they'd entered the war.

Three weeks later, almost to the day, Bettina was notified that her husband had been killed in France during training exercises. She was going to give birth to a father-less baby in four months. The house felt like a tomb after both young men were killed in Europe.

Blake and Sybil found some relief when they took Andy to Edinburgh to settle him in. They took Caroline and Charlie with them, and they found it a charming city. Andy was wildly excited to be going to college at a foreign university, and he joined them in London for five days, and then Blake and Sybil took Charlie and Caroline to Paris, and then Blake, Caroline, and Charlie flew back to San Francisco. Sybil went to New York for the opening of the show at the Brooklyn Museum. She hadn't touched the book she'd been working on since they moved to San Francisco. She just hadn't had time. Between her children, the Butterfields, and her work, she never had the quiet hours she needed to continue the research and work on it, but she had promised herself and her publisher that she would finish it that winter. She was in New York for two weeks, and pleased that the reviews of the design exhibit in Brooklyn had been excellent. Based on the event's success, she was asked to do a show at the Los Angeles County Museum of Art. It had been a very fruitful trip. And when she got home, she found Blake coping well. Alicia had stayed at the house to help Caroline and Charlie while Sybil was gone. Alicia was the only one at home when she arrived in the early afternoon. The black wreath was off the door, which Sybil was pleased to see.

"How is everyone?" Sybil asked her, and she shrugged when she answered.

"They talkin' to themselves a lot." But they all did. Sybil too. Alicia thought they were all a little odd, but nice people, and they were good kids. "They do their home-work every night, and Mister Gregory, he take them out to dinner a lot. Chinese, pizza, Thai, Mexican." This told Sybil that they hadn't dined with the Butterfields while she was gone, and she wasn't sure why. She wondered how they were doing after all the shocks of the summer, and how Bettina was. And she was excited to see her chil-dren when they got home from school. Charlie let out a whoop and threw himself into his mother's arms.

Caroline's boyfriend had left for college, but she had met another boy she liked, a fellow senior, and Charlie said he had seen Magnus almost every day.

"How are they?" Sybil asked with a look of concern.

"I don't know. He says his mom cries all the time, and Bettina throws up a lot." Sybil winced when she heard it. Magnus showed up a few minutes later and gave her a big hug too. He felt just as solid and real in her arms as Charlie did, and he was happy to see her. He told her he had missed her, and she said she had missed him too.

"My mom told me to ask you for dinner tonight." She nodded.

"How is everybody?"

"My grandma was sick for a while, but she's fine now.

And Bettina is really fat." Sybil knew that they hadn't told him about the baby yet, but they would have to soon. Magnus knew she had gotten married and was a widow now. Sybil didn't ask him if Josiah was back yet. She'd have to see that for herself.

When the four of them joined the Butterfields in the dining room that night, it was obvious that he wasn't, and Bettina was almost transparent, she was so pale. Lucy seemed healthy by comparison, but they all greeted Sybil warmly, even Augusta, and she had brought back little presents for all of them. A scarf for Augusta, a pipe for Angus, a light cashmere shawl for Lucy, a book for Bert she thought he'd enjoy, perfume from Paris for Gwyneth, a box of lace handkerchiefs for Bettina, two sweet little nightgowns for the baby with matching caps and booties, and new videogames for both boys. And she could see immediately how much Bettina's pregnancy had grown. She couldn't hide it anymore.

"She won't be able to go out for much longer," Gwyneth said with a look of concern. "A few more weeks maybe. From the beginning of November, she'll stay home." She said it as though that were a normal occurrence, and Sybil realized that Bettina would have to stay out of sight and literally be "confined" at home, like other women in her condition at the time. "Maybe even before," Gwyneth added. It sounded depressing to Sybil, but was accepted behavior for women of her day.

They talked about Sybil's trip and the exhibit and how much Andy loved school. She had been FaceTiming with him from New York, while Blake and the children were Skyping with him from San Francisco.

They stayed at the table longer than usual, to catch up on each other's news. Bert still seemed very down about Josiah. The loss of his oldest son had been a terrible blow. Gwyneth whispered to Sybil that she had been doing artwork on the computer the whole time Sybil was away, and they exchanged a smile.

"How do you feel?" Sybil asked Bettina when they got up from the table, and she saw that Bettina's eyes looked inconsolably sad. She had lost a husband and a brother, and was having a baby she wasn't ready for and would have to bring up alone. Her mother had whispered to Sybil at dinner that it would be nearly impossible to find her a husband now, especially during a war. Her fate as an unmarried woman in future was nearly sealed, and with a child.

"I'm all right," Bettina answered in a thin voice. Sybil had noticed that she'd eaten almost nothing at dinner except some clear broth and a piece of toast. But Augusta appeared to be in robust health, and so was Angus, and he was very pleased to hear how much Andy loved school, and how he was traveling around Scotland on weekends.

"I'm amazed he got over there without a problem. Give the dear boy my love," Angus said, with Rupert at his feet.

"I will," Sybil promised. It felt good to be home with all of them. As odd as it seemed, she knew that this was where she belonged, even if her best friends now were all ghosts. At least they had Bettina's baby to look forward to, but Sybil seemed like the only person in the house who was excited for it to arrive.

Chapter 9

By the end of October, as was proper for her time, Bettina no longer left the house. It wasn't considered appropriate for her to be seen in public in her condition, and she accepted it without complaint. But she looked profoundly depressed whenever Sybil saw her at dinner, which wasn't often. She remained very ill and violently nauseous throughout the pregnancy. Her mother said she still threw up several times a day and could barely eat. It sounded awful to Sybil, who'd had easy pregnancies with all three of her children.

"I don't think I could have done that," Sybil said sympathetically when Gwyneth came to visit her in her office. Sybil was trying to work on her book, but still with little success. There was always too much going on with Blake, the kids, or at night with their friends they shared the house with. They had dinner with the Butterfields two or three nights a week, and usually went out once a week to a restaurant with clients or one of Blake's associates from work. They had a full life.

"I was very sick with Josiah," Gwyneth said and looked

sad as she said it; she missed him so much. They were having a beautiful portrait done of him in his uniform, from a photograph that had been taken right before he left. "I had less trouble with the girls," she commented. "And I was in bed for six months with Magnus so I wouldn't lose him. He came early, and hopped around all the time. He was in such a rush to be born." She smiled at the memory.

"Do you think Bettina's baby is all right? She eats almost nothing. She can't be getting much nourishment."

"The doctor has come to see her several times, and he says she's fine, and the baby is quite small." That didn't sound good to Sybil, but she didn't say anything. She didn't want to worry her friend. They had their own way of dealing with things, according to the times they lived in. And a small baby would make for an easier birth. She would have the baby at home with a midwife in attendance, and a nurse who would stay on. It was how Gwyneth had given birth to her babies too. She said Magnus had almost fallen out, he was so anxious to arrive, and had come three weeks early, which could have been dangerous, but all had gone well, and she was sure it would for Bettina too. She was young and strong, in spite of how ill she had been for months.

"Is Bert feeling better about it?" Sybil asked Gwyneth, handing her the cup of tea Alicia had brought for her. She couldn't justify asking for two cups of tea when she appeared to be alone.

"Not really," she said honestly. "But he's relaxed a little. He feels sorry for her. Apparently, her husband's family wants nothing to do with her. They were afraid she'd ask them for money. And they're devastated over their son. So are we over ours," she said simply. "They're not going to help Bettina or the baby. We'll take care of both of them, of course, but no man is going to want her." She had said it before. But Sybil knew differently and wanted to give her friend hope without telling her the future.

"There are going to be lots of young widows with children after the war. That will change things. And the baby will be legitimate – they were married." For five months. An illegitimate child would have been much harder for a new man to accept, or even impossible in their social world.

"I suppose so," Gwyneth said, looking out the window with a sad expression, thinking about Josiah. "How's your book?"

"Slow." Sybil smiled.

But, much more exciting than her book, Blake's business was going extremely well. They had a new influx of money from a group of venture capitalists, and they were broadening their goals, since the model was working well. It was liable to be a huge hit, with enormous profits for them all.

Blake discussed it with Bert again that night, who

warned him about the risks. "Don't be too greedy," he said seriously. "Don't stretch farther than you should."

"It's hard to resist," Blake said sincerely, but he knew Bert was right. They talked about it for a while, and Bert expressed his opinion as best he could, based on his understanding of their plans, which he said were foreign to him. But it always surprised Blake that many of the principles and the dangers were the same, no matter the century.

*

The two families spent Thanksgiving together, and Angus came down the grand staircase before dinner, playing the bagpipes, with Rupert following him, howling. It was hard to decide which sound was worse. The entire group sat waiting for him, and he walked around the table three times, with ear-shattering results. Violet, Augusta's pug, jumped into her lap and buried her head in Augusta's arms to avoid the noise. It was a blessed relief when he stopped.

"Wonderful, Angus, thank you," Augusta praised her brother, and Phillips walked in with an enormous turkey on a silver platter. There was stuffing, sweet and mashed potatoes, half a dozen different vegetables, popovers, cranberry jelly, and all the trimmings, and excellent wine from Bert's cellar.

It was the Gregorys' first Thanksgiving with the Butterfields. They were going to spend Christmas together too, and then the Gregorys were planning to go to Aspen between Christmas and New Year's. They had rented a house there. And Andrew was coming home for three weeks. They were all looking forward to it. Angus had sent him a list of his favorite pubs around the campus, with no understanding that they might not still be there seventy years later in his own time, not to mention a century later for Andy.

The food was delicious and everyone was in good spirits, despite the heavy losses they had suffered that year. Bert led them in prayer before they began eating, and they still found things to be grateful for, especially their close friendship. Bettina was beginning to look a little healthier as her pregnancy came to an end. She had five weeks left. Gwyneth was frantically knitting little sweaters and caps, while Augusta embroidered tiny night-gowns with white rosebuds on them that would work for either sex. They would put the baby in dresses for the first few months whether she had a girl or a boy.

Caroline and Lucy were excited about the baby, and so was Sybil. Magnus and Charlie showed no interest in it at all.

"I suppose it will keep us all up yowling at night," Angus commented. "I'll play the bagpipes for it to calm down," he promised.

"Please don't," Augusta said firmly, as they all winced at the thought. Bert still hadn't made peace with the idea of his daughter having the grandchild of an immigrant fish-restaurant owner who wanted nothing to do with his daughter, for fear it would cost them something. And they had never gotten over the slight of the Butterfields thinking them unsuitable, and were taking it out on Bettina as revenge, and punishing her. Bert wondered if they'd feel differently if she had a boy, and he suspected that would be the case. It made him think of Josiah, and he wished they had a child of his now, but there had been none. It made them regret he hadn't married, although he was young.

Their Thanksgiving meal was a long one, with warm feelings of friendship among them, and at the end of the evening, they all hugged one another, and Augusta even embraced Sybil, although most of the time she ignored her or complained about what she wore, which was never right according to Augusta. She always said that Caroline looked like a dancer on a music box with the outfits she had on at dinner.

Bettina could hardly move when she got up from the meal. Her belly was huge now, in a red velvet dress Gwyneth had had made for her, although she wore black most of the time, suited to her being a widow. Gwyneth had worn black for Josiah since he died. She had done the same for Magnus for a year when he'd died twelve years before.

They said good night to each other, heavily sated by the

meal and good wine. Bert and Blake clapped each other on the back, and Sybil and Gwyneth hugged, and then they quietly left the room and vanished, as the Gregorys wandered up the stairs, groaning about how full they were.

"I feel like Bettina," Sybil said, laughing, and Blake said nostalgically that he wished it were them having a baby, and she looked surprised. He had always wanted a fourth child, although he hadn't said it for a while. But Sybil felt that three was enough.

"One more would be nice," he said wistfully. "A little girl." But at nearly forty, she didn't want to do it again. "It would keep us young."

"Speak for yourself," she said, as they walked into their bedroom, after a really wonderful evening with their friends.

They lay in bed a little while later, talking about nothing in particular, and feeling close to each other. And then he mentioned Bettina again.

"I feel sorry for her, having that baby alone. It won't be easy."

"I don't think she's happy about it," Sybil said thoughtfully. "I think she realizes she made a mistake and acted in haste to defy her parents, and she regrets it. But it's too late now. Maybe the baby will cheer her up."

"Her father thinks no one will want her now, with a child," Blake said, thinking about it.

"Gwyneth says the same thing, but we know that's not true. And there will be lots of young widows with children after the war. This war will change things for everyone. It will even make it all right for women to work, if the bread-winners are gone."

"You're beginning to sound like them," he said, and she laughed.

They fell asleep and woke up late the next morning, and had a relaxing weekend with their children. The Butterfields did the same. It was a perfect Thanksgiving for them all.

*

December was busy for Sybil, getting ready for Christmas and for Andy to come home. She had presents for every-one, including the Butterfields. The two families got together to decorate an enormous tree in the ballroom, as the Butterfields had always done. Charlie and Blake went to pick up a tree, and they all worked on it, hanging decorations they found in the garage. Bert had told them where they were. Alicia's husband, José, helped them, as the Gregorys chatted with each other and people he couldn't see. He decided that Alicia was right and they were all slightly crazy.

"They all have imaginary friends," she had told him, "even the grown-ups." But the Gregorys paid them well and were kind employers, so he didn't care if they talked to themselves, and told Alicia not to pay attention to it either. It was none of their business if they were eccentric.

*

On Christmas morning, they all gathered in the ballroom, and everyone's presents had found their way there. The Gregorys had exchanged a few presents on Christmas Eve as they always did, but they'd decided to follow Butterfield tradition this year, and exchange their presents with them on Christmas Day. Phillips served eggnog, with the adults' portions laced with brandy, and Magnus and Charlie took a sip before they got caught, and Phillips pretended not to notice. He was very fond of the boys.

Both sets of parents had told them that Santa Claus had left the presents during the night, and they still believed it. Charlie got a new bicycle from his parents, and they had bought one for Magnus too, a bright red one, and he loved it, and rode it around the ballroom and the Christmas tree as fast as he dared.

Everyone else loved their gifts too. Bettina received a number of them for the baby, all handmade by her female relatives. Augusta and Gwyneth were in a frenzy of knitting and sewing these days. She said she felt like an elephant now, and the midwife had said the baby was a good size and could come at any time. Bettina just wanted it over, and the baby in her arms and out of her body. It felt as though it had been there forever, making her feel sick.

The two families shared another big dinner that night, and the next morning, the Gregorys left for Aspen, with all their ski equipment and clothes. They planned to come back the morning of New Year's Eve, so they could see in the New Year together. They had received other invitations, but they wanted to spend it with the Butterfields, who had become like family to them now. And Sybil had bought a new silver dress for the occasion.

They had a wonderful week in Aspen, and skied together a lot of the time. Andy was full of stories about school in Scotland, and he picked up lots of girls on the slopes and went out at night. And he and Caroline talked about colleges a lot. She had applied to ten of them, and wanted to stay in the west if she could. Stanford was her first choice, and then UCLA. She wasn't ready to go as far afield as her brother, although he loved Edinburgh.

*

Their faces were tanned with goggle marks from skiing and they were happy and rested when they got back to San Francisco at noon on New Year's Eve.

When they came downstairs that night, Sybil was wearing her new silver evening gown, and Blake said she looked spectacular. Gwyneth was in black lace with jet beads all over it and looked like a John Singer Sargent

painting with her upswept hair and a long string of dia-
monds around her neck and at her ears. Augusta had worn
black velvet and was very dignified. And Blake had surprised Sybil and bought a set of tails. He had decided he
could use them for dinner at the house, and wore them for
the first time that night.

"Finally!" Augusta said with approval when she saw
him. "It took you long enough," she teased him, and then
she told him how handsome he was, and Sybil agreed.
Augusta liked Blake. He was always respectful and attentive to her.

They played charades after dinner, and then adjourned
to the ballroom to dance. They used the music system the
Gregorys had installed, and Blake swept Sybil away for the
first dance, as the children watched and giggled. Bettina
felt like a whale in a black velvet gown she could barely
get into. She had outgrown everything she owned, but
she looked pretty and young, and very maternal, with her
enormous round belly under the dress. Gwyneth and Bert
danced, and then stepped out onto the terrace in the
moonlight, and they were both thinking of their son. They
walked back into the ballroom to join the others, and as
they did, Josiah came through the ballroom doorway in
his uniform, waving at everyone. He was back! Everyone
gave a cheer to greet him. It was cause for celebration, and
Blake and Sybil smiled at each other, happy for their
friends.

"There is something so perfect about their world," Blake said as he danced with her again. "It all comes full circle in the end. You don't have to wait to find out what happens and how it all turns out. We already know. Maybe the secret is that we can't influence their world, in the past, but they can still influence ours, by what we learn from them. Maybe that's right and the way it should be."

They all kissed each other at midnight, and embraced Josiah, who looked more handsome than ever in his uniform. Everyone was thrilled to have him home. It had taken him four months to get back to them. Sybil wondered if Bettina's husband would join them too. But this wasn't his home, and he knew he hadn't been welcome here. There was no mention of ghosts in Bettina's book, and almost no mention of Tony, although he was her daughter's father. But since her second husband had adopted her, Tony had faded rapidly from her life. And she wasn't alone for very long, before Louis de Lambertin appeared.

Josiah danced with all of them, his sister Bettina too, in spite of her enormous shape, but she only danced to celebrate his return for a few minutes before she sat down. And then he danced with Lucy, and Caroline, who looked lovely in a midnight blue satin dress and high heels, with her blond hair piled on top of her head.

"They'll have to marry her off soon," Augusta said to Gwyneth, watching her. "She's growing up fast." She had just turned seventeen, and Augusta thought the time was right, and said as much to Gwyneth, who laughed. She knew that Sybil wouldn't have agreed. Their ideas about when girls should marry were very different from what Gwyneth and her mother were used to.

Everyone was exhausted when they left the ballroom at three A.M. A new year had begun. Bert had toasted 1918 at midnight, and he hoped it would be an exceptional year for all of them. It had been the perfect way to see in the new year, and Josiah was home again. What more could they ask?

Chapter 10

They all looked a little rough around the edges on New Year's Day. A great deal of champagne had been poured the night before, especially since Josiah was home. They had all felt very festive. And they were quiet at dinner that night, still recovering. Everyone wanted to talk to Josiah, and tell him what they were doing. They were careful not to ask him any questions about the war. But Sybil noticed that he seemed more mature than when he left. His portrait was complete by then, hanging in the front hall, and was a perfect likeness.

Bettina said very little, and she excused herself at the end of dinner and said she didn't feel well. Gwyneth went upstairs to check on her, and nodded at Sybil before she left the dining room, and whispered to her that it had started. They had just called the midwife. She was coming right over, and was bringing the nurse with her.

"You don't think she should go to the hospital, or have a doctor come here?" Sybil asked, worried.

"Why?" Gwyneth smiled at her. "She's not ill, and there have been no complications."

"Will they give her anything for the pain?" Sybil asked, dreading the experience for her without it.

"Some laudanum drops, if she needs them, but she probably won't. I never did," Gwyneth said bravely. But the baby wasn't as small as it had been a few weeks earlier. It had grown exponentially, and her belly looked twice the size it had a month before. It was no longer such a small baby.

Gwyneth glanced at Sybil with a warm look in her eyes. "Do you want to come?"

"Would Bettina want that?" Sybil hesitated. She didn't want to intrude—she wasn't a relative, after all.

"She'd be grateful to have you with us," Gwyneth said sensibly. "You've had babies too. It will help her get through it." Sybil nodded then, and told Blake what she was doing. And then the group disbanded and Blake left with their children. Sybil followed Gwyneth up the grand staircase to the floor above theirs, and found herself in an enormous bedroom she didn't remember seeing before, and then she realized it had been Bettina's bedroom in the past, and still was.

Phillips let the midwife in half an hour later, and escorted her to Bettina's room. Bettina was in bed, in a freshly pressed nightgown, when the midwife came in, and the nurse was folding sheets and towels, getting things ready for the birth.

Bettina was glad to see Sybil with her mother, and

smiled at her. There were beads of sweat on her brow, and a moment later she was panting and couldn't talk. Everyone in the room was calm. Gwyneth sat down on a chair, and a little while later the midwife and the nurse checked the baby's progress. Bettina gritted her teeth in stoic silence, as Sybil winced for her. She could see how much pain she was in, and couldn't imagine how she would get through it without the benefit of modern medications, but no one in the room looked concerned. The midwife listened to the baby's heartbeat regularly with a stethoscope she kept around her neck, and a little while later, they pulled back the covers, slipped sheets under her that they had brought with them, and covered her with another sheet after they took off her nightgown. They were getting ready, and Bettina looked dogged as she beckoned to her mother and Sybil. They each stood on a side of the bed and held her hands, and her mother smoothed back her hair and wiped her brow with a cloth dipped in lavender water.

"Mama, this is awful," she said in a raw voice and clenched her jaw so she wouldn't scream. Sybil had never seen anything so brave in her life, and couldn't bear the thought that it could have all been so different, but this was what they expected and how they did it at the time. All of Gwyneth's babies had been born at home, in the bedroom Sybil and Blake now slept in. She had no idea where Bert and Gwyneth's room was now, or if they had one. She had never asked.

"It won't be long," the midwife said after she looked between Bettina's legs, then pulled them back and she and the nurse each held one and told her to push.

"I can't," Bettina said. "It hurts too much." And then she couldn't keep the baby from coming and she had to push it out, as all four women encouraged her while Sybil and her mother held her hands. She worked hard for half an hour, and finally the baby tore through her, and nothing could stop it or slow it down. With one long shattering cry, the baby she hadn't wanted and that had made her so ill lay on the bed between her legs and gave a soft wail, and looked up at all of them, as Sybil felt tears roll down her cheeks. She had never seen a woman as courageous as Bettina.

It was a girl. The midwife picked the baby up and cleaned her, cut the cord, and handed her to the nurse. She did some repair work on Bettina, and gave her some drops to make her sleep, and then they cleaned her up and put her daughter in her arms. Bettina was already a little groggy but no longer in pain. The infant stared at her mother. The room was quiet and peaceful. It was so different from what Sybil remembered from when her own children were born. There had been frenzied activity, people and noise, and incredible joy. The baby made small snuffling sounds, and Bettina had been silent for most of it. She leaned down and kissed the top of the baby's head as she held her. And then the midwife put her to Bettina's breast, and covered them both with a light blanket. They made it all seem so simple and natural. Gwyneth was smiling down at her first grandchild, and kissed her daughter and told her what a good job she'd done. A few minutes later, Bettina drifted off to sleep from the drops. And as she watched her, Sybil was sorry that Bettina's husband wasn't there, and that there hadn't been great love or joy in the room. She deserved so much more. But there was a sense of peace, as the baby drifted off to sleep too.

"What are you going to call her?" the midwife asked Bettina when her eyes fluttered open again.

"Lili. Lili Butterfield," she said clearly, and drifted off again. She had decided not to give the baby her father's name, since his family didn't want either of them, and Bettina realized now how little she had known him. She preferred to give her child her own name, and Gwyneth nodded her approval. Sybil realized how alone Bettina had been at that moment, when the baby was born, even with four women in the room to help her. The baby's father should have been somewhere in the house, pacing and waiting for news. But Bettina looked content as she fell into a deep sleep. A little while later, Gwyneth disappeared to her own room to tell Bert, and Sybil went downstairs to the room where Bettina had been born, and found Blake was sound asleep. Sybil got into her nightgown and slipped into bed beside him, and was surprised to see the sun coming up. The night had gone quickly, as they watched Lili come into the world. The baby still felt like a miracle to Sybil, even without a father to love her. Life would somehow provide what she needed. Lili's journey had begun.

Chapter 11

There was champagne at the dinner table the night after Lili was born. They had each been to see her that afternoon, except Angus, who said he preferred to wait to meet her until she was old enough to drink champagne with him. After a careful inspection of every inch of her, including her fingers and toes, Augusta pronounced her "very pretty" and added "surprisingly," given who her father was. She said she was relieved to see that she didn't look Italian. The baby was very fair like her mother. Gwyneth could see that the baby was going to be a towhead like both of her own daughters. And Gwyneth liked to say that Sybil looked related to them, and Caroline was just as fair. Bert finally relented when he saw his oldest daughter holding his first grandchild. Bettina suddenly seemed older and more mature as she held her daughter. She kept staring down at the tiny, perfectly formed features, as though wondering who she was and wanting to get to know her. She was responsible for another person now, and it had subtly changed her, even overnight. She thought about what it would have been like if Tony were alive, if he would have been happy, or disappointed it wasn't a boy. Bettina was happy the baby was a girl; it would be easier for her.

When Sybil came to visit her, Bettina wanted to get up and walk around the room. She felt stiff in the bed after the rigors of the night before, but the nurse wouldn't let her get up, much to Sybil's surprise. They all insisted that mother and infant stay in bed and keep warm. There was a roaring fire in the grate, and Bettina looked restless. She was healthy and young, and felt better than she had for all nine months of her pregnancy, which had been miserable. The one thing she knew was that she never wanted to go through it again. Even the agony of childbirth had been worth it to get the baby out of her, and be free of her at last. It had been a time of unhappiness and deep grief for her, with her family's stern disapproval and Tony's death.

The next day, Bettina wrote a letter to Tony's family, telling them that the baby had been born, and that it was a girl, and asking if they would like to see her. It was a respect she felt she owed the man she had married, however briefly the marriage had lasted and how slightly they knew each other. She had been carried along on the wave of girlish emotions and romantic illusions, and she saw now that there was no reality to them. She had married a man she barely knew, and borne a child after one night with him. He felt like a stranger to her now, in spite of Lili, although she was sad that he had died. She wondered if they would have loved each other, after they knew each other, had he lived, or if their families would have prevailed and pulled them apart. Fate had done it for them, and now she had his child.

She felt no bond to the baby yet, and had confessed it to her mother, who said she would in time. She said that the pain of childbirth often made for a slow start, but Bettina's memory of it wasn't that it had been terrible. It had been worse than she'd expected, but she already felt better, and what shocked her was that she and Lili were bound to each other for life. It was an awesome responsibility, for a stranger's child. She wondered who Lili would be when she grew up, who she would look like, what sort of person she would become. Augusta had said that she looked like a Butterfield, and Bertrand agreed.

Bettina had Phillips drop her letter off at the Salvatores' restaurant. She had written it to his father, Enrico, as the head of the family, essentially asking if they wished to see the child, since she was their son's daughter. His response came by mail several days later and was harsh. His granddaughter's arrival didn't change his feelings toward her, Bettina, or the Butterfields, and he said he wanted nothing to do with any of them. He was still furious over Bert calling Tony and his family unsuitable, and the elder Salvatore would never forgive them for it. And even the baby didn't alter his decision.

He told Bettina in his response that his son hadn't been

good enough for them when he was alive, and now she and her daughter weren't good enough for them. He told her there would be no money, which she hadn't asked for, and not to contact them again. He said that he had four grandsons and no interest in a granddaughter. Bert's rejection had cut deep and now Tony's father was retaliating in kind with angry words. It made Bettina glad that she had decided not to give the baby their name. She owed them nothing more. He had rejected her and Lili in every possible way, beyond any doubt. It gave Lili a lonely start in life, with no link to her father, but in the end it was easier that way. Bettina could leave any sense of obligation to them and the past behind. The letter was ugly, but also a relief. She had written to them out of a sense of duty, wanting to do the right thing. The Salvatores had been expunged from her life now, and her daughter's. Bert was relieved too when she showed him the letter, which only confirmed to him how vulgar they were.

"It's better this way," Bettina said to Sybil when she told her about the letter from Tony's father. "I don't want to see them again either. I only wrote to him to be fair to Tony. I thought he would want me to do that. Lili doesn't need them. She has us. And they're not nice people." He had been almost as clear about it when she went to see them and told them she was pregnant. They had made it obvious that they didn't care. And Enrico had spoken for Tony's mother too. She had never reached out to Bettina after Tony's death, almost as though they blamed her for stealing him from them, instead of destiny.

Sybil was sorry for her. It was a sad thing to bear a child without a father, and the future wouldn't be easy. Lili would always wonder about her father's family and why they didn't want to see her. Bettina would have to come up with some excuse or explanation. At dinner, Sybil told Blake that the Salvatores had rejected Bettina and their grandchild, and he thought it was simpler too.

"I was afraid they might be a problem, or want money," Blake told her honestly.

"They were afraid of the same thing," she said with a sigh.

"She never should have done it," Bert said, looking stern again, thinking about it, when he mentioned it to Blake.

"She's not even twenty-two, Bert, she's young, and we're all foolish at her age," Blake said gently.

"Her foolishness has produced a child," Bert said soberly, "a responsibility and a burden she will have to shoulder forever, for the rest of that child's life, and hopefully hers." Having lost two children himself, he did not wish that on her, no matter who the child's father was, or how unsuitable. "I suppose we'll have to invent some respectable story about who Lili's father was. It's easier to do after a war. A lot of girls married too quickly, and proper young men too. At least Lili wasn't born out of wedlock." That would have been an unpardonable stigma the child and Bettina would have carried forever. He was grateful they didn't have that to contend with, and could put it behind them now. Lili was a Butterfield, and that was that.

"How is she?" Blake asked about Bettina. He hadn't seen her at dinner yet, since the birth, and it had been a week.

"She seems fine. She'll rest for the next month, and then she'll be back among us," her father said.

Blake was sure that lower-class working women got back on their feet more quickly. But not women in their world.

Augusta was pleased with her first great-grandchild. Bettina had chosen "Augusta" as Lili's middle name to pay homage to her, and her grandmother was flattered.

"Shame it wasn't a boy," Angus had said regretfully, when told of the baby's arrival, but on the whole it was a happy time, and Gwyneth was enjoying her grandchild. She had stopped her computer sessions when the baby was born, so she could help Bettina adjust to motherhood, which didn't seem to come naturally to her, and she was outspoken about not wanting more children. Gwyneth told Sybil she'd be back on the computer soon, once Bettina was up again in about a month.

It seemed like forever to Bettina before she was allowed to come downstairs for dinner. She had been permitted to walk around the garden with the nurse a few days before, and she had admitted to Sybil with a grin that she wanted to leap over the wall and run away. She felt like she was in jail in her room with the baby. Lili was four weeks old by then, and Bettina was finally released. It had been a long convalescence for a healthy young girl her age, after a natural event. She had almost regained her figure by then, and wasn't nursing. They had hired a wet nurse a few days after the baby was born, and Lili was fat and healthy, and had just produced her first real smile. And so did her mother as soon as the doctor pronounced her free and she was allowed to leave her room.

She still had trouble feeling close to the baby, and Sybil wondered if it would have been different if she had nursed, but she had been adamant about not wanting to. She wanted her body back now, and her life. She and Lili would be linked forever, but she showed no signs of being maternal and was perfectly content to let the nurse and wet nurse tend to all of Lili's needs. The last ten months had been too traumatic, and she wanted to get back on her feet.

The first time Bettina rejoined the family for dinner, Caroline announced that she had been accepted at UCLA and would be going to college there in the fall. She had been wait-listed at Stanford, but was satisfied with her second choice. Andy was already back in Edinburgh after the Christmas break. He was dating a girl there, and Sybil had the feeling it was serious, or could be. Caroline was still seeing the same boy at school, but he had been accepted at Princeton and was going east, so they had agreed to break up in June.

Blake was looking strained. They had some financial issues at the start-up, with the founders losing a great deal of money with some high-risk decisions that had gone badly. He was discussing them intently with Bert, who always gave him good advice. And he had made Sybil aware of it too.

And for the Butterfields, there was still a war on. They no longer had a son in it, but the news from the front was devastating, and the boys were dying like flies in the trenches. Things were going better for the Germans than the Allies. There were gold star banners in the windows of homes all around the city, and across the country, indicating sons who had died. America had been in the war for only nine months, but the death toll was alarmingly high, and it showed no sign of being over yet. And stories of the revolution in Russia were depressing too.

But the mood at the Butterfield Mansion was lighter with Bettina back in their midst, the baby to admire, and Josiah home. Sybil was working on her book again, and hoping to finish it by the end of the year. She kept adding more material to it, and Blake called it the never-ending book. Gwyneth returned to Sybil's office to create art on the computer. The two women worked side by side for many hours in companionable silence, with an occasional smile or comment.

Sybil was sorry Gwyneth couldn't show anyone her art; Gwyneth was still keeping it a secret from Bert and didn't think he'd approve. And Sybil didn't disagree with her. She was not only challenging the time barrier, but defying the social rules of her world and class, by trying to be a modern woman, which was forbidden to her. Sybil often chafed for her more than Gwyneth did, but it bothered Gwyneth too, to be so restricted from the natural order of things, in a world run entirely by men.

*

That summer the Gregorys rented a house in Santa Barbara for a month, instead of the one they used to rent in the Hamptons when they lived in New York. It was fun to do something different, and have a change of scene. The summer before, their first in San Francisco, Josiah had been killed and they hadn't wanted to abandon the Butterfields, and canceled their vacation, but this year things were peaceful. The Butterfields were going to Woodside, and Bettina was taking the baby and the nurse with them. Lili was six months old in July, and a happy, easy baby.

Caroline had broken up with her boyfriend in June as they had agreed to do. She had been ready to let him go by then anyway. She met someone new while they were in Santa Barbara; he was going to UCLA in the fall too. He came to dinner at the rented house in Santa Barbara several times, and he took her out for dinners and movies, and he got along well with her brothers. They went out on his parents' sailboat a few times, and Sybil and Blake liked him. His name was Max Walker, and he wanted to major in film, which he already seemed very knowledgeable about.

While they were in Santa Barbara, Andy texted a dozen times a day with the girl he liked in Edinburgh, Quinne MacDonald. He asked his parents if she could visit in San Francisco over Christmas, which was an interesting dilemma, since they spent their holidays with the Butterfields, and they weren't easy to explain. Sybil and Blake had no idea how they would deal with a stranger or if the Butterfields would even appear if someone else was there. And they didn't want to spoil things.

"I already told her about them," Andy said blithely.

"You did?" His mother looked stunned. "How did you manage that?" She had never told anyone herself, except Michael Stanton at the Berkeley Psychic Institute, and she wouldn't have known where to start, without having people think they were on drugs or insane.

"I just told her how it happened in the beginning, and what it's like," Andy said simply. "Her parents have a castle in the north of Scotland, and she says it's full of old ghosts and relatives who died there and people they don't know but everyone thinks they see. It's not exactly like us and the Butterfields, but she said it sounds like fun." It was fun, for all of them, in both families, that was the odd part. And after a year and a half, they were all used to it and had adjusted. They seemed to have no trouble living together and straddling two different centuries under one roof.

"I'd like to meet her," Sybil said about Quinne, and told Blake. Andy seemed serious about the girl.

When the two families were reunited after their vacations, they had lots to talk about: family news, the baby had grown, and Bettina seemed to be bonding with her a little more with some effort. She had spent most of her time in Woodside riding, and looked happier than she had in a year. She was an expert horsewoman, and Josiah was an excellent rider too. They had spent hours on horseback together in Woodside that summer—and she wanted Lili to ride too when she was older. She had lots of plans for her, which Sybil thought was a good sign. Bettina was having a hard time adjusting to motherhood. She didn't have the maternal instincts of her own mother. In some ways, Bettina was more like Augusta, and was close to her. She and Angus had been in Woodside too, and she complained about the heat there when they returned, and said she was delighted to be back in the fog in San Francisco.

Sybil thought Angus looked tired and was getting more confused, but his sister kept a close eye on him. Augusta was still clear as a bell, at whatever great age she was. She kept it a dark secret. Sybil suspected she was in her mid- to late eighties, and could even be ninety, judging by the way she looked and the events she talked about.

At the end of August, after Andy had returned to Edinburgh for his second year, Sybil took Caroline to UCLA to settle her into the dorms, and she connected with her new friend Max within an hour of her arrival. He helped Sybil carry Caro's trunks and bags into the dorm, along with her computer, her music system, and the small refrigerator she had rented. He had already been there for two days and knew where everything was. By the time Sybil left the next day, Caroline barely had time to see her. She and Max were having dinner with friends from other dorms that night. She was off and running in her college life.

It was a lonely feeling as Sybil drove back to San Francisco that night, and she was particularly glad that she still had Charlie at home. She wasn't ready to become an empty nester just yet, and for a minute she wondered if Blake was right to want another baby. But at forty now, she wasn't sure about it. What if there was something wrong with the child? And it would be hard starting all over again. She loved playing with Lili, but a baby was so much work and needed so much attention. She couldn't see herself doing it again. Bettina had a full-time nurse and her mother to help her. Sybil would do most of it herself, as she had before. Charlie was easy now, at seven. He'd been lording it over his friend that he was a year older than Magnus, which Magnus had complained about to his mother and she laughed. Sybil knew that was going to continue happening, because Magnus would be six forever.

The house seemed empty without Caroline when Sybil got back to San Francisco, and she sat down to work on her book in earnest. Gwyneth was spending a lot of time with Lili, and working on her computer during the baby's naps. Bettina had started writing a family history, and asked Augusta for pertinent information, without explaining why. Her grandmother remembered all the details and gossip that no one else did, who was related to whom and how, whom they had married and who died when. Bettina drew a family tree from what Augusta told her, which helped her keep it all straight while she was writing. Sybil knew it would be a fascinating book, and Bettina said it would take her years to finish. Longer than she knew, Sybil realized as she listened to her talk about it, since she had only completed it when she was eighty, in the final years of her life, so she had obviously stopped writing it for a while at some point.

For the next few months, both Bettina and Sybil spent most of their time writing, and the house was very quiet. Blake was staying late at the office, wrestling with the financial ups and downs of his start-up, and consulting with Bert on it for advice.

The battles in Europe had been fierce that fall, but by October there was some hope that the war was drawing to an end. More than eight million men had died and twenty-one million had been wounded on the battlefields of Europe, and on November 11, 1918, the armistice was finally signed, nineteen months after America had entered the war and lost over a hundred thousand men, Josiah Butterfield and Tony Salvatore among them. Tony had never returned as a ghost to join the others at the house. Sybil thought it was better that he hadn't. Bettina was young and alive, and needed to meet someone from her own world, whom her family thought suitable, and who would be willing to be a father to Lili. From reading Bettina's book, Sybil knew it would happen in time. In December, Bettina made a shocking announcement at dinner that no one had expected. She had exchanged letters with friends of her parents in Paris, and they had invited her to come over in a few months, after the dust settled, now that the war was over. They were aware that she had been widowed and had a baby, and they thought a change of scene would do her good, and so did she.

"The Margaux?" Gwyneth said, looking shocked. "We haven't seen them in years. What made you write to them?"

"I have nothing to do here, Mother," Bettina said sensibly. "I can't just walk around our garden pushing Lili in her pram for the rest of my life." And she didn't do that anyway, the nurse did. Bettina spent very little time with the baby, and most of her time writing. "I won't stay forever, just a few months."

"Will you take the baby?" Gwyneth looked disappointed at the news, because she was having so much fun with Lili, and Sybil squeezed her friend's hand when she saw how sad she looked.

"I think I should. It will be good for her too, to see new people and new places." It was obvious that she'd given it considerable thought and made up her mind before she told them.

"When are you thinking of going?" her mother asked her.

"I haven't decided. February maybe, or March. The war's only been over for a few weeks. We'll see how it goes." Lili would be a year old by then, and Bettina was going to take the nurse with her.

"I think it's an excellent plan," Augusta chimed in. "She's never going to meet a husband here, locked up in this house. And no one's entertaining these days."

"They will now that the war is over," Gwyneth added, and Bettina looked annoyed.

"I'm not looking for a husband, Grandma. Just a change of scene."

"There's nothing wrong with having both. A nice Englishman perhaps, or a Scot. Please God, no one French. Will you be going to London?"

"I might. I haven't figured it out yet. Father, may I go?"

She looked at her father imploringly, and he nodded. She wanted to get out of San Francisco for a while. She felt stifled in her life as a widow and a mother sequestered in her parents' home. She was desperate to get out again.

"I don't see why not, as long as you wait for things to calm down over there, and all the soldiers to muster out and go home. You wouldn't want to be there now." Bettina agreed. "I think it's a very good plan. Just don't stay too long." He smiled at his eldest daughter. "It's nice of the Margaux to have you. I've always liked them."

Gwyneth reluctantly agreed, although she hated to lose her daughter and her grandchild even for a week, let alone several months. But it was obvious to all of them that a trip would do her good, and there was nothing better than Paris for a change of scene. What woman wouldn't want to go there? Just thinking about it, there was a new spring in Bettina's step as she ran up the stairs to her room after dinner, to work on her book. And even if it was a few months away, she could hardly wait for Paris.

Chapter 12

Andy startled everyone when he sent his mother an email saying he was bringing his girlfriend, Quinne MacDonald, with him when he came home for Christmas. He had mentioned it to Sybil casually over the summer, but she had forgotten all about it. And when she got the email from him, they were due to arrive in a few days.

They had plenty of room for her, and she was going to sleep with Andy anyway, but Sybil still wasn't sure how it would work to have a stranger in their midst. Andy had told her before that he had explained the Butterfields to Quinne, but did she really understand that they were all existing at some kind of crossroads of time, and the Butterfields, however lively, were all actually dead? It was a real-life ghost story, based on psychic phenomena that none of them were able to explain. But Andy insisted she was fine with it and that they would all love her. Sybil hoped he was right.

Out of courtesy and concern, Sybil discussed it with Gwyneth, who was startled too. They never appeared when there were strangers afoot or if the Gregorys were entertaining guests or Blake's business associates. The two families wanted to spend Christmas together. Gwyneth promised to discuss it with Bert, and got back to Sybil with his response, which had surprised her.

"He said it's fine for us, as long as she can handle it and Andy has explained it to her. We can't predict my mother of course, or Uncle Angus. That could go either way. She might not want to meet strangers or she may be curious about her." She smiled at Sybil, who was relieved to have their permission for a guest staying at the house. It was still their home too, and the Gregorys treated it that way.

But when Sybil picked up Andy and Quinne at the airport, she was less sure it would work. Everything about Quinne MacDonald shrieked "modern woman." She had several noticeable tattoos on her hands and arms and some kind of flower tattooed on her neck, and she was wearing knee-high lace-up military boots with a micro-mini leather skirt. She was a beautiful girl with a lovely face, a graceful figure, and electric blue hair. But she was well spoken and intelligent and had perfect manners, and Andy said she was an excellent student and wanted to go to medical school. She was from a very fancy family in Scotland, and her father was an earl. Sybil hoped that would carry some weight with Augusta and compensate for the blue hair, if Augusta appeared at all. Quinne had six tiny diamond studs in each ear but, fortunately, none in her nose. She had no facial piercings at all. Thinking of

Augusta again, Sybil was grateful for that. As the Gregorys became closer to the Butterfields, Augusta had become their matriarch too.

Their conversation on the way to the house was easy and pleasant, and Quinne thanked Sybil very politely for allowing her to come. She admired the house as they drove into the courtyard, and looked at the Butterfield portraits with interest when they walked into the front hall. And then she turned to Sybil with a questioning look.

"So where are they?" she asked, referring to the members of the family in the portraits, with an expectant look.

"We usually meet them for dinner," Sybil said quietly, although Gwyneth and Bettina often came to her rooms now, which worried Alicia.

She had noticed her employer talking to herself more and more in the past year, and thought she should be on medication. She thought it might be Tourette's, which she had read about on the Internet. Charlie seemed to have it too. And Blake once in a while. They all did. They talked to themselves whenever they felt like it, and sometimes they even laughed for no reason. She thought it was very sad that they were mentally ill. They weren't hurting anyone, but Alicia felt sorry for them anyway. And they dressed up like the Addams family for dinner. She'd see their evening clothes in their dressing rooms the next day. Sybil wore more evening gowns than an opera singer or a movie star. At first Alicia had wondered if they were vampires, which Alicia firmly believed in. It was all crazy behavior to her. Sybil had no idea the housekeeper was observing them so closely and coming to such dire conclusions.

"If you brought a nice dress with you, you could wear it tonight for dinner," Sybil told Quinne. "We are not sure if they will appear or if you will be able to see them. But I mentioned you, and I think most of them will come to dinner. They're quite formal. The men wear white tie and tails for dinner, but Andy's dad usually wears black tie. Caroline and I try to wear evening gowns, or something long anyway. Caro wears short cocktail dresses too, although I warn you, Uncle Angus is a bit of a lech." She sounded crazy even to herself as she said it, but Andy didn't seem to mind, and nodded agreement with what she said. He had told Quinne pretty much the same thing himself.

"If you didn't bring anything, don't worry," he told her. "Just wear whatever you have." Sybil agreed, as they set Quinne's bags down in Andy's room, and she noticed the sparkling blue nail polish that matched Quinne's hair. It was a complete look.

"Actually, I did bring some dresses for dinner," Quinne said quietly. "My grandparents are quite formal too, when we stay with them. And they're alive, which is worse." They all laughed. Sybil realized, as she left them to settle in, that she had now become officially eccentric herself.

She was living with dead people who seemed to be alive, in a mansion, in a time warp. There was no way she could ever feel normal again, or explain it to anyone sane, although Quinne said she thought it was fine. Maybe one had to have electric blue hair to feel that way.

Andy and Quinne went out shortly after to have lunch; he wanted to show her around the city. He borrowed his mother's car and gave Sybil a big hug, happy to be home with his parents and to have Quinne with him. He was in love with her, which was easy to see. She was a sweet girl, and seemed like a bright one, and despite the punk-rock style she exhibited, she was obviously very well brought up. Sybil could hardly wait for Augusta and Angus to see her, if they chose to appear, and hear what they'd say about her. It would do them good to be mildly provoked; the thought of it amused Sybil.

They had that opportunity at dinner, when Quinne appeared in a tight black evening gown that showed off her figure, startlingly high black suede platform shoes, her tattoos in full evidence, and the electric blue hair brushed straight up and gelled, a bit like the bride of Frankenstein, but blue and much prettier. And Andy was wearing black tie. Sybil was wearing a dark green velvet evening gown. Blake had come home from the office on time, met their guest, and changed into his dinner jacket, and Caroline was due back from Los Angeles the next day, for the Christmas break. Quinne and Caro had already met on

Skype and followed each other on Instagram to share photos.

Quinne walked into the dining room blended among them, and Augusta's eyebrows nearly shot into her hairline when she saw her. There were no words to describe the look on her face, and Gwyneth and Sybil had to turn away so Augusta didn't see them laugh.

"Oh, my dear," Gwyneth whispered to her, nearly choking.

"I warned both of them," Sybil whispered back, "but she's actually very nice, very polite, and seems very bright." When Sybil turned around, Augusta was interrogating their guest by then. She noticed her accent instantly, and knew she was Scottish. "And where are you from?"

Quinne told her, and Augusta narrowed her eyes. "What is your father's name?" She supplied it and the dowager stared at her intently, as though to discover if she was an imposter. "Castle Creagh?" Augusta asked pointedly, and Quinne nodded with a smile. She wasn't afraid of Augusta and thought her remarkably like her own grandmother, which amused her. It was a breed she understood and knew well, whatever the century, ghosts or not.

"Ian MacDonald and my late husband went to school together," Augusta said, smiling benignly at their visitor.

"He's my great-grandfather," Quinne said, smiling back,

and Augusta looked shocked for an instant, not remembering that in Quinne's world, he'd been dead for sixty years.

"What are you doing here?" she asked, and didn't comment on the hair, the tattoos, the shoes, or any part of her outfit. She looked delighted to see her.

"I'm visiting Andy," she said demurely with a smile, and Augusta told Angus who she was. He looked pleased too, although he didn't seem to remember who her great-grandfather was, but Augusta reminded him that her father was the current Earl of Creagh, and they lived at Castle Creagh.

"Your family hasn't sold it, have they?" she asked, looking concerned.

"No, ma'am, they haven't." Quinne addressed her formally in a thick Scottish burr that made Andy smile. She put it on when she wanted to, and knew that it would be a winning card with Augusta. After that, she sat down at the table next to Bettina and they chatted. Andy had told her that Bettina was leaving for Paris soon, and Quinne said she loved Paris and had studied at the Sorbonne for six months. "Though my accent is awful, pure Scot," she confessed, and Bettina laughed. She'd been brushing up on hers ever since she'd decided to go. And she wanted to hire a French governess when she got there, in addition to her American nurse, so Lili would learn to speak French.

Considering Quinne's exotic appearance, the dinner

went remarkably well. The fact that she was Scottish, and the daughter of the Earl of Creagh, had won Augusta over immediately. He was as eccentric as his daughter. Quinne had told Andy that her father had attempted to be a rock star at one time, but Augusta wasn't aware of that obviously, although she did say later, when Andy and Quinne left the table to go out so he could continue showing her the town, that the Creaghs had always been a little odd. But she thought Quinne was a pretty girl with good manners from a good family.

Sybil added that Quinne wanted to go to medical school, and Augusta looked shocked. "Why would she want to do that? How unsuitable for the daughter of a peer," she said grandly. "You'll have to talk her out of that." The electric blue hair didn't bother her, but the possibility of her becoming a doctor did. They lived in a mad world, Sybil thought to herself, and she and Gwyneth exchanged a look.

The next day Caroline came home from school. She didn't bring Max with her, but he was coming up after Christmas to spend New Year's Eve with her. He had gone to Mexico first, to meet his parents for Christmas.

Everyone had a good time at dinner, and they all played charades afterward, after Quinne and Andy went out. Josiah was exceptionally good at it. Andy and Quinne came back early to join the young people again. Josiah told Andy how much he liked her. Lucy did too, although

she was a little jealous of her, but Andy was always attentive to Lucy and treated her like a sister. It was the same
way Josiah felt about Caro now. And they all recognized
that they needed to spend time with their contemporaries
too. They couldn't exist solely in the Butterfields' rarefied
world, in a dimension accessible only to the two families.
The Gregorys needed more than that, although the Butterfields and the mansion were home base.

"As soon as my grandmother knew you were a countess, she didn't even notice the color of your hair," Josiah
teased Quinne when they sat in the drawing room playing
cards.

"My mother is still alive, so I'm not a countess yet,"
Quinne corrected him. "And her hair is shocking pink. It
was purple for a few years. She just changed it. My father's
is blue too. It's genetic." She grinned at him.

"You're a Scot. That trumps all," Josiah added. "That
means you're perfect."

"Of course," Quinne agreed. She fit right in, and Andy
had been right, she was perfectly at home in a family of
Victorian ghosts. Sybil couldn't imagine another girl who
would be. They had lucked out. And Andy was happy with
her, and was talking about staying in Scotland while she
went to medical school, but that was still a few years away,
and Sybil didn't want to think about it.

It was late by the time all the young people went

upstairs, and Quinne and Andy went back out for a night-cap at a bar in the Mission that stayed open late, and they slept in the next day. When Quinne emerged from Andy's bedroom, Alicia got a fright when she saw her hair, but Quinne was very polite, and she whisked down the stairs in denim shorts with a leopard sweater and camouflage combat boots.

"Madre de Dios," Alicia said, shaking her head. And when she went to vacuum the third floor, she could hear Sybil talking to herself again in her office. Gwyneth had come by for a few minutes, to gossip about Quinne, and both women agreed that they liked her. Other than the hair, she seemed perfect, and Andy was crazy about her. The only thing Sybil didn't like about her was that she was afraid Andy would stay in Scotland to be with her.

"Can't he convince her to come here?" Gwyneth asked her.

"I don't know. I think he likes it there. I'm going to blame Angus if he stays."

"You just have to convince her to move to the States, if he marries her," Gwyneth said.

"He's a long way from that. But you never know." There was always something to worry about with kids. Gwyneth was equally worried about Bettina staying in France.

"I don't think she will," Sybil reassured her. "She'd miss all of you too much."

"She's bored here," Gwyneth said realistically, "and if

she meets a man there . . ." Gwyneth's voice drifted off, and Sybil tried to forget what she already knew, that Bettina did meet a man there, and married him. But she and Blake had agreed that they had no right to tell them the future. It had to unfold, and if destiny changed it, that was different, but they couldn't influence what would happen. They didn't have that power anyway. And why upset Gwyneth?

*

Quinne had brought small, thoughtful gifts for everyone, and they all spent a beautiful Christmas Eve together. Christmas Day was sunny and warmer than usual. They sat in the garden together and talked, and had dinner again that night, informally. All the men wore black tie. Andy took Quinne away for a few days after that, to the Napa Valley and Lake Tahoe to show her the sights, and have some time alone together. They shared a lovely few days in beautiful places. Sybil liked Quinne more and more. She got along with everyone, and Augusta was enchanted by her. Angus was not entirely sure who she was, but commented that she had great legs and a very handsome bosom, which made everyone laugh except his sister, who scolded him soundly when they left the table, and told him he sounded like a masher.

*

Their New Year's Eve together was exceptionally nice too. It wasn't as dramatic as the year before, when Josiah had returned from the war. Max Walker arrived to spend the evening with Caroline, and Sybil had warned Gwyneth. Neither of them was sure how Augusta would react to all these strangers coming and going. But they were young and guests of the Gregorys, so Augusta came to dinner and ignored Max completely. He wasn't Scottish and his father didn't have a title, so he was unworthy of her notice. But the other Butterfields were there too and welcomed him warmly. Caroline had explained to him that they were ghosts, which he found hard to believe at first. But once he met them, he loved them. They celebrated Lili's first birthday two days later. Bettina had decided to leave for France a month later, in February, and had booked passage on the White Star Line's *Baltic.*

At dinner after Lili's birthday party, Gwyneth noticed that Augusta was coughing and looked feverish.

"Are you all right, Mother?" she asked, as she observed her through dinner. She didn't look well, and Sybil agreed.

By the time they left the dining room after dinner, Augusta seemed unsteady on her feet. Sybil remembered then from Bettina's book what it was, and suggested to Gwyneth that they call a doctor immediately. She nodded, and asked Bert to do it. The doctor came an hour later. He was the same doctor she'd had for fifty years, and he looked serious when he came downstairs. They were all waiting for him in the drawing room, which they seldom used.

"Is she all right?" Bert asked. He and Blake had been drinking some very fine brandy they'd found in his wine cellar.

"I believe it's the Spanish flu," he said ominously, "but hopefully a very mild case." The Spanish flu had been ravaging the United States and Europe for several months. Some survived it, but many didn't, and the death toll was beginning to compete with the war dead, and people feared it would exceed it. It was an epidemic of epic proportions, and none of them wanted Augusta to become one of its victims or fatalities. She was not a young woman.

The doctor recommended bed rest, keeping Augusta warm, and what medicines they had to combat it. But so far, little was known about the disease. Death could occur very quickly, even in healthy young people, and particularly among the elderly or infants, so Augusta was at serious risk.

Gwyneth volunteered immediately to nurse her, as did Bettina. They forbade Lucy to go near her, and Sybil volunteered her services too. There was no danger for her, and all three women were adamant about wanting to care for her. They wouldn't allow Angus to enter his sister's room, and when Quinne and Caroline offered to help too, the older women declined. But Sybil knew there was no chance of their catching any illness from a ghost.

Moments later, they began the first shift to nurse her. Gwyneth went first, and her mother got steadily worse through the night. She stayed with her until noon, and then left her in Bettina's care. There was no change when Sybil took over at midnight. She stayed on duty until the next day. The doctor came and went and brought a nurse with him, but there was nothing they could do. They just had to wait it out, as the flu tore through Augusta like a tidal wave, weakening her as the fever raged, and she began to cough blood.

Augusta was barely conscious on the third day when Gwyneth came to nurse her again and relieved Sybil. Bert came to check on them, and Gwyneth sent him away. She didn't want him to get sick too. Bettina kept her mother company that afternoon, before she relieved her, but Gwyneth didn't want to leave her mother's side. They were each sitting on one side of her, when Augusta sighed deeply, looked from one to the other and smiled, thanked them for nursing her, and then closed her eyes and exhaled her last breath. It was quiet and peaceful. She didn't struggle, but it was all over. Her body had suc-cumbed to the dreaded Spanish flu. Gwyneth and Bettina sat looking at her in shock, with tears rolling down their cheeks, as Augusta lay on the bed, an empty shell with a spirit that had flown.

Sybil and Blake were deeply saddened when Bert told them and their children. The entire house went into mourning, and Phillips put a black wreath on the door. They had had too many of them in recent years, and Alicia saw it when she came to work the next day and wondered what it was for. She'd seen them there before, and they always looked creepy to her. She wondered at times if the Gregorys were into witchcraft. But at least none of them were talking to themselves that day, as she perceived it. The Butterfields were in seclusion. Gwyneth was organizing her mother's funeral, and Bettina was helping with the details.

Bert told Angus the day after it happened, as gently as he could, but he didn't seem to understand what Bert told him, and rambled for a long time about people Bert didn't know. He didn't appear to comprehend that his younger sister had died, or what Bert had said. He took to his bed that afternoon, and refused to get up the next day. He said he was tired, but his mind was clearly rejecting the information he'd been given. It was too much for him to bear. He played his bagpipes in the middle of the night, and Bert had to ask him to stop.

He wouldn't get up to dress the day of the funeral, and after discussing it, Gwyneth and Bert agreed to let him stay home. His consciousness was refusing what had happened. He didn't have the Spanish flu, but he was clearly not well himself, in body or mind. It was as though someone had pulled the plug, and he was simply fading away on his own.

The funeral Gwyneth organized was solemn and beautiful and respectful, but the Gregorys couldn't go with them. They couldn't travel back in time to events outside the house, so they waited quietly for them at home. Quinne said she was happy to have met her, even for a brief time. They all sat in the drawing room afterward, had a light dinner together, and went to bed. And in the morning, Angus had died in his sleep, and joined his sister. Sybil wondered how long it would take them to return, since she knew they would, and that Augusta's spirit was strong. But no one could say, and Sybil didn't want to ask.

Andy and Quinne left for Edinburgh the next day, to go back to school, and Caroline flew to Los Angeles that night. Max had gone back just before Augusta got sick. It was a sad time for all of them, but they knew she had led a good life. Sybil went through the box of photographs the bank had given her. She found pictures of Lili as a little girl in France, and Bettina with her, and a man Sybil didn't recognize. They were all there with dates on the back, and there was a beautiful one of Augusta in her youth, which she set aside to frame and put on her desk. When Gwyneth saw it there a few days later, she asked how Sybil had gotten it, and she said she'd found it in a drawer, not wanting to tell her about the box of photos from the bank, or

Bettina's book. Gwyneth nodded. It was how her mother had looked when Gwyneth was a young girl.

The house was in deep mourning for several weeks, and Bettina thought about postponing her trip to Paris, but Gwyneth told her she should go. There was nothing more she could do at home. Only time would gentle the loss, but the house was too quiet without the indomitable matriarch who had terrorized them all.

Bettina went back to her packing, and Sybil and Gwyneth both knew how lonely it would be when Bettina and Lili left. The only young people in the house would be Lucy, who rarely emerged from her room except on particularly good days, and Magnus and Charlie. The others had all flown the nest or would soon. Gwyneth dreaded that moment, and so did Sybil for her.

Chapter 13

On the tenth of February, Gwyneth and Bert took Bettina, Lili, and the nurse to the train station, and watched the steamer trunks loaded into the first-class freight car, and helped her settle into the two first-class compartments they would occupy on the trip to New York. Bettina had their passports, their tickets, a letter of credit for a bank in Paris that her father had given her, foreign currency, and more than she needed in U.S. cash. She had enough clothes with her to stay away for ten years, and she was wearing an elegant midnight blue wool traveling suit with a mink coat over it, from her mother, and a very elegant black hat and long black gloves. She looked like a stylish young matron leaving on a trip, and she would board the RMS *Baltic* in New York for the trip to Liverpool, then Cherbourg, and from there by train to Paris, to stay with her parents' friends the Margaux. Gwyneth couldn't hold back the tears when she said goodbye to her daughter.

"Come back soon," she managed to choke out. Bert kept an arm around Gwyneth's shoulders as they watched the train pull out of the station. Bettina waved from the window in her compartment until she could no longer see them. She felt guilty for leaving, but like a bird that had been set free. It was exciting to be traveling across the country and stopping in cities along the way. She couldn't wait to get to New York and stay at a hotel for a night and then board the ship for the transatlantic crossing. It was the most thrilling thing that had ever happened to her. She felt very grown up, as she settled down on the train with a book, while the nurse took Lili to their own compartment for a nap.

*

Bettina was smiling with pleasure as the train picked up speed, but her mother cried all the way back to the house. Having lost her own mother a month before, now having Bettina and the baby leave was almost more than she could bear. Sybil was waiting to hug her when she got home. They were sitting in Sybil's office while Gwyneth cried, when they both heard a huge commotion on the stairs. Sybil thought she was imagining it, but she could hear Augusta calling orders to Phillips, and Angus in the background. Both women rushed to the landing to look down the stairs in time to see Phillips dragging her trunks up the stairs and Augusta in an enormous hat, ordering Angus around too. She glanced up and saw Sybil and Gwyneth, and they both started to laugh. Her trunks were everywhere and she was pointing at them with her cane, telling Phillips where to put them. Sybil and Gwyneth ran down the stairs to help her and hugged her. She was back! It hadn't taken long to return at all—she had the strongest spirit of all of them, even more so than her grandson Josiah, who had taken four months to return after he died. Augusta had taken four weeks, and had probably bullied her brother into joining her. She was in full command. Bert appeared to help Phillips with the trunks, as Augusta took off her hat with a victorious expression. Angus disappeared to his room.

She asked about Bettina and they told her she had left for France that morning.

"Sorry I missed her," she said, and then asked about Quinne, whom she had liked and who was there when she died.

"She's back in Scotland with Andy," Sybil told her, as they all stood on the landing together.

"Nice girl, unsuitable hair for a countess," she commented tartly.

"Welcome back, Mother Campbell," Bert said to her and smiled, as Gwyneth accompanied her to her room. It took the sting out of Bettina's departure. Her daughter and grandchild had left and her mother had returned. Violet and Rupert came running down the stairs to greet them, barking frantically. They had been mournful for the past month without their masters, and made up for it now. It was good to see Augusta and her brother again, at full strength, their spirits recharged and in fine form. They looked ready for another century at least.

"It's wonderful that they all come back," Sybil said to Blake that night. She hated the thought of people leaving whom they'd never see again, as happened in real life. With the Butterfields, in the dimension where they had taken refuge for the past century, they all came back to the home and people they loved. It was comforting to know that they would. But Sybil knew that she would miss Bettina's baby. It had been so sweet to hold Lili on her lap, or sing to her at bedtime, smell her hair right after it had been washed, or listen to the little snuffling sounds she made when she was sleeping. Lili reminded Sybil of her own babies. It made her sad to think about it, and even more so for Gwyneth. She knew just how terribly she would miss Lili.

*

After the small towns Bettina's train passed through, where they stopped just long enough for people to board the train for the trip east, the first big city was Chicago. They had the whole afternoon to look around. And after that, they would travel to New York, where Bettina was going to spend the night at the Plaza hotel, stay for a day or two, and then board the ship to France.

Chicago had been interesting, but New York was throbbing with excitement when Bettina checked in to the

Plaza. There was a telegram from her father waiting when she arrived to say that her grandmother and Uncle Angus were back, and Bettina smiled. She hired a carriage to take her around to look at the sights. She had a wonderful time and felt quite safe alone. She had dinner in her suite that night, and the next morning she boarded the ship with all her steamer trunks and bags and got settled in her stateroom. She had a second one for Lili and the nurse. The crossing would take nine to ten days to Cherbourg, with a stop in Liverpool. The *Baltic* was back in passenger service after her wartime activities carrying troops. She had been attacked by German U-boats but escaped undamaged. There would be entertaining things to do on the ship every day and night: games, teatime, elegant evenings, and the captain's dinner. Bettina was a beautiful young widow, and her eyes were wide with anticipation when the ship pulled away from the dock. The nurse was standing next to her, holding Lili. Bettina had sent her parents a telegram from the hotel to assure them that all had gone well so far.

It didn't frighten her at all to be making the trip unescorted. Other young women her age might have shrunk at the thought, but not Bettina. All she wanted now was to see the world, get to Paris, and escape her quiet life. Waiting for the war to end so she could leave San Francisco and travel had seemed endless, and nine months of pregnancy before that. She felt like she'd been released from prison.

She was twenty-three years old, it was 1919, and she couldn't wait to spread her wings and fly. And contrary to her family's wishes for her, the last thing she wanted now was a husband. That would be just another form of jail, with a man as her jailer. Bettina wanted freedom! With the wind on her face as the tugboats guided the ship out of New York Harbor, she knew that she had done the right thing leaving, and she was in no hurry to go back.

The crossing on the RMS *Baltic* was as entertaining as Bettina had hoped it would be. She met interesting people dining at the captain's table. There was an illustrious journalist, a famous writer, a very distinguished couple from Boston, a young couple from New York on their honeymoon, and well-known socialites. Bettina was just a young woman from San Francisco, but she was very pretty and was staying in two of the most expensive staterooms, which assured her a certain amount of attention and a place at the captain's table every night for the duration of the crossing. She wondered what her grandmother would say if she could see her conversing with elegant strangers and dancing in one of the ship's nightclubs with handsome bachelors who flirted with her at night. But she knew she was perfectly safe on the ship. Her daughter and the nurse established her as a respectable young woman, and not some wild single girl hoping to meet men in Europe or on the ship. She was a beautiful young war widow, like so many young women then.

She was sorry to see the trip end, said goodbye to her new friends, and was fascinated when they reached Cherbourg. She watched her belongings loaded on the boat train for the four-hour trip through the countryside on the way to Paris. She was happy to have the fur coat her mother had given her. It was still chilly in late February, and she noticed that there was light snow on the ground as she boarded the train in yet another first-class compartment. Her father had seen to it that she would travel in luxury and comfort at all times. For an instant, she was sorry that Lucy and Josiah weren't with her. She missed them, but she was looking forward to seeing her parents' friends in Paris. The letters they had sent to her, in response to her own, had been warm and welcoming, and promised good times.

The Margaux wanted to console her in her widowhood after the war, and said they didn't mind her bringing her baby. They had an enormous house on the Left Bank, an eighteenth-century *hôtel particulier,* with carriage barns, stables, and gardens, even larger than her parents' home in San Francisco. They had no children of their own, and said they'd be delighted if she and Lili would stay with them for several months. They invited her to bring as many servants as she chose with her. She would be occupying an entire wing of the house.

When Bettina arrived at the Gare Saint-Lazare, the Margaux had a car and driver waiting for her, and an entire carriage for her steamer trunks and bags. Once her belongings were loaded, they drove through Paris, and crossed the Seine to the Left Bank, down the rue de Varenne, and the chauffeur stopped the car in front of imposing double doors the guardian opened for them, and they drove into the courtyard. Bettina hopped out onto the cobblestones and gazed at the magnificent house as Angélique de Margaux came down the stairs to greet her with her husband, Robert, right behind her. They had been waiting for her all afternoon, and they put their arms around her, and admired Lili when the nurse emerged from the car holding her. Lili had been sound asleep and looked confused about where she was, as their benevolent hostess kissed her cheek and spoke to her in French.

For the Margaux, taking young friends like Bettina and her daughter under their wing had long since dulled the ache of not having children of their own, and they were delighted to have them. They led the way into the house and showed Bettina to her quarters as two footmen and a porter brought their bags upstairs. They had put Lili and the nurse on the floor above her, so Bettina wouldn't be disturbed but could have her close at hand whenever she wanted. It was the ideal setup, and several of their maids volunteered to babysit Lili so the nurse could go downstairs to the servants' hall to meet the others and eat with them. Lili's nurse looked excited. She had already noticed several handsome young footmen. Bettina laughed, remembering all her grandmother's warnings and the aspersions she cast liberally on the French. Bettina shared none of her opinions on the subject.

She dined with her gracious hosts that night, in a dining room even larger and much more elaborate than the one at home. There were exquisite boiseries, lush satin curtains, and impressive paintings, some of which had been in Versailles before the Revolution and they'd bought at auction, or had in their château near Bordeaux. The meal was delicious, and they wanted to hear all about the crossing and her parents. They discreetly offered their condolences for her late husband. She explained that he had died before Lili was born, a few months after he left to fight in the war.

Bettina was looking forward to visiting the museums and galleries of Paris again. She had been to France once as a young girl with her parents and Josiah, and she was startled to discover that the Margaux had much more planned. They had already organized several dinner parties to introduce her to their friends and the young people they knew, and Angélique de Margaux said to her in an undervoice that she had several possible suitors for her to meet. Out of the kindness of their hearts, they had taken her future in hand and wanted to help her. The thought of their friends' daughter languishing alone as a widow with an infant daughter seemed too cruel to them. And just as the Butterfields did for them, the Margaux had a great fondness for her parents. In a sense, it was their gift to them as well, to relieve them of one more worry, particularly as they had lost their son. The war had been hard on everyone, with so many young men who had died. There were too few to go around now, so young single women needed help, and they were determined to provide it. Bettina was quite shocked to hear their plan. It hadn't been the purpose of her trip, but once they described it to her, it seemed like an amusing idea. They had even planned a weekend at their château when the weather got warmer.

Bettina felt like a princess in her room that night, in a canopied bed with pink silk brocades, worthy of Marie Antoinette, and it might even have belonged to her, knowing the opulent taste of her hosts.

The next morning, after breakfast with Angélique, when Robert had left for the bank he owned and ran, Bettina borrowed the car and driver and went to the Louvre. She walked in the Tuileries Garden after that, and felt quite racy being alone. She returned to the house in the late afternoon and visited with Lili for a few minutes, then went back to her own rooms to rest before dinner.

They dressed as formally for dinner as her own family did, and she had brought a number of evening dresses to wear when she dined with her hosts. She had brought some ball gowns too, in case they invited her to grand parties, and her mother had lent her one of hers, which she said suited Bettina better.

Five days after she arrived in Paris, they began her Paris social life with a dinner party for a dozen guests, all carefully chosen to further her life there. There were two sisters her age with their parents, a charming young couple with a child Lili's age, and three handsome bachelors from excellent families whom their hostess said were the most desirable men in Paris. It was everything her parents would have wanted for her, and Bettina didn't normally think about. But she had a fantastic evening, and managed to speak French all night, much to everyone's delight. She knew her parents would have been extremely pleased and very grateful to her hosts. It more than made up for the two extremely boring and depressing years she had just spent at home in San Francisco during the war and her pregnancy. It had been five years since she'd come out, and she'd had no social life to speak of for the past three. She loved her family, but now she was ready to explore the world on her own.

Bettina thanked her hostess again profusely the morning after the dinner. Angélique assured her that she had another one planned for her the following week. And two of the men she'd met sent her flowers that afternoon. She had a feeling they were both practiced flirts, and the third one seemed like a fortune hunter, but they had certainly been fun for an evening. Angélique wanted to know if any of the men of the night before had struck her fancy.

"I'm not really looking," Bettina said honestly. "I just

wanted to get away from San Francisco for a while. I didn't have any plan to find a husband." And she wasn't sure she wanted one either, which she didn't say. She didn't want to appear ungrateful.

"But why not let us try? It's so much fun. And you deserve a handsome man." Bettina felt like a schoolgirl as she blushed, and she had to admit, it was entertaining to be the object of their attentions.

From then on, they gave a dinner party once a week to introduce her to suitable men and potential husbands, and Bettina had never seen so many good-looking men in her life. She had no idea what her grandmother had against the French, but Bettina thought the men were devastatingly handsome. And people she met at the Margaux dinners started inviting her too. Two months after she'd arrived, Bettina had a wide circle of friends in Paris. It was early May by then, and the weather was beautiful. She was invited to a lovely garden party one afternoon, to play croquet, and afterward she sat down on a lawn chair with a glass of lemonade and was surveying the scene when a man approached her. He was quite serious, and, as she recalled, he was a banker like her father and Robert de Margaux. He looked less playful than the men who had been pursuing her, but he was handsome and seemed pleasant, and was older than the others by several years.

"How are you enjoying your stay in Paris?" he asked her. He had come to one of the Margaux dinners for her, so she assumed they approved of him, or he wouldn't have been there.

"Very much so," she answered in French. She remembered that his name was Louis de Lambertin.

"How long will you be here?" he inquired quietly.

"I don't know. I needed a change of scene," she said honestly.

"Heavy losses during the war?" he asked, curious about her. He knew she was from a prominent American family in California, but nothing else about her.

"A brother and a husband," she answered his question. It was true, although Josiah was back in their midst. But Tony wasn't.

"I'm sorry. The war was so hard on everyone. I don't know of any family that wasn't touched by it," he said sympathetically.

"Particularly in Europe," she said softly, and they exchanged a smile.

"Do you have children?" he asked her, since she'd been married.

"A little girl, sixteen months old. Her father died before she was born." She didn't know why she was telling him all that, but he had asked. "Do you have children?" she asked, turning the tables on him, and he laughed.

"No, I don't. I've never been married." It surprised her, since he looked almost as old as her father, though not quite. She correctly guessed him to be around forty. In fact, he was forty-one, eighteen years older than she, but he seemed younger in spirit. She couldn't imagine her father having anything to say to a girl her age, particularly a single woman.

"Were you in prison?" she teased him, and he laughed.

"No, but perhaps I should have been. All bankers should be in prison." They chatted for a while, and then she went to look for the Margaux among their own friends, and Louis de Lambertin joined his. He didn't appear to be in a flashy group. They seemed like solid, aristocratic people, rather like her parents. Some of the Margaux family's friends were more glamorous.

Angélique commented on her talking to him, on the drive home, and Bettina asked about him.

"He's very quiet. I think he had a serious romance when he was younger that didn't work out, and then he never married. I'm not sure he's in the market for a wife. He strikes me as a permanent bachelor now. After a certain point, they don't care," Angélique said.

"That's perfect." Bettina smiled at her. "Because I'm not shopping for a husband." But a friend would have been nice, someone to explore Paris with her.

She was surprised to hear from him a few days later, and he invited her to Le Pré Catelan in the Bois de Boulogne for lunch.

He picked Bettina up in his enormous Citroën, drove her there, and they never stopped talking all through lunch. He wasn't a practiced flirt like many of the men Angélique had been introducing her to. He was just a nice person who was easy to talk to, and he thought the same about Bettina, and in addition he thought she was very beautiful. He invited her out again, the next time to dinner, and she had a good time with him once more.

She continued going to dinner parties, and the Margaux persisted in entertaining for her, but she managed to go to the ballet and the theater and the opera with Louis, and he took her to a dinner party to meet his friends. He met Lili and they went to the park together and he was very sweet to her, and Bettina realized that she had never been as comfortable with anyone. He was part father, part brother, part friend. She tried to explain that to Angélique after they had been seeing each other for over a month, and she smiled at her young friend.

"That sounds like a husband to me," Angélique said sensibly.

"Does it?" Bettina looked surprised. "I thought it was supposed to be much more romantic," she said innocently, and it had been with Tony, for one night.

"Not really." Angélique explained the ways of the world to her. "Eventually the romance goes away, most of the time anyway, and you want to be sure you're left with something you can live with. Friendship isn't a bad way to start, especially if it's what you wind up with in the end." It made sense to Bettina, and apparently to Louis too. He continued asking her out, and planning excursions that she enjoyed, and at the end of June, before he left to visit his family in Dordogne for the month, he proposed to her, on one knee. It had been quite different with Tony. They had just rushed off to city hall to get a marriage license and get married before he shipped out, and spent a night in a cheap hotel. In retrospect, it seemed tawdry, and she knew her father had been right. It would never have worked. Their worlds were too far apart.

"I never thought I'd get married again," she said in a soft voice after he asked her. "I'm not even sure I want to, although I like you very much." He smiled at the choice of phrase.

"I like you very much too. In fact, I love you, Bettina. I think we could be happy together. Why don't you want to get married again?" She found that she could always be honest with him and could say anything to him, and she liked that too, like a best friend.

"I don't want more children. It wasn't a good experience for me. In fact, it was awful. I was sick the whole time. I hardly knew the man I married, and I didn't think about what could happen. We were barely more than children, and got swept up in the drama and romantic illusions right before the war. But in terms of a baby, I don't think I'm very maternal. I love Lili, but I never really feel like a mother." He was touched by her honesty, as he leaned over and kissed her.

"Then we won't have children," he said simply. "I'm not sure I want any either. If you marry me, may I adopt Lili? Then she will be my daughter, and that's all the children we need." He made it all seem so easy. Everything was effortless with him, and she knew he'd protect her, like her father.

"Yes, you could adopt her. Her father's family isn't involved with us. They've never seen her."

"Never?" He was surprised when Bettina shook her head. "How long were you married before he went to war?"

"One night," she said with a sheepish grin. "We eloped. His family has a fish restaurant and my father was furious with me for marrying him. I think I got carried away with a lot of girlish delusions because he was leaving." Louis nodded, and understood the situation better than before.

"When are you going back to the States?" Louis asked her, thoughtfully.

"I'm not sure. Maybe sometime this summer, or in the fall. My parents have been asking me to." But she was in no hurry to leave Paris and go home. She was having too much fun.

"I'm leaving for Dordogne. I have to spend a few weeks with my parents and my grandmother, who's very old. But if you wait a few weeks, I'll go back to the States with you, and I can ask your father for your hand properly. How does that seem to you?"

"Very nice." She beamed at him, realizing that she loved him too, and how well he treated her. He was a kind, patient man, and would be a wonderful father for Lili. Angélique said he had a very considerable fortune, and was an only son. He wasn't showy in any way. He was substantial and solid, which was so much better. And he was handsome, in a dignified fatherly way, which she liked. He wasn't a boy, he was a man. She could suddenly see herself married to him, and the idea pleased her very much. It was not a wild romantic love, like her youthful passion for Tony. This was a very stable love, which seemed better to her, and Angélique said would last longer.

"You've forgotten one thing," he reminded her, with a warm light in his eyes that made her feel happy and safe.

"What did I forget?" She looked puzzled.

"You haven't said yes yet to my proposal. Should I get down on one knee again?" She blushed in embarrassment as she laughed, then put her arms around his neck, and he kissed her.

"Yes. Yes, I will marry you, Louis, and . . . I love you," she whispered and he kissed her again, very pleased with what they'd agreed to.

They made all the arrangements for her trip back before he left for Dordogne. He booked their passage on the ship for three staterooms, and she wrote to her parents that she was coming home. She said she was bringing someone with her, a friend of the Margaux, and her family assumed it was a woman when they received her letter. She didn't say his name, and she didn't mention that they were getting married, since Louis didn't have her father's permission yet. Bettina wanted to do it right this time. Her family had no idea that she was bringing her prospective husband home. And she didn't tell Louis that both her brothers and her grandmother and great-uncle weren't actually alive, and were ghosts whose spirits had returned to their home after their deaths. She hoped he didn't figure it out while he was there. There were some things he didn't need to know.

While Bettina spent her last weeks in Paris, anxiously waiting for Louis's return from Dordogne, Angélique was jubilant that she had found her a husband after all. He seemed like the perfect one to her. The Margaux were very pleased with their matchmaking, but Louis and Bettina were the most pleased of all. She could suddenly envision a bright future with him. And she laughed thinking of what her grandmother would say when she told her she was marrying a Frenchman. That was going to rock her grandmother to the core.

Chapter 14

Bettina would have been sadder to leave the Margaux after staying with them in Paris for five months, but she knew she would be returning soon. She and Louis were planning to stay in San Francisco for a few weeks, long enough for him to meet her family and ask her father properly for her hand in marriage, and then they would travel back across the country and return to Paris by ship. It was a long journey to make, and Louis needed to be back for work at the end of August. When they got back, Angélique wanted to give a party for them, to celebrate their marriage. Louis was a discreet person, but he was well liked and had many friends, and Bettina had met a number of people in Paris that she liked too.

Louis's parents had a house on the Place François Premier that they no longer used since they had retired to their château in Dordogne, and Louis wanted to move into their old home in the city with her. He was living in a small bachelor apartment now. His parents' house was perfect for them and Lili.

And in the meantime, Bettina was leaving two of her

trunks with Angélique and Robert. All she was taking was what she needed for the boat, and a few things for when she was at home in San Francisco. They would be away for only five or six weeks, and after that, Paris would be her home forever. She missed her parents, but her life in France was so much more interesting and more exciting, and she liked knowing that Lili would grow up there. Louis spoke English, but he preferred speaking to both of them in French. It seemed hard to believe that she had left San Francisco five months before, and her whole life had changed.

She hoped that her father would approve of Louis and the marriage, and that her grandmother wouldn't make a fuss because he was French. She had warned him that her grandmother was very opinionated and eccentric, and that her great-uncle lived with them and was even more so, but she didn't tell him that the house was full of ghosts and the people who lived there never seemed to leave. Even if they died, they came back, and nothing changed. She didn't want him to think that her family was strange before he met them. This was her chance to have a normal, happy life, and she didn't want anything to spoil it. And there was always the risk that the ghosts wouldn't appear at all, which might be simpler.

Their crossing to New York on the ship was almost like a honeymoon for them, except that they were in separate staterooms. He was very respectful of her. Having understood that her previous conjugal life had lasted for exactly one night, he didn't want to press her for more than they had until they were married. There would be time enough to discover each other then. He could hardly wait. She was so young and beautiful that he felt like a very lucky man. And he was acquiring a daughter too. He was wonderful to her as well.

On the ship, they dined with the captain, talked to people on deck, played shuffleboard, lay in the sunshine, swam in the pool with Lili, talked for hours on deck chairs, and went dancing every night. Bettina had never been happier in her life. She even enjoyed Lili more, knowing that she had provided a father for her who would love them both. The burden of motherhood that had seemed so weighty to her before seemed lighter now that she knew that it would be shared. And she was relieved that he didn't want more children. He was the perfect spouse for her.

When they docked in New York, they stayed at the Plaza again, and took the train to California the next morning, in three first-class compartments, as they had done on the ship. The journey was tedious and long, and Lili was fussy. At nineteen months, she was running everywhere, and hated being confined in the small compartment. Louis walked her up and down the passageway with the nurse when Bettina took her afternoon rest.

In San Francisco, they were getting ready for her return, thinking she was coming home to stay. She had given them no warning that she was going to be there for only a short time, and that the guest she was bringing home was important. They wondered who it was, but all Gwyneth could think about was Lili. She couldn't wait to have her granddaughter home again. Their five-month absence had seemed interminable to her. It had been a long summer. The Gregorys had rented a house in Maine for two months for their annual vacation, and they weren't due back until the end of August. Andy was going straight back to Edinburgh from the East Coast, and Caroline was flying directly to Los Angeles. Quinne was with them, and Magnus missed Charlie terribly. Everyone at the Butterfields' house had been bored without the Gregorys and Bettina, particularly Josiah, who had been reading novels to Lucy at night, for lack of anything else to do, and missed his conversations with Bettina.

The family had gone to the house in Woodside briefly in July, but it was tiresome there too. They'd been happy to get back to the city, and Gwyneth wanted the house to look beautiful when Bettina got home. The day they were due to arrive, she put vases of fresh flowers everywhere, and the house was fragrant with the scent. She had cut them from the garden and arranged them herself.

"You'd think we were expecting a royal visit, instead of your daughter," Augusta complained, but she was excited too. Angus had offered to meet the train and pipe them in, but Augusta had convinced him not to, and to wait for them at the house. It was a foggy day and chilly, as San Francisco tended to be in the summer, and she didn't want him to catch a cold. "Who's she bringing, by the way?" Augusta asked her daughter again, thinking she might know by then, but it was a mystery to them all. Bettina had just said "a friend," and her mother assumed it was some nice woman she'd met in Paris who was coming to stay for a month or two, as people did from Europe, because it was so far to come for a shorter visit.

Gwyneth was pacing the halls around the time Bettina was expected to be there. She had wanted to go to the train station in Oakland, but there would be so much confusion with all their trunks and bags that they had sent the chauffeur with the car, and the carriage and coachman, and had agreed to meet at the house. Bert had come home early, and was excited too. Augusta and Angus were playing a card game in the drawing room, Josiah and Lucy were watching, and Magnus was up to some sort of mischief in the garden. The whole family was there, waiting for her.

And then, finally, they heard the car pull up in front of the house, and the carriage wheels, and they all ran outside to greet her. Bettina was the first one out of the car, wearing a white linen suit and a huge hat she'd bought in Paris. She looked very stylish. The nurse was carrying Lili and stepped out right behind her, as Gwyneth rushed forward to hug them, and Bert was beaming. Louis stepped out of the car last in a dark suit and a homburg, looking very much like the banker he was, and he smiled, watching the scene of Bettina in the arms of her family. They hadn't even noticed him until the grande old dame stood at the top of the stairs to the house and stared him into the ground, her fierce scowl suggesting he didn't belong there. She normally would have disappeared with a stranger among them, but she stood visible and undaunted.

"Bettina!" she said in a booming voice that would have carried for miles. *"Who is that?"* As Bettina heard her, she looked up and smiled at her grandmother, pleased to see her so clearly, and ran up the stairs lightly to hug her, and then hugged her brother and sister and great-uncle right after her father. She turned to glance in the direction her grandmother was pointing and saw Louis behind her, waiting discreetly before he approached. Bert gazed at his daughter and then at the man in the hat and dark suit with a question in his eyes.

"I'm sorry." Bettina remembered her manners immediately, beckoned to Louis, and introduced him to her parents. "Louis de Lambertin, may I present my parents, Bertrand and Gwyneth Butterfield." She smiled proudly and Gwyneth took her in her arms again and held her, to make sure she was real. "I wrote to you that he was coming," she reminded them, because the entire family looked stunned to see Louis. They just stood there and stared.

"You didn't tell us you were bringing a gentleman," her mother said gently, "you only said 'a friend.'"

"I thought it was better for you to meet him," Bettina said, since she wanted the reason for his being there to be a surprise.

Louis shook Bert's hand, and Angus's, and bowed low over her mother's and grandmother's hands to kiss them, and then he shook hands with Josiah, who greeted him warmly. Nothing about their appearance or behavior would have suggested that Josiah, Angus, Augusta, and Magnus were not alive. They looked, felt, and behaved entirely real. Only if they did their disappearing act would one know, and Bettina was going to warn them not to while Louis was there.

"Why don't we go inside and have some tea?" Gwyneth suggested, smiling politely at Louis and engaging him in conversation as they walked in. Bettina could see that the house looked beautiful and was filled with flowers. She was very proud of her home, just as Louis was of his family's château in France. And his father had agreed to let them move into the house on the Place François Premier in Paris once they were married. He couldn't wait to show it to Bettina when they went back. It wasn't a palace, or as large as Bettina's home, but Louis's city home was a very handsome house. And the château was huge, daunting, ice cold, and nearly impossible to heat. But his parents lived there, and Louis only went there a few times a year.

"Is he French? . . . He must be French," Augusta was saying. "Did you see him kiss my hand? No self-respecting Englishman would do that." Louis was smiling at what he overheard, and was tempted to do it again to shock the old lady. Despite his restrained exterior, he had a sense of humor.

Gwyneth handed him a cup of tea as they sat in the drawing room, and she asked if he took milk and sugar or lemon, and he said plain. The moment Bert observed him more closely and how he and Bettina spoke to each other, he knew why Louis was there. There could only be one reason why he had come so far. And now Bert wanted to know who he was. He whispered a question to Bettina, and she smiled and nodded.

"You could have warned us," he scolded her.

"I wanted it to be a surprise," she said innocently and looked very young.

"Well, it certainly is." He took her aside and led her into the library, while Gwyneth chatted with Louis in conversation with the others. So far, it was all polite, banal repartee.

Once he had her alone in the library, Bert looked at his daughter seriously. "All right, who is he and how do you know him? How did you meet? Who are his parents, and does he have any? He seems rather old for you," he said sternly.

"He's a lovely person, Father. You'll love him. He's a banker like you. He's French. He has a house in Paris, and a château in Dordogne, or his family does. I met him through the Margaux. They like him very much, and I love him. We want to get married."

"You didn't ask me last time," he reminded her. "Why now?" he asked, still a little miffed over Tony.

"Louis wants to ask your permission," she said seriously, and Bert could see all that it meant to her in her eyes. He was pleased that she was doing it the right way this time, with the right man. It was his only concern.

"How old is he?"

"He's forty-one, Father. But he's not old," she insisted.

"He's eighteen years older than you. That's a lot."

"He's very good to me. He'll take care of me." She was pleading with him. Bert had already seen that he was a kind, proper person, and approved, particularly since the Margaux had introduced them. They would never have introduced them if he were unsuitable.

"And where would you live? Here or in France?" He guessed the answer before she said it. She hesitated for a long moment, knowing he'd be sad.

"He has to work there, Papa," she said in a soft voice. "At the bank. We'll have to live in Paris. But you can come to visit us anytime. And he wants to adopt Lili."

"That's a long way for us to go," Bert said practically, knowing Gwyneth would be upset. "And we can't leave your grandmother and Magnus."

"Yes, you can," Bettina insisted. "Nothing can happen to them now," she reminded him with a grin, which reminded her of her warning. "And please don't let them do anything weird while he's here, nor Uncle Angus." She knew Josiah would behave.

"I can't control your grandmother, but I'll say something to the others. When are you thinking of getting married?" he asked her.

"That's up to him, and whatever he works out with you," Bettina said demurely. "Where are the Gregorys?" She wanted them to meet Louis too.

"They're in Maine till Labor Day."

She looked disappointed. She knew they had to leave before that.

"Well, I'll wait for him to speak to me," Bert said, as they left the library and walked back to where the others were. Louis was engaged in a lively exchange with Augusta, which worried Bettina.

"What are you saying, Grandma?" Bettina asked her, as Augusta looked at her.

"I was telling your friend that he has excellent manners for a Frenchman." Bettina rolled her eyes and suggested they show Louis to his room. It had been a long day. They'd been up since dawn on the train. And a few minutes later,

Phillips took him to one of the large guest bedrooms. Gwyneth wanted him to have the best one.

"We dine at seven-thirty. It's early, I know," Bert said pleasantly, and Louis asked him politely if he might have an audience with him before dinner, and Bert said he could. He wasn't wasting any time. Gwyneth overheard them, and raised an eyebrow at her daughter.

"Is it what I think?" she asked Bettina in a whisper as she followed her upstairs to her bedroom. It had stood empty for five months while she was gone.

"Yes, Mother, it is," Bettina said, turning to her, as tears filled Gwyneth's eyes. She tried to restrain them but couldn't.

"I should never have let you go to Paris," she said sadly. "Now you and Lili will live there." Tears rolled down her cheeks as they hugged each other.

"I'll come to visit you, and you can visit us too, I promise. He's such a fine man."

Gwyneth nodded, pained that she was leaving the nest again. But Bettina looked so happy. She had never hoped to meet anyone like him. "Is it really what you want?"

Bettina nodded in answer. Gwyneth didn't want to stand in her way, and knew she had been miserable in San Francisco for several years. With Tony, and the baby, and a life that was too quiet for a young girl, with more responsibility than she had wanted, on her own. Her life in Paris would be better for her.

They chatted for a while as Gwyneth helped her unpack, and tried to adjust to the idea of losing her daughter. She had thought she was coming home to stay, but she had only come to say goodbye.

Louis and Bert came to a satisfactory understanding when they met before dinner. Bert granted his permission for them to marry. He was impressed by what a serious man Louis was, and satisfied that he truly loved Bettina. Bert was sure she would be in good hands, and he had liked all of Louis's answers to his questions. And he was obviously a person of substantial means.

Louis was waiting for Bettina at the bottom of the stairs when she came down dressed for dinner in a pale blue satin dress and the tiara she had worn when she came out. This was a special occasion, and she hadn't worn it since.

"What did he say?" Bettina whispered with stars in her eyes.

"He said yes." Louis beamed at her. "Now what do you say, my darling?"

"I say yes too," she whispered back, and he kissed her, and slipped a small old black leather box out of his pocket. It had been his grandmother's, and his parents had given it to him when he went to Dordogne. They were anxious to meet Bettina, and they had given him his grandmother's ring to take to California when he got engaged. He gently put it on her finger, and put the little black box back in the pocket of his tails. The stone was quite large and Bettina was amazed. It fit perfectly, and they walked into the dining room together with it sparkling on her finger. It looked huge on her slender hand. She had never expected her life to turn out so well.

It took exactly two minutes for her grandmother to pick up her lorgnette and stare at her granddaughter's left hand.

"What is *that*?" she asked, and looked from Bettina to Louis.

"We have something to tell you," Bettina said softly, and her father interrupted her immediately.

He stood at the head of the table and smiled at all of them. "I would like to welcome our guest, Monsieur Louis de Lambertin," Bert said in perfectly accented French, although it had been a long while since he'd spoken it. "And I have an announcement. Monsieur de Lambertin and Bettina are engaged," he said proudly with a warm glance at his future son-in-law, who was only eight years younger than he was.

"As of when?" Augusta demanded to know, furious not to have been told before.

"As of twenty minutes ago, Mother Campbell," her son-in-law informed her with a bow. "We wish them well. They will live in Paris, unfortunately for us, and Monsieur de Lambertin will adopt Lili and be her new father. This is a very happy day." He beamed at his daughter, as tears rolled down Gwyneth's cheeks. It was all so bittersweet.

"I can't believe you and Lili are going to be French," Augusta sniffed at Bettina. "I find that quite shocking." But she had to admit, he seemed like a very well brought up person, and a nice man. "And when is the wedding?"

"I don't know. We haven't set a date yet," Bettina said shyly.

"You'll have to do it here. I'm too old to go traveling on trains and boats to France," not to mention the fact that she had returned to the house from the spirit world six months before and Bettina had no idea if she could travel, nor Josiah or Magnus, or her great-uncle. It was a complication she hadn't thought of, but she did now. She, Louis, and Lili were leaving in three weeks, and they couldn't easily return to get married. She looked at Louis and whispered something to him during dinner, and he nodded. She spoke to her parents after dinner. They were delighted at the idea, and gave their permission instantly. It was the perfect solution for a number of reasons she didn't want to mention to Louis. Bettina wanted to get married at the house, before they went back to France. They could have a reception for their friends in Paris. The Margaux had already offered to give them one. And she just wanted her family at the actual wedding. She wanted the Gregorys there too, but they were in Maine and not returning in time. Louis was very pleased at the idea. That way, they would already be married when they went back to France, and could live together immediately, and travel as man and wife on the ship.

"I'll arrange everything," Gwyneth promised. And she was going to see if the Gregorys could be home in time.

The next day, she and Bettina got busy with all the arrangements. They needed a minister, a caterer, and flowers. Bettina needed a dress, but there was no time to have one made. They had decided to have the wedding the following weekend, which was barely more than a week away, two weeks before they went back to France. The next afternoon, Bettina and her mother went up to the attic and began opening boxes, where the family wedding dresses were stored. Gwyneth had broader shoulders and was taller, and her wedding gown looked too old-fashioned and would have taken time to alter. Augusta had always been a much bigger woman. Bettina would have drowned in her wedding gown. But Augusta's mother had been very much the same size and build as Bettina, and they carefully took out her white satin dress that was entirely encrusted with tiny pearls. It had a beautiful headdress, which looked like a pearl tiara, and Bettina very gently tried it on, mindful of how delicate and old it was. And when she put the dress on, it looked as though it had been made for her.

Louis was visiting Bert at the bank, so Bettina tiptoed down the stairs to her grandmother's room to show her, and Augusta just stood there and smiled with tears in her eyes.

"May I wear it, Grandma?" she asked, and Augusta nodded.

"Of course . . . although it's a shame to waste it on a Frenchman," she said, but she was smiling, and Bettina knew she liked him and was happy for her.

They put the dress away again carefully, and Bettina had white satin shoes that were perfect for it. It needed no adjustment or alteration, and she was going to wear her hair swept up, with the little pearl tiara and the long veil, with pearls on it too. And the dress had a very long train.

"You're going to look exquisite in it," Gwyneth said when they got back to Bettina's room. A few minutes later, Gwyneth went to Sybil's office and sent her an email. It was the only way she could think of to contact her with the obstacle of their being a century apart. She told her about the wedding and the date and that Bettina and the entire family hoped they could be there. She went to the office an hour later to see if Sybil had responded, and she had. She explained that there was no way they could come out in time. They had to get Andy off to Edinburgh and Caroline to Los Angeles, Blake had business in New York after that, and then they'd return to the house in Maine and a sailboat they'd chartered, although she hated to miss the wedding. Gwyneth emailed back that she understood.

Gwyneth told Bettina later that the Gregorys had sent

a message that they couldn't get back to San Francisco in time for the wedding. They had too many plans they couldn't change. They hated to miss it, but it was going to be strictly a family affair. But all Bettina wanted was Louis there, and all he needed was his bride.

*

When the day came, it was brilliantly sunny, without a wisp of the usual summer fog. The weather was warm, and they were going to be married in the garden, under an arch of white roses. And Gwyneth had filled the house with white orchids from their hothouse. She was wearing a royal blue gown, and Augusta was wearing purple. And Lucy had a pink silk dress she'd never worn. The men looked serious and elegant in morning coats, striped trousers, and top hats. Magnus was the ring bearer, Josiah the best man at Louis's request, and Lucy her sister's maid of honor. The ceremony was brief and very moving, and Louis gasped when he saw Bettina come down the grand staircase in her great-grandmother's gown, with the train stretched out behind her the length of the staircase. Lucy kept it in good order for her, and felt well enough to do it.

Every minute detail of the wedding was perfect. And the lunch in the dining room was delicious. Angus insisted on playing the bagpipes and they couldn't stop him, but he got winded very quickly. Even Rupert and Violet attended the wedding. Louis said he had never seen such a magnificent bride, and Bert had a photographer take formal portraits. There was a problem with his lens, which he was upset about. The photographer said his camera malfunctioned every time he tried to take photographs of the bride's grandmother, her two brothers, and her great-uncle, and he just couldn't record them. It had never happened to him before. But he got beautiful shots of the bride and groom, her parents, and her younger sister, and everyone was satisfied with that. Bettina knew why it happened. They all did, but said nothing.

Bettina told Louis it had been the most perfect day of her life.

"Really, Madame de Lambertin?" he asked with a satisfied smile. "As a matter of fact, mine too." He had promised her a honeymoon in Venice when they got back to Europe, or Rome if she preferred it, or both. But that night, they slept in Bettina's room, in her parents' house, where she and her sister and brothers had been born. She wouldn't have wanted to get married anywhere else. She was going to miss it terribly. She had always felt that the house had a soul of its own.

"You love this house, don't you?" he asked her gently, and she nodded.

"I will always love it," she said sadly.

"Perhaps one day we'll spend time here when we're very old." But he had his château in Dordogne, and the house in Paris. And this was her home, and always would be. "If your brothers don't want it, it might pass on to you," he said, but she didn't want to think about it. Neither Josiah nor Magnus could inherit it any longer, and Lucy wasn't well. But Bettina couldn't bear thinking about a time in the future when her family wouldn't be there.

"Have I told you how much I love you?" he whispered to her, as he put his arms around her. "I love you much more now that we're married." And that night she discovered mysteries with him that she had never known. She felt as though she had waited her whole life for him, and belonged to no one else. She was his now, and their story was just beginning.

Chapter 15

It was excruciatingly difficult for Bettina to tear herself away when it was time to leave, knowing that she wasn't coming back, or not for a long time. She had to say good-bye to her parents, brothers, and sister. And even her grandmother was very tender with her, and wished her a happy life with Louis. Bettina promised to come home when she could, but she had no idea when that would be. She wanted her parents to visit her, but she knew they had responsibilities in San Francisco that made it hard for them to travel far away.

As the car pulled away from the house, they were all waving, and Uncle Angus was playing the bagpipes. She knew she would remember that sight of them, waving to her, and her wedding day forever. Their visit to San Francisco had been perfect, and everyone had behaved impeccably. Louis had no idea that there was anything unusual about the family or the house. And he had no reason to suspect.

"You warned me that they're eccentric and like to play tricks on people," Louis said on the way to the train station. "They don't seem eccentric to me at all, and your grandmother was quite charming and almost forgave me for being French," he laughed.

"That's because you charmed her." Bettina beamed at him. She was still sorry that he hadn't met the Gregorys, but hopeful that he would in the future. "My whole family loves you," Bettina said, sitting close to him with his arm around her.

They settled on the train, and she had asked the others not to come to see them off. It was too emotional and would have made her too sad to see her parents shrinking away on the platform as the train pulled away. Now Lili was in her compartment with the nurse, and Louis held Bettina in his arms as she watched her city disappear from sight, as they began their new life together.

*

The voyage back to Europe was delightful, and especially nice as Louis's wife. Once in Paris, they moved into his parents' old home on the Place François Premier, and Bettina tried to make it feel like their home now. The house was a bit gloomy, but with new curtains, moving things around a little, and fresh flowers, she thought she could improve it. She felt very grown up as she tended to her household and waited for Louis to come home every day. They made love more than she ever could have imagined, and she was so happy he didn't want a baby and felt Lili was enough. Bettina would have hated to have another child, and he knew that and didn't mind. He was a loving, caring husband and lover. And their three-week honeymoon in Venice and Rome was idyllic.

She wrote to her mother almost every day, and when Blake and Sybil and Charlie got back to San Francisco, Gwyneth told them all about the wedding.

"It was gorgeous," she said dreamily, with tears in her eyes.

"I wish we had been here." Sybil had been sad to miss it.

"So do I." And even though Bettina had been gone for five months before that, and had been back for only a few weeks, the house seemed so empty now without her and Lili. Bettina had written that Louis had started the adoption process for Lili as soon as they got back to Paris. It meant that Lili would inherit a sizable fortune from him one day, and be safe for life, no matter who she married. Bettina would also be set till the end of her days, in addition to what she would inherit one day from her parents. She hated to think about it, but it was nice to know that her future was secure. And best of all, she and Louis were madly in love with each other, and everything about their life together felt right. It made up to Gwyneth for how much she missed her, knowing how happy Bettina was.

"You never know how things are going to turn out, do you?" Sybil mused, as she and Gwyneth walked in the garden. "You think you do, but there's always a little surprise, or a big one, good or bad." Bettina hadn't expected to meet her husband in Paris, or to spend the rest of her life in France as she knew now that she would. Her home was no longer San Francisco. It was wherever he was. After the unhappy years before Lili's birth, and her rash marriage to Tony Salvatore, destiny had taken the upper hand. No one could have predicted that. In some ways, it was reassuring that things turned out right in the end.

*

Andy had gone back to college in Edinburgh from New York before Blake and Sybil came back to San Francisco with Charlie. Quinne had been with Andy, and Caroline had flown back to Los Angeles in time to start her second year at UCLA. Charlie started school again in Marin County as soon as he got home. And Magnus was overjoyed to see him.

Sybil was working hard on her book. She had made good progress, and was trying to finish it by the end of the year. And Gwyneth did her artwork on the computer to fill her days after Bettina left. She had gotten very skilled at it and produced beautiful work.

Sybil was in her office when she heard Blake come home early one afternoon. She found him in their bedroom.

"What are you doing here?" She was startled to see

him. He'd been sitting on their bed, with his head in his hands, and she was instantly worried. "Are you sick?"

"Maybe." He stared at her, his face pale, and she could see that something was very wrong. She'd never seen him that way before.

"What is it?" She sat down next to him and took his hand in hers, and he had no choice but to be honest with her. He had never lied to her, and wouldn't now.

"The business is in trouble. We took too many risky positions. Our two brilliant geeks who've made billions with their other ventures didn't know what they were doing with this one. They started leveraging it heavily a few months ago. They figured they could cover it, but they can't now. And I sank a lot of my own money into the business to try and save it. More than I should have." He had always had money of his own set aside, to make investments with, sometimes risky ones. He had never taken chances with their joint investments, and he hadn't this time. But his own money was in the business he had believed in, and the *Titanic* was about to go down, with all of it. "I talked to Bert about it, and he gave me some good suggestions a few months ago. I should have listened to him and pulled out then, but instead I put more money in, and we're going to be up to our ears in lawsuits, personally and in the business, if we can't cover our loans."

"Could you go to jail?" she asked him, terrified, and he shook his head.

"I don't think so. But I could lose everything we have. I might have done that already." He looked panicked.

"What can I do?"

"I want to talk to Bert again, when he gets home from work." He had already talked to his investment adviser too, but he wanted to go over it with Bert. "But, Syb, I want to warn you, we may wind up totally out of money." She nodded, trying to understand just what that would mean to them and their children. What she made curating museum shows and writing articles wouldn't make a difference. Even her book wouldn't when she finished it. She had always had the luxury of not worrying about how much she was paid, because he made enough money with his work to support them.

"Do we need to sell this house?" she asked him quietly, although she would hate to lose it, and the whole family that came with it. They were part of that family now, their lives woven together like a tapestry of past and present. But Blake looked grim when she asked him the question.

"I think we have a decision to make," he said honestly. "This is an unusual house and it could take time to sell, to find the right buyer. And we haven't owned it long. Tribeca would be a faster sale, for more money, but I know how much you love it and the city." It was like asking her to give up a kidney. But they knew that they could sell it well. Apartments in Tribeca sold for a fortune.

They both heard the front door close then, and Blake

stood up. He knew it was Bert and he wanted to see him. Blake left Sybil alone in their bedroom, as she looked out the window and wondered what would happen now.

*

Bert spent hours with Blake that night going over the numbers and agreed that he had to sell the loft in New York or the house in San Francisco to give him the money to cover the shortfall of several million that he was on the hook for.

"I hate to sell it," he said about the apartment. "Sybil's money is in it too."

"You might be able to get some of that money back later, but right now you have no choice." Blake knew he should have listened to Bert months before, but he hadn't. And now it might be too late to salvage anything. "The men you're in business with are high-stakes players. Too high. The numbers don't work, and their assumptions and judgment aren't sound. Get out of it now, if you can. You can always do something else without them later. You'd be better off without them risking your neck." Blake knew it was true. "You know what you're doing." Blake had been impressed with them, and he had been foolish and naïve, dazzled by them, and now he knew it. And when his gut had told him to get out, he hadn't followed his instincts, and stayed.

He thanked Bert for the time he spent with him, and

went upstairs with a heavy heart to discuss their options with Sybil. She had the right to make the decision too. But he had to sell something and cover his part of the debts.

Sybil was waiting for him in their bedroom when he walked in, and she said she had something to tell him.

"Me too," he said grimly. "You first?" He was going to tell her that Bert agreed they had to sell the house or the apartment, but he knew that ultimately she wanted to go back to New York.

"I want us to sell the apartment in Tribeca," Sybil said. "We're not going back, even if the business fails. We love it here, and this house. The Butterfields are family now. And we'll get more money for New York." She looked totally calm as she said it, and he stared at her in disbelief. She had made the decision while he was with Bert.

"Are you serious? You won't regret it?"

"I *want* to sell it. I don't want to go back," she repeated. "Let's do it." He put his arms around her, feeling like an utter failure, but selling their New York apartment would save him. The apartment would give him what he needed to swim free. There were tears in his eyes when he thanked her.

They called the realtor in New York the next morning and put it on the market at a hefty price, but it was worth it. Blake just hoped it would sell quickly. He wanted to get out of the business now while he still could.

The New York realtor was delighted to list their Tribeca

apartment, and by sheer miracle, it sold in five weeks for a good price. Blake managed to keep a lid on things at work, and Bert helped him almost daily. Blake knew that Bert's own downfall had come due to a national disaster, not through errors of his own. And with his advice, Sybil's support, and the sale of their New York apartment, within two months Blake had managed to extricate himself from a potentially disastrous situation and leave the firm. He had lost a considerable amount of money, but he hadn't lost everything, and they still had the house. And after some careful thought, he decided he wanted to start a business of his own. The damage he had escaped could have been infinitely worse. By Thanksgiving Blake knew he had much to be thankful for, and was enormously relieved. He and Sybil were closer than ever, and he and Bert were almost like brothers.

Blake told Bert again how grateful he was to him. He was going to let things cool off for a while, and then try something of his own, based on sound principles. He might not make as much as he could have with the geeks, but he wouldn't lose as much either.

The apartment in New York was gone, so this really was their home now. Sybil had flown to New York and packed everything at the height of his crisis, and had shipped it all to San Francisco. She had never complained once about the mess Blake had gotten them into, and he was deeply grateful to her too. It had been a harrowing time for both of them. Spending Thanksgiving with the Butterfields was even more meaningful this year. Andy hadn't been able to get home from Edinburgh since it wasn't a holiday for them, but Caroline was home with Max, and Andy and Quinne were coming home for Christmas. And Blake was thankful they still had a home to come to. He had escaped total ruin by the skin of his teeth, with Bert's advice.

Chapter 16

After Thanksgiving, Sybil was organizing papers in her office, as she was in the home stretch of her book, and she noticed the box the bank had given her about the Butter-fields, with the photographs and Bettina's book in it. She smiled when she saw it. Nearly three years after they'd bought the house, she knew so much about them, prob-ably even more than Bettina had known when she wrote it. Sybil had the benefit of the present to add to the past, while Bettina could only guess at the future. And she was blissfully happy in Paris with Louis.

She glanced through the photographs and saw pictures of Lili as a baby, and with Bettina shortly after she was born. Bettina looked so serious and unhappy. She had been so worried about the responsibilities of being a mother, and now she was in love with a wonderful man and protected by him. Her letters from Paris were only happy, after three months of marriage. She felt totally separate now from her life in the States, and believed she would never live there again.

Sybil found other photographs too, of Magnus and

Josiah, Bert and Gwyneth. They'd looked so young when they were married. There was one of Bettina after she bought the house back, after Louis died, in 1950. It was jarring to see it, knowing that they had just gotten married that summer. But in real time, she had married him in the summer of 1919. Sometimes Sybil forgot that she was reliving history with them because the present times she lived with them were so vivid. They existed in another dimension together in addition to the one each family was in, a hundred years apart.

There was a picture of Gwyneth too, after Bert died in 1930, when Bettina took her to Paris to live with her after they sold the house in San Francisco. Gwyneth looked so ravaged, so lost without him, that it pained Sybil to see it. And when she looked at the date on the back of another photograph, she knew that Gwyneth had died a few months later in 1932. After that, the only ones still alive were Bettina and Lili, and there were no more pictures. And then Sybil thought of something. Bettina had written that Lili got married in France to Raphael Saint Martin, a doctor, after the Second World War. She had a son named Samuel, born in 1946. As far as Sybil knew, Samuel Saint Martin was the last descendant of Gwyneth and Bert. There were no other heirs, as Bettina had been their only surviving child, Lili Bettina's only issue, and Samuel Lili's. He was the end of the line. Sybil wondered what had happened to him, and if he'd had any interest in the house or knew anything about it. His mother had sold it after his grandmother's death in 1980. Sybil wondered what had happened to him since.

The bank had said that Lili had sold the house from France without even coming to see it, because she was in ill health. She had inherited it from her mother and disposed of it. Michael Stanton of the Berkeley Psychic Institute had said that Lili probably wasn't alive when he visited the house. She would have been a hundred and one years old now, and if Samuel was still alive, he would be seventy-three. For the first time, Sybil felt a duty to try to contact him and share his family history with him. Maybe he never knew anything about them, since Lili had no real bond to the house, and in everything Bettina had written in her lifetime, she had admitted that she and Lili had never been close. She blamed herself for it, and Lili's ties were all in France, and she would have had none of the Butterfield history to pass on to her son.

Suddenly Sybil knew what her mission was and what she owed them, and wanted to give them. She wanted to reach out to Samuel and tell him about the Butterfield Mansion and the wonderful family who had lived there, and were his heritage too. It was a gift she could give to him, and to Bert and Gwyneth. Samuel Saint Martin was the last link in the chain. She and Blake were the guardians of their history, but Samuel was the rightful heir to it and their stories, their victories, and their broken dreams.

He had a right to know the truth about all of it, and even to meet them, since the strange phenomenon that existed in the house would allow him to, if he wanted to and was willing. And if they were. He could meet Augusta, his great-great-grandmother, and his great-uncle Magnus, his great-great-uncle Angus, and Bert and Gwyneth, his great-grandparents, and Sybil knew she had to pass it on to him. She could be the bridge between the Butterfields she knew and their last descendant. All she had to do was find him, if she could. And then he had to believe it was possible for him to meet them, and not that she was some lunatic who had imagined it, or was lying to make herself interesting. She wasn't sure how to convince him, if she found him, but she wanted to try. She had a strong sense that when Bettina had bought the house back after Louis's death, she had lived with her family around her in the same spiritual dimension where they existed now, and where Sybil saw them every day. They had probably populated Bettina's final years in the same way until she died. So she was never alone or lonely in her final years, and had returned to the comfort of her youth.

And somewhere in the world was Lili's son, who had a rich history he probably knew nothing about, but deserved to at least learn as the Butterfields' final blood relative. She felt powerfully that Bert and Gwyneth and even his grandmother Bettina would have wanted that. Sybil was the only one who could give him that now, or at least offer it to him. She not only knew their history, she had lived it with them. They had entrusted it to her by being so open with her and her family, and she wanted to share it with Samuel now.

Chapter 17

With a feeling of trepidation, and after thinking all night about it and whether it was the right thing to do, Sybil started searching for Samuel Saint Martin the next day. All she knew about him was the minor mention of him in Bettina's book, as Lili's son.

His father, Raphael, had been a doctor, and if he and Lili had other children, Bettina didn't mention them in the book.

Sybil didn't know what was pushing her to look for him, and she didn't tell anyone about it. It might be a dead end, anyway. He might have died. Or the Butterfields could refuse to meet him. Lili hadn't been part of their lives once Bettina moved to France and she was a baby then. Her seventy-three-year-old son might just seem too remote to them. They lived within the confines of the house and the grounds and the world they had known, with the family members they had lived with for more than a century. Samuel might not seem part of the family to them. But Sybil could feel something beckoning her as she began her search.

She found him on Facebook in less than an hour, if it was the right person. It had been startlingly easy, and his age matched up. She had nothing else to go on. His Facebook page said that he was a history professor at the Sorbonne, he lived in the fifth arrondissement on the Left Bank in Paris, which wasn't far from Saint-Germain, and Sybil was desperately curious about him and wanted to know more. She had a burning sense that this was important without knowing why.

She was composing an email to him on her computer that afternoon when Gwyneth walked into the room. She had come to finish a drawing she had started.

"What are you doing?" She was bored and missed Bettina, and hadn't had a letter from her in a week. Bettina was busy reorganizing her new home and enjoying their busy social life. She had written that she loved being married and having a home of her own, and not just living with her parents.

"Looking for your great-grandson," Sybil said seriously, looking distracted.

"Very funny." Gwyneth thought it was a joke.

"No, really. I know that makes no sense, but it's one of those time-dimension things I can't explain, it just is."

Gwyneth nodded. She knew it happened to them, but it confused her, so she tried not to think about it, about who was dead and who wasn't, and who wasn't really the age that they seemed, who was past and who was future.

It was much easier to take it at face value. And Sybil was more interested in it than she was. Bert didn't like her to talk about it, and had forbidden her to tell anyone.

"So I have a great-grandson?" she asked, looking uncomfortable. Bert wouldn't have liked her asking questions about the future, even if Sybil knew the answers, particularly if she did.

"Yes, you do. Lili's son," Sybil said. It seemed harmless to tell her, as long as she didn't warn her of the tragedies that would come and no one could alter.

"Shouldn't you be working on your book?" Gwyneth said to change the subject.

"Don't remind me. I'm taking a break." Sybil smiled at her. "I'm almost finished."

"Do you know where he is? My great-grandson, I mean." Gwyneth was curious about it, even if she knew she shouldn't be. They both knew it was dangerous to pry into the future, and they were usually careful not to and respectful of the privilege they had.

"Sort of. If he's the right one, he's a history professor at the Sorbonne. That's all I really know. The rest is guesswork. And maybe he won't give a damn about any of you or your history if I find him, but I figured that you or Bettina or someone, maybe your mother, would want me to reach out to him, to tell him about all of you, so you could meet him if you want to." And he'd have to be willing to come to San Francisco if so. It was all a long shot for now.

"I think that would be nice," Gwyneth said, smiling at her. "We're all still here. He might as well know about us." And then she looked shyly at Sybil. "Sometimes I think we're here because of you. Maybe without you, if you and Blake hadn't bought the house, we wouldn't be in our home anymore." It was one of those rare times when one of them admitted that the way they all existed, including her and Blake, wasn't entirely normal, and had defied what was possible for other people.

"I don't think that's true. I think you'd be here anyway. I think you're all so attached to the house and your life together, you'll never leave," Sybil said honestly. "You were all here when we arrived. We just found you. We didn't bring you back." Sybil took no credit for it, and what she said was true. She smiled warmly at Gwyneth. The two women had a powerful tie of love and friendship and had been through a lot together.

"Do you ever get tired of us?" Gwyneth asked, since they had opened a forbidden subject, and Sybil laughed.

"Never, except when Angus plays the bagpipes." They both laughed. Sybil turned back to her computer then. "I'm trying to find this guy's phone number. Maybe I should just call Paris information." She did, as Gwyneth listened to her, marveling at modern communications when they gave it to her, as simple as that. A moment later, when Sybil turned to say something to her, Gwyneth had vanished, to check on Magnus and make sure he wasn't up to mischief. And she didn't want to intrude on the call.

Magnus had been rambunctious lately. Charlie was getting more homework and couldn't play as often, or for as long. It made Sybil wonder if she was damaging her children, allowing them to grow up with people who no longer existed in the present, and facilitating their living together as friends. But the Butterfields had enriched their lives in so many ways. She didn't know what they would tell their children about it. What had Bettina told Lili? Did Lili know? Or did Bettina simply live with her family and never tell her daughter of the unusual phenomena in the house? And would Lili have believed her or thought her senile and dismissed it as an old woman's fantasies or some form of dementia, living in the past? Sybil was sure that Bettina had come back in order to find them all again, after Louis died. And now Sybil didn't want to leave the house either, nor did Blake or their children. She couldn't imagine living without the Butterfields anymore. They were an important part of each other's lives.

Sybil wanted to call Samuel Saint Martin in Paris, but she realized it was one in the morning there, and she'd have to wait until morning for him, and midnight for her.

She went back to her research papers but couldn't focus as she thought about Samuel Saint Martin, curious if he was even the right one. Thinking about him made her wonder if she should be writing the Butterfields' family history instead of her book on design. She was curious what kind of history Samuel was interested in. Maybe he should write the family history, using Bettina's original book as a base. Maybe that was why she felt compelled to find him, so she could give him all the material and he could write it. She knew there had to be a reason why she felt so strongly that she had to reach out to him. The idea had come from somewhere. She sensed that someone or something was pushing her to find him.

Neither she nor Gwyneth said anything about it that night at dinner. They talked about their plans for Christmas, which was only a month away. Everyone would be home except Bettina, who had written that she would be spending the holiday in Dordogne with her husband and in-laws. Gwyneth commented to Sybil how much they were going to miss her.

"You never should have let her marry a Frenchman," Augusta said from the other end of the table. "I told you that. She'll bring Lili up as a French child. She'll never even know us." Augusta looked disapproving as she said it.

"You liked him, Mother," Gwyneth reminded her.

"I did," she admitted. "But, still, she should have married an American. A *suitable* one," she said pointedly, referring to Lili's father and Bettina's regrettable transgression with the restaurant owner's son. They had never heard from any of the Salvatores again. The match had been reciprocally undesirable, and Lili was the only fortunate result. And now Louis had adopted her, so the Salvatores could be entirely forgotten. "Will the little countess be joining us for Christmas this year?" Augusta asked Sybil, and she laughed. She meant Quinne.

"I'm not sure." Andy was very serious about her, but they were so young, and she had her family in Scotland to go home to, although they seemed to be a bit disorganized about making plans, and so was she.

She went upstairs with Blake after dinner, and once he was asleep, she went to her office to call Samuel at midnight, which would be morning for him.

Sybil had gotten his number from information and hoped it was the right one. The phone rang several times before he answered. He had a young voice in spite of his age, and answered in French, which Sybil had expected, and she asked him immediately if he spoke English. Her college French was too rusty to even attempt.

"Yes, I do," he said, sounding puzzled about who she was, and for an instant, she wondered where to start and then jumped in before he could hang up.

"I know this is a bit unusual, but I'm a friend of the Butterfield family, your grandmother Bettina's family, actually. My husband and I bought their home in San Francisco three years ago, and I have a book written by your grandmother about the family and the house, and quite a lot of photographs of all of them. And I wondered if you would be interested in seeing them, or would even like to visit the house," she said cautiously. It seemed like a safe opening, although a little forward. She had no idea how he'd react.

"I really know nothing about them. My mother came to France when she was a year old. She never had any interest in my grandmother's family. She was closer to my grandfather's family in France. And my American grandmother moved back to the States when I was four years old. I only saw her a few times in my life. I don't think my mother and her mother were very close. But thank you. You can send me a copy of the book if you wish. I'd like to read it. Were they interesting people, or just rich Americans?" he asked, and the question annoyed Sybil. They deserved far more respect than that. But at least she had found the right Samuel Saint Martin. That was something.

"*Very* interesting." Sybil defended them immediately. "Your great-grandmother and her family were actually Scottish. And they were all quite colorful. Your great-uncle was a war hero in the First World War, and your great-grandfather was a very respected banker."

"And lost all his money in the Depression, as I recall," he said succinctly. "My mother got her fortune from her father on the French side. Her mother's family had lost everything, except what she inherited from my French grandfather, from what she always told me. Her mother was only able to buy her family home back with what her husband left her. She went back to the States as soon as he died." He had a very cut and dried way of talking about it, which ignored entirely who they'd been as people, and what they went through. "My mother always said that her mother became a recluse when she went back, living with her memories. She sounded like a sad woman. She never returned to France. And my mother's health deteriorated and she couldn't travel shortly after her mother left. She was only able to visit her a few times. She developed severe Parkinson's when she was quite young. As a result, I really never knew my grandmother. I'm much closer to my French relatives. The American ones were all gone when I was a child, except for my grandmother. She sent me a check every year for Christmas and my birthday until she died, but I had no other contact with her. She left everything to my mother. And my mother never went back to see the house. She had no history there, and she was quite ill by then, so she sold it. Are there ghosts there?" He laughed as he said it, and she almost wanted to say yes, to jolt him out of his supercilious attitude about the Butterfields, as though he believed them to be lesser people than his French relations. It made her feel that Augusta was right about the French.

"They were a wonderful family, and their spirit and history are certainly here. We love the house. It's a beautiful place. And they gave so much of themselves to it." She sounded emotional as she said it.

"It's very large as I recall, from what my mother said." But their château in Dordogne was larger, and older. He had inherited it but was thinking of selling it. It was too much trouble and expensive to keep up, and his parents and grandparents were long gone. His daughter wanted him to keep it, but it didn't make sense for her either. "My daughter might like to see it," he said thoughtfully then. "She's an architecture student at the Beaux-Arts and fascinated with old houses." It surprised Sybil that at seventy-three he had a daughter young enough to be a student. "Her mother is an art professor, and I teach art history," he said, and then answered Sybil's unspoken question, as though he'd sensed it. "I married very late. It's a tradition in my family. My grandfather married my grandmother when he was older too. I married at fifty, to a younger woman. My daughter, Laure, is twenty-two. She's a terrific girl. Her mother and I are divorced, but she spends a lot of time with me, and we share a passion for art and history. My father was a doctor, and my mother a nurse during the war, but none of the medical genes seem to have come through. The artistic and historical sides have won out." He laughed again as he said it, and Sybil couldn't decide if she liked him or not. He sounded a little pompous and very French, but he had softened considerably when he mentioned his daughter. "Unfortunately my mother didn't live long enough to see my daughter, since I married late. She died six years before, ten years after her own mother." He was filling Sybil in on all the more recent details she didn't know. It told her that Lili had died in 1990, if it was ten years after Bettina. And Michael Stanton had been right when he said that he had the feeling that Lili was no longer alive when he toured the house. She had died at seventy-two, which wasn't very old in that case. And it was clear to her that although Samuel didn't know much about the Butterfields or the house, he had a passion for history.

"I think you would love the house," she said to him, trying to interest him in coming to see it. And he could meet his ancestors, if they were willing, or at least see where they had lived and learn more about them. She wanted to encourage him to do that, but wasn't sure how.

"I probably would," he said, "but it's very far away. San Francisco is a long way from Paris." It was an eleven-hour flight, and a nine-hour time difference. "Maybe my daughter will come sometime. I have a heavy teaching schedule right now, and I'm about to start a new book," he said, sounding pompous again.

"I'm just finishing one," Sybil said. So there. Match point. But that wasn't what the call was about.

"You're a historian?" he inquired, curious about her. She seemed to know a great deal about his relatives, the previous owners of her house.

"No, I curate exhibits on mid-century modern design for museums, and I write about design. Sybil Gregory." In case he wanted to check her credentials on the Internet and make sure she wasn't some crackpot calling him. Their interests were not very different, and overlapped to some extent, since her book was about a more extended period of design history than just mid-century.

"You should write about the Butterfields, if they're interesting enough. Or at least the house, if it's still handsome," he suggested.

"Very much so. But I was thinking you should write about them, since you're a historian. I don't know why, but I thought you would be intrigued by the house and should know about it, and your family." She tried to make it more personal for him, to pique his interest, which seemed to be her mission. And even Gwyneth had looked interested in the idea of a great-grandson through Bettina. None of their other children had lived to marry and have children, and Bettina had only had one, Lili. Samuel was the last surviving member of a wonderful family and a great legacy, and his daughter, Laure, whom Sybil had just discovered when he told her. She was Gwyneth's great-great-granddaughter, which seemed amazing to Sybil. And even more so if they could meet each other. It was an extraordinary opportunity for both Gwyneth and Laure, and the others.

"I can't imagine writing about a family I'm related to but really never knew, but send me the book. I'd like to read it. You've sparked my interest. You're a good ambassador for them, posthumously," he added, and Sybil smiled. Not as posthumously as he thought, but there was no way she could explain that to him, certainly not on the phone, the first time they talked. He would have hung up on her immediately if she'd told him, and she wouldn't have blamed him.

"One feels them very strongly in the house. It was a very important place to them," Sybil said, trying to entice him, but not give too much away.

"That's what my mother always said. She said that as my grandmother got older, and especially once her husband died, she was more attached to her history, her own family and her parents' home, than the live people in her life, like my mother, her daughter. But I think they must have been very different. And my mother was very French. She said her mother always stayed very attached to all things American. And that can be a clash sometimes, culturally. My own daughter likes the idea of having some American ancestry. She thinks it's exotic." He laughed. It was interesting to Sybil too that Lili considered herself entirely French, since she was entirely American by blood, and her French father had adopted her. She wondered if that was why Lili was so adamant about it, to establish her identity and dispel the idea of her biological father's family rejecting her at birth, which Bettina must have told her at some point as an adult.

By the end of the conversation, Sybil was beginning to like Samuel. He had relaxed on the phone, and had been generous with his time, and open about his own family and their quirks. "I only have one very old copy of your grandmother's book," Sybil told him then. "I'll have it copied for you and send it," she promised.

"Can you scan it to me? That might be simpler."

"Of course. I hadn't thought of it. I don't think there are any other copies of the book than the one I have. She really only did it for the family, and if there were other copies, they must have gotten lost. The bank gave me this one, along with the plans and a lot of old photographs when we bought the house."

"I can't promise you when I'll read it," he said honestly. "I'm retiring at the end of this semester, and I have a lot of things to wrap up here at the university. After the first of the year, I'll have more time." He sounded wistful as he said it. A fifty-year career as an academic was about to end. She suspected he was finding it hard to retire, and was wondering how he would fill his time, other than with the book he said he was starting, which sounded as dry as hers on design. The Butterfields were a far more intriguing subject.

She thanked him again for his time. They had been on the phone for more than half an hour. He was an interesting and intelligent man, and he hadn't hung up on her, as she had feared. But she hadn't told him about the psychic dimension to the house either, which no one would have understood or believed, unless they'd experienced it, as she and her family did, and had for three years. They had been living with the entire Butterfield clan since they moved in, and sharing their lives and experiences of a hundred years before, at the same time as their own in current time. But somehow it worked, and the parallel time frames had brought them together as one family under one roof.

Sybil scanned the book for him an hour later, and had just pressed the send button when Gwyneth materialized out of nowhere, as she did at times. It was easier than walking up two flights of stairs, and Sybil teased her about it. Magnus liked doing that too, just popping in, usually in Charlie's room. Augusta was more circumspect about it, and lumbered up the stairs with her cane, on Angus's arm, with the two dogs behind them, panting heavily, since both dogs were old and had short snouts.

"Did you call him?"

Sybil had jumped when she turned around and saw Gwyneth right behind her. She was wearing a pretty dark blue velvet dress she'd worn at dinner, and her hemlines had recently gotten shorter and were showing her ankles. Gwyneth was a beautiful woman. They were both up late, thinking about Samuel.

"You scared me!" Sybil scolded her.

"Sorry! Did you?"

"Call who?" Sybil was distracted for a minute, and looking for something on her desk.

"My great-grandson, in Paris." Sybil looked up and smiled at her, as Gwyneth settled comfortably in a chair in Sybil's office.

"Yes, I talked to him. I didn't like him at first, but he warmed up after a while. You have a twenty-two-year-old great-great-granddaughter too, who is studying architecture at the Beaux-Arts. She loves old houses."

"How interesting," Gwyneth said, impressed by what Sybil had been able to find out, and so quickly. "I wonder what she looks like. She would be Lili's granddaughter, since he's Lili's son and Bettina's grandson."

"He's retiring shortly, and starting a book on some dull subject. He's crazy about his daughter, and sounds very proud of her. He got married at fifty, and he's divorced." Gwyneth took it all in. Sybil had already put Bettina's book away. She had never shared it with Gwyneth and felt strongly that she shouldn't since it revealed far too much about what Gwyneth didn't know. There were too many painful things in it about their future, and it wouldn't be fair.

"I wish they'd come to visit. I'd love to see them," Gwyneth said longingly.

"I wish they would too. I don't know if they have the money or the time. Let's see what he says." She didn't tell her she'd sent him Bettina's book, since she'd never discussed it with her. "Maybe he'll think about it and want to come. I could send him a photograph of you, maybe that would do it. Or one of your mother. Or a recording of Angus playing the bagpipes," she teased her, and they both laughed.

"You're a wicked woman," Gwyneth said, and they chatted for a few minutes, and Gwyneth left, via the door this time, as Sybil smiled and went back to work on the final chapter of her book, since she was too wound up to sleep now. She was almost there. She wondered if she'd hear from Samuel. She had sown what seeds she could to inspire him to want to know more, and hopefully even see the house.

*

The weeks before Christmas were as busy as they always were. They got the giant Christmas tree up in the ballroom, which was a major feat. It had to come in through the windows, and it just grazed the eighteen-foot ceiling. And then they all decorated it, with tall ladders and much consultation with one another about which ornament should go where.

It was their third Christmas together. Andy and Caroline were coming home the next day, and Max and Quinne were joining them right after Christmas and would be with them for New Year's. She had Bert and Gwyneth's blessing for their visit. They liked them, and Augusta loved Quinne. It would compensate a little for Bettina and Lili's absence. It would be their first Christmas without them, and Sybil knew that Gwyneth was sad about it. Sybil was grateful that with Bert's help, Blake was pulling out of the financial disaster he'd been in, without too much damage, but it had been a very bad scare. He still wanted to open his own start-up, but was waiting a few months to do it. And he was exploring some new ideas on the subject.

Sybil was wrapping gifts in her office late one night when Samuel Saint Martin called her from Paris. She didn't recognize his voice at first, until he identified himself.

"I'm sorry to call you so late," Samuel apologized. It was eleven o'clock at night in San Francisco, and eight in the morning in Paris.

"It's fine," she said easily. "I'm wrapping Christmas presents. My children are coming home tomorrow."

"How old are they?"

"Almost the same age as your daughter. My son Andrew is twenty, my daughter, Caroline, is nineteen, and my son Charlie is nine. They're just a little younger than yours." But he was thirty-one years older than Sybil since he had married and had his daughter so much later. "Andrew is at the University of Edinburgh and Caroline goes to UCLA," she filled him in. "Have you read the book yet?" She hadn't expected to hear from him for a month or two, till after he retired, and it had only been a few weeks now.

"I have, and so has my daughter. That's why I'm calling you. She's obsessed with it, with the house and the family. And I have to admit, I find them quite haunting too, if you'll forgive the expression. We have all kinds of old legends about ghosts in my family's château in Dordogne, and Laure is fascinated by them. She's convinced there must be some in your mansion too." He laughed as he said it, and Sybil grinned. He had no idea what he was getting into with the Butterfields. But that was precisely why she had contacted him. And he, or at least his daughter, sounded hooked, or intrigued at the very least.

"She's spending Christmas with her mother in Normandy. But we have quite a long Christmas break at the university. She wants me to come over with her to visit you, sometime during the holiday. Perhaps around New Year's. Would that be terribly inconvenient for you?" he said apologetically. "We would stay in a hotel of course, but it sounds like you have family plans."

"It wouldn't be inconvenient at all," Sybil said, thinking about it and trying to decide just how far she wanted to go. And then she decided to go further. She owed it to Gwyneth and her family, to all of them, to make the meeting possible, and comfortable for them. She was the liaison between their two dimensions, and it was very important to her to do this right. "You can stay with us.

You don't need to stay at a hotel," she said bravely, hoping that he and his daughter were up to it. "We have plenty of guest rooms, as you can imagine."

"Your husband and children won't mind? We're strangers, after all." He sounded cautious and polite.

"No, you're not. You have more right to be here than we do. Ancestrally speaking, you're Butterfields. We'd love to have you." And so would all the others, once they met them. She knew Gwyneth would be happy.

"You're very kind." It was one thing he'd always liked about Americans. They were always so hospitable, even to strangers, if they had some common connection. But in his mind, this was a thin one, and Sybil had been charming to him since the beginning. And he had found the book riveting, as he read about all his distant and not-so-distant relations and how their lives had turned out and the challenges they'd faced at interesting times in history, the Great War, the Spanish flu epidemic right afterward, the Crash of '29, the Great Depression that had swept away their fortune. Samuel knew the more recent history, about when his grandmother had bought the house back, and when his mother had sold it again, but he had known none of it from before that, until he read the book.

And Laure, his daughter, was even more excited about it than he was. Although he had insisted to her that Sybil had said there were no ghosts in the house, Laure was sure there had to be, with such an intriguing family once living there. She loved the idea of being related to them. And, despite his initial reluctance, so did he. He wanted to meet Sybil, and thought her a very interesting person too, for being so dedicated to them, simply because she and her husband had bought their house. He had looked Sybil up on the Internet, and was very impressed by her professional credentials as a writer and curator. And she had obviously researched the Butterfields carefully, since she knew so much about them. He had been moved by that too when they last spoke.

"Do you have the exact dates that would work for you?" Sybil asked him, wanting to pin him down.

"Perhaps we could arrive around the twenty-eighth or twenty-ninth? We won't stay for more than a few days." It was six or seven days away, but it worked well for her too. She didn't think Blake would mind, or her children. They would have Christmas *en famille*, with the Butterfields, and then Quinne and Max were coming anyway. The more the merrier, as far as Sybil was concerned, and she could hardly wait to tell Gwyneth that her great-grandson and great-great-granddaughter were coming. She just hoped the others would be willing to welcome them too.

"That's perfect. Let me know your flight, and we'll pick you up at the airport," she said warmly.

"There's no need to do that. I'll rent a car. We'll need one anyway, so we can see the city, and we don't want to be a burden on you. I'll let you know what time we'll arrive at the house, and on which day."

"I look forward to meeting you and Laure," Sybil said, excited about it. "Have a lovely Christmas in the meantime."

"You too, and your family. And thank you again for allowing us to make this pilgrimage," he said, laughing. It was Sybil who had started it, and she was glad she had. Calling him had been so much the right thing to do. It would complete everything to have the last of the Butterfields come to meet their family. And maybe he would write the next book about them.

Sybil was excited about their visit, and she knew Gwyneth would be too. It hadn't been a crazy idea after all. It had been inspired. She couldn't help wondering what had impelled her to do it. Maybe even Bettina herself. But whatever the reason, her efforts had been successful so far. She sat in her office smiling after they hung up. Their visit was the best Christmas gift of all. And after that, she wanted him to write the book.

Chapter 18

When Sybil told Blake that Samuel Saint Martin and his daughter were coming to visit, he was dubious at first, and wanted to know how it had happened. The coincidence was too great, and the connection too slim. He questioned her intensely, and she admitted to having contacted him, and he expressed strong disapproval.

"You're not supposed to meddle with these things," he reminded her. "I thought we agreed to that in the beginning. It's their lives and their destinies. We're just the observers here, by virtue of a very strange freak phenomenon that none of us understand."

"I'm not trying to change anything, or warn them," which was what she and Blake had agreed not to do. They behaved at all times as though they were on real time, whatever the event, date, or century. They did not interfere or tell them the future. They felt they had no right to do that, whatever the outcome, or however hard it was to watch it unfold, like when Josiah went off to war, or knowing that Bettina would remarry and leave San Francisco.

"If they were meant to meet their great-grandchildren,

they would have, without your help. What if they don't want to and refuse to appear? Or it traumatizes them? Bert has no idea that the crash and the Great Depression are coming. He thinks they are secure for life. If he knew now that they were going to lose everything, it would break his heart. What if finding out about it now precipitates his death earlier?"

Sybil hadn't thought about that and it panicked her. "I can warn Samuel if he meets them, and tell him he has to live by the same rules we do. They may not even see each other. The family may not want to include anyone else in that circle, and not appear."

"I don't think they have that choice," Blake said to her seriously. "They didn't decide to meet us. They were as shocked as we were. It just happened."

"Supposedly it happened because we were open to it. Maybe Samuel and his daughter won't be. We can't predict that."

"You're playing with fire, Sybil," he said sternly, and she felt mildly guilty about it after what he said, particularly about Bert and the stock market crash and the dire results for them. In fact, the consequences of it had killed Bert and Gwyneth within a very short time, and it was slowly approaching in the dimension they were in now, though it was still ten years away. "I think what you're doing is very dangerous," he reproached her.

"I don't want to do anything to hurt them. I love them,"

Sybil said with feeling. "They're our family now too. I just want to help them complete the circle, and to know their children's children, just like they know us and our kids, and love them. I want them to see that it came out all right in the end, in spite of the hard times they went through, and the end of the story is a good one. It does have a happy ending. We're all together now. And they're still together. It didn't end with Bert, or Gwyneth, and losing everything. Don't you think they should know that?"

"They've gone back to a comfortable time in their lives. Think about it. We met them in 1917 for them, before the war, when everything was still all right," Blake reminded her.

"Yes, but Josiah was killed in the war anyway, and Magnus had died before we met them. We can't protect them from the bad things that had to happen, any more than they can protect us."

"But they teach us things that we wouldn't know otherwise," Blake said soberly. Bert had literally saved him from financial ruin in the past few months, sure disgrace, bankruptcy, and maybe even prison, with his experience and sage counsel. "I just don't want you to break the rules we all respect, or hurt them. I think you're taking a tremendous risk and I don't like it. What if their great-grandson is an asshole and ridicules them, or exposes us or them in some way, and turns our lives into a freak show? That could happen. Reality TV at the Butterfields', with Uncle Angus in a ghost costume playing the bagpipes."

She laughed at the suggestion. "I don't think Samuel is a jerk, and what I'm hoping for is that he'll write a book about them. They deserve to have a really great book written about the family. They were important at the time, and it could be done with insight and dignity."

"Why don't you write it?" Blake suggested. He knew Sybil would do it lovingly and well. He trusted her, not a great-grandson he didn't know.

"I've thought about it, and I'm not sure I'd do it justice. Their great-grandson is a historian, and a good one." She had looked up his credentials too, and read a translation of his writing, and it was excellent. He'd had impressive reviews on all his books. They were said to be historically accurate and respected. A writer like Samuel Saint Martin was not going to exploit the emotional aspects of their tragedies. He would weave the important historical facts of the times into their story. They had lived at a key time in American history, when everything had changed dramatically socially, economically, industrially, and scientifically. She was sure Samuel would do justice to that, and to them.

"You may be right," Blake conceded, "but I'm worried. I just don't want anything to go wrong for them, and it could. I don't care about him or his daughter, but I do care a great deal about the family we know and love, whom we live with. The privilege we've been given of knowing them, seeing them, and living with them in their time frame and ours is an enormous gift from an unknown source. Let's not damage that, or hurt them."

"I won't. I swear," she promised him, and reported the conversation to Gwyneth that night at dinner, in a whisper. She told her that Blake wasn't in favor of the meeting, which was disappointing.

"I'm sure Bert wouldn't be either, but I won't tell him. Hopefully, it would just happen the way it did with you. Naturally, even if it surprised all of us." Sybil smiled at the memory of their first dinner together, and how shocked they had been. And Gwyneth did too. "Are you going to cancel their coming?" She looked dismayed at the thought and Sybil shook her head.

"Blake will be furious with me if something goes wrong. But I think it's important to do. And if you're not meant to meet them, you won't. It won't happen. You can't force it." Alicia and others who came to the house had never seen them. No one entered their common dimension unless they were meant to. And for the past three years, that had been only the Butterfields and Gregorys, with very rare exceptions, and with their approval. It reassured both of them to know that. In some way, they were all protected. And the bond they shared linked them closely to each other, which kept them safe too. It was very much what Michael Stanton had said in the beginning.

Others just could not see them, which was as it should be. It was extremely selective. And Sybil felt privileged that her family had been chosen. None of them knew why it had happened or who had ordained it. And there was no telling if the great-grandson and his daughter would be included in the magic circle. It was entirely possible that they wouldn't be, in which case they could tour the house and learn the family's history, but it would go no further than that and they wouldn't see them. Both women found that reassuring.

No one had noticed them whispering at dinner, because Andy and Caroline had come home that afternoon and there was much chatter at the table, and a volley of questions aimed at both of them about school, their friends, and their romances.

"When is the blue-haired countess joining us?" Augusta asked him.

"In three days, Grandma Campbell," Andy answered. It was what Sybil's children called her now, and Augusta liked it. She had taken them into her heart long since, particularly Charlie, whom she thought was an endearing imp, and she liked Andy and Caroline too.

"She'll have to give up that hair color when she inherits the title. Are you engaged yet?"

He guffawed. "We're too young, Grandma." Sybil smiled. Her children finally had grandparents after all.

"Nonsense," Augusta responded. "How old are you

now? Twenty? You should be married by next year, and she'll wind up a spinster if she's not careful. I was engaged two weeks after I came out, and married at eighteen. You young people are too slow these days. You'll all wind up spinsters and fussy old men who never marry," she warned him and everyone at the table laughed, thinking of Angus, who was just that. "I like her," Augusta added. "You should get engaged. And you too," she said pointedly to Caroline, who still had to finish college and wanted to go to graduate school. None of them had the least bit of interest in getting married, which was appropriate for them—but wouldn't have been for the Butterfields in 1919, which was where they were. In nine days, it would be 1920 for them.

*

Christmas was as beautiful as it had been for the last three years together. Both families blended perfectly, exchanged presents, played charades, looked elegant at dinner, danced in the ballroom, and spent a memorable holiday with each other. And two days later, Quinne arrived from Scotland, with her hair slightly bluer, and a shocking pink streak in it. She looked a little more grown up, and had two new tattoos, and if possible her skirts were a fraction shorter. Everyone was delighted to see her, including Augusta. Quinne had just spent Christmas at Castle Creagh with her parents and siblings, which she said was very boring. She said even the ghost in the chapel tower hadn't bothered to show up, and had probably died of boredom. She was delighted to join the Gregorys and their extended family in San Francisco. She and Andy were going to go skiing in Squaw Valley for a week on New Year's Day, but they were planning to spend New Year's Eve with everyone at home. And so were Caroline and Max, whom the Butterfields had graciously included in the group for Caroline's sake. After that, Caroline and Max were joining his family in Mexico for a few days before they went back to school in Los Angeles.

Sybil told her children, but not the others, that they were expecting guests from Paris, and she hoped that they would show Laure around the city while she and Blake entertained her father. So far, no one had complained, and the kids said they would take Laure under their wing. Sybil and Gwyneth still had not warned the others about Samuel yet and had decided to see what happened when they arrived. And Blake still disapproved of the plan.

*

The day that Samuel and Laure arrived in San Francisco was bright and sunny, as San Francisco often was in December, although it was cool. But it had been snowing in Paris when they left, so the weather was a pleasant change for them. Sybil was home waiting for them anxiously, when Samuel pulled up at the gate in a rented white station wagon, and Sybil went out to the courtyard to let him in herself. He parked the car and got out, looking very French in a tweed jacket and turtleneck with a windbreaker over it, jeans, and hiking boots, and his salt and pepper hair was tousled after the flight. He was taller than Sybil had expected him to be, looked ten years younger than he was, and didn't seem like a professor to her. He smiled as soon as he saw her, while a pretty young girl got out of the front seat. She was petite and very delicate looking with long blond hair and big blue eyes, and she looked instantly familiar to Sybil, but she wasn't sure why. Sybil shook hands with both of them, as they gathered up their bags and followed her into the house. They were tired from the flight.

"You're so kind to let us stay here," Samuel said warmly, as Laure looked around the long front hall with interest, and glanced up at the Butterfield portraits. And before she could say another word to the Saint Martins, Sybil saw Angus walking toward them, with his enormous English bulldog trotting along at his side. He smiled when he saw Sybil, and glanced at her guests. He was wearing a velvet smoking jacket and matching slippers, and smoking the new pipe she had given him for Christmas.

"Sorry, dear girl, I can't find my bagpipes. Have you seen them somewhere?" He seemed slightly confused, as Sybil walked hastily toward him and gently turned him around toward a door to the back stairs, just as Phillips emerged carrying his bagpipes. Phillips was in full livery, and Sybil was taken aback. She had never seen him around the house in the daytime, only serving dinner at night.

"Found them, sir," he told Angus, ignoring Sybil.

"Excellent!" Angus said, and followed him through the door with a wave at Sybil and her guests. She was stunned to have seen Angus and Phillips in the front hall, and turned to Samuel and Laure to see their reaction and if they had seen them too. Samuel was smiling and it was obvious he had, which answered her question about whether they would choose to be visible or not. Decidedly they were going to be open with him, or Angus was. It was a start.

"Sorry, it gets a little chaotic here at times," she said, trying to be nonchalant. Angus normally never wandered around the house either, and certainly not in the daytime with his dog.

"Your father?" Samuel asked, looking amused, although the elderly gentleman looked more like her grandfather, and had seemed ancient but good-humored.

"Actually, no. Not really." She dodged the question, and they had just walked past Angus's portrait on the way to the grand staircase, but neither Samuel nor Laure had noticed. "Are you hungry?" she stopped to ask them. "Would you like something to eat?"

"We ate on the flight," Samuel said, still grinning about

the old gentleman looking for his bagpipes. "You run a very formal home," he commented to Sybil, referring to Phillips's white tie and tails. There was no way to explain it to him, so she just nodded, and they headed up the stairs, and passed Alicia and José, who were in jeans and T-shirts, carrying cleaning utensils, which made Phillips's uniform when they'd seen him seem ever more incongruous. Her guests said nothing as they looked around.

She took them to two large, beautiful guest bedrooms on the third floor, made sure they had what they needed, and said she'd be in her office down the hall, and told them which room it was.

"It's a beautiful home," Samuel complimented her, and Laure smiled at her shyly.

"Thank you." She was still feeling unnerved by Angus's unexpected appearance, as well as Phillips's.

She left them and went to the room she used as an office and sat down to catch her breath, and as soon as she did, Gwyneth appeared, looking excited, and startled Sybil. She had simply materialized with a big smile, in a lovely dress.

"Are they here yet?"

"Yes," Sybil whispered, so they wouldn't hear her talking if they walked down the hall. "And Angus came down the front hall as soon as they arrived."

Gwyneth was surprised at that. "He did? He's not supposed to do that."

"I know." And Gwyneth had appeared out of nowhere too. They all seemed to be lively today.

"Did they see him?" She was whispering too, in case they could hear her.

"Yes, they did. Samuel asked if he's my father."

"What did you say?" Gwyneth looked amused and Sybil didn't.

"I said no, he isn't. He even had the dog with him, and Phillips came for him. He was looking for his bagpipes."

"Oh, I hope he didn't find them," Gwyneth said fervently, and Sybil laughed.

"Phillips did, worse luck."

"Oh, dear." And then she turned her attention to her great-grandson again. "What's he like?" She was curious about him.

"Very handsome, young for his age. Quite distinguished actually." And then something struck her that she hadn't realized at first. "Actually, he looks a lot like Bert."

"Really? How interesting!" She was pleased.

"And his daughter looks like Lucy. I just thought of it, but she does." Gwyneth was happy about that too. Laure was healthier than Lucy, and stronger, but she had the same delicate features, big blue eyes, and blond hair. She'd been wearing jeans and a down jacket. Sybil wanted to introduce her to Caroline and Andy, but she knew they were out.

Gwyneth chatted with her for a few minutes and then

left to see what Magnus was up to and have tea with Lucy and Augusta. Sybil answered some emails, and a little while later, there was a soft knock at the door. It was Samuel, and he said Laure was asleep.

"Do you mind if I explore a bit?" he asked her, and she offered to accompany him. He was carrying a camera, and seemed to be interested in every detail as they walked down the long hall. Sybil explained that there were children's and guest rooms on that floor. It had been the nursery floor in the early years of the house, but that had been changed a long time ago, long before she and Blake bought the house. And she told him the top floor was all servants' rooms that were no longer used, and then they walked down the grand staircase, to where she and her children slept, and they could hear Magnus and Charlie talking in his room, so she didn't go in. She could tell they were playing videogames.

"I'll introduce you to my youngest son later. I think he has a friend over."

"You have a busy household." He smiled at her.

"Only when my older children are home. The rest of the time it's very quiet. My two oldest are in college," as she had told him on the phone. "Charlie is nine."

They continued down the grand staircase, and on the main floor she showed him the drawing rooms and the ballroom, and he studied the beautiful carvings, the exquisite curtains, the high ceilings, the furniture and chandeliers. He seemed vastly impressed and was silent for a moment.

"It's much grander than I thought it would be," he said, looking deeply affected, which touched her. "I thought it would be an interesting house, but I didn't expect to be moved by it. I never knew these people. I barely knew my grandmother, and my mother and I weren't very close. There's no reason why the home of my great-grandparents should mean anything to me, and yet it does." He was silent for a moment, out of respect. "You can almost feel them here, as though they never left it. You've preserved it beautifully, Sybil. It seems like a home and not a museum, and yet it's so pure and so warm that I feel transported back into the time when the house was built. I am very touched by it," he said as they walked past the dining room, where the Butterfields and the Gregorys ate dinner every night. She could see Phillips setting the table with the silverware and crystal, and wondered if Samuel could see him again since he didn't react. As they walked back into the main living room with the enormous Aubusson carpet and antique furniture that Sybil and Blake had retrieved from storage three years before, Laure found them, looking sleepy but pretty, with her long blond hair and a white sweater and boots with her jeans. She and Sybil exchanged a smile, as her father pointed out important details to her, typical of the period when the house was built. They were looking carefully at the moldings when Sybil saw Charlie and Magnus run down the stairs and into the kitchen. And just at that moment, she heard Andy, Quinne, and Caroline walk in. They came to find Sybil, and she introduced Samuel and Laure to them, and they invited Laure to join them, and she left happily with the younger group.

"She's a lovely girl," Sybil complimented him and he looked pleased.

"She's very impressed by the house. I've never seen her so quiet. But I am too. It's truly the most beautiful home I've ever seen. And we have some very important homes and châteaux in France. But this has a soul, and it's not so big you can't feel at home here. You must enjoy living here. I can see why you fell in love with it."

"We do love it," she admitted, as they continued their tour, and everything he'd said about it was true. She could tell that he already felt a bond to it.

"I'm so glad we came," he said, and thanked her again for having them. They walked into the library and sat down, and talked about his work, and leaving the university, and how strange it was going to be after being at the Sorbonne for so many years. Blake came home a little later, and enjoyed meeting Samuel, and the three of them sat for a long time, talking, and then Samuel went out to the garden to look around.

"How's it going?" Blake asked her when Samuel went out a side door. "He seems nice."

"They're lovely people. The house has been crazy today. Angus wandered through the front hall. Phillips came after him. The boys ran down the stairs screaming, and were playing in Charlie's room. They must think we're nuts. And I'm not sure what to do about dinner. Should we take them out, or eat in the kitchen, or tell them to dress for dinner and then maybe no one will show up?"

"Is this some sort of a test or experiment?" her husband asked her, a little confused himself.

"I don't know. Maybe they'll want to see him, and they'll just come in as usual. Gwyneth is dying to meet him. I don't know about the others. Maybe that's why Angus turned up. I've never seen him in the daytime before."

"Maybe we should just do what we always do, and see what happens," Blake said, suddenly feeling brave. "Maybe they're up for it and so is he. And what can he do if he sees them? Call the police and say he saw a bunch of ghosts having dinner? Let's just do it." After opposing their visit initially, he was willing to throw caution to the wind now. The Butterfields were Samuel's ancestors, after all, not Sybil's and Blake's.

"Okay," Sybil said, feeling nervous now and less confident than Blake. She didn't want to explain it to Samuel, in case the others didn't appear. And if they did, he'd be unprepared and confused. And Blake was right in a way, it was a kind of test. Did the Butterfields want to meet him or not? Were they willing to accept the French branch? And were Lili's child and grandchild acceptable to them? Would they consider them Butterfields at all? Or simply ignore them and refuse to be seen?

As Blake and Sybil left the library, she asked him if he had noticed Samuel's resemblance to Bert, and Blake laughed. "It's funny that you said that. I thought so too, but I figured you'd think it was hokey if I said it. They have strong genes."

"And his daughter looks like Lucy," she said as they walked into the kitchen to see the young people. They were having a snack at the kitchen table, and Charlie had joined them, but not Magnus. And Max, Caroline's boyfriend, walked in a minute later. They were a happy, lively group. Samuel followed the noise and joined them a few minutes later.

"Would you like to join us here for dinner tonight?" Sybil asked Samuel, trying to sound casual, and he looked pleased as he accepted for him and his daughter. "I should have warned you. We dress for dinner, but you don't have to. You can wear whatever you want."

"I can lend Laure a dress if she needs one," Caroline volunteered, and Laure thanked her.

"When you say 'dress' for dinner," Samuel asked cautiously, "that means? Tie and jacket?"

"We follow some of the old traditions of the house, and

we wear black tie," Blake said, embarrassed at how ridiculous he knew it sounded, like a costume party. But it seemed run of the mill to them now. And they even wore white tie on some nights, but Blake didn't say so.

"How amazing!" Samuel looked surprised. "It's a nice idea actually, and must have been then. And now that I've seen the house, I can see it, but if you had told me that on the phone, I would have thought you were mad. But the house is so perfectly of the period, I actually understand it."

Samuel walked around the ground floor again, taking pictures, and Sybil joined him and pointed out some details, which Laure found fascinating too, as an architecture student.

"I'd love to see some of the photographs you said you have," Samuel said after a little while, and Sybil walked him back upstairs to her office, and took them out of the box where she kept them. She went through the photos, explaining who was who, and he was fascinated. There was one of his grandmother Bettina holding his mother, Lili, when she was only a few months old, and all the dates and many of the names were on the back. And then he noticed the resemblance between Laure and Lucy. "What happened to Lucy again?" he asked Sybil.

"She always suffered from ill health, and she died of pneumonia right after the Crash of '29, when she was twenty. I think it totally disheartened her father, particularly with the reversals they had. He had a heart attack and died about six months later. They sold the house for the first time when he did. That was when your great-grandmother Gwyneth went to live in Europe with your grandmother Bettina. Your mother must have been about twelve then."

"I think she said something about it," he said, jogging his memory, "about her grandmother coming to live with them, my great-grandmother, but she died soon after. My mother always said that her grandmother died of a broken heart after her husband died. Somehow that sounds very sweet. I don't think women do that these days. If I had died during our divorce, my wife would have celebrated, although we're good friends now." He laughed ruefully and Sybil smiled. "We divorced a long time ago, when Laure was five. The relationship didn't last very long. Now we're fine just as friends and co-parents, but it took a while."

"Did she marry again?" Sybil asked him, and he shook his head.

"No, but she has two children with the man she lives with, and she's very happy. I think I cured her from marriage," he said and they both laughed. It sounded very French to Sybil. And she remembered that Bettina hadn't wanted to marry again after Tony, until she fell in love with Louis in Paris. So maybe Samuel would feel that way one day too. He had said he had never remarried either and didn't want to. He was content with his daughter and his work, which Sybil thought was too bad. He seemed like a nice man.

They walked downstairs to the next floor together to Sybil's bedroom, so she could dress for dinner. The young people had stayed together downstairs, and Andy was showing the guests the antique pool table in the playroom in the basement.

"I'm so sorry I don't have a dinner jacket for tonight," he said apologetically.

"Don't even think about it," she reassured him. She was convinced by then that the Butterfields weren't going to appear anyway. The Saint Martins were strangers, after all, so all he'd see were the Gregorys overdressed and they'd eat in the kitchen and look silly.

"I have a tie and a blue shirt," he offered, "but I didn't even bring a white shirt." She couldn't give him one of Blake's because he was taller and broader than Samuel, although Samuel was tall too, but Blake's shirts wouldn't fit him.

They met in the hall again an hour later, and Samuel looked very nice in his tweed jacket, pale blue shirt, and navy blue Hermès tie, with proper shoes and black jeans, and Sybil was wearing one of her less dressy evening ensembles, a long black velvet skirt with a black cashmere sweater, and he complimented her on how nice she looked.

They all reached the stairs at the same time, and headed down toward the dining room. Blake and Sybil exchanged a glance and were almost sure they would find the dining room empty, but as soon as they reached it, Sybil saw immediately that the silver and crystal were gleaming, the candles were lit, Phillips was standing at attention, and all of the Butterfields were in place, as though they knew precisely that guests were expected. Augusta looked them over as they walked in, like a drill sergeant inspecting the troops.

"What on earth are those on your feet, Countess?" she asked Quinne, who burst out laughing. She was wearing shocking pink velvet Doc Martens with matching fishnet stockings under a black velvet miniskirt, with a hot pink angora sweater. "Did you steal them from a soldier?" Augusta asked her, and Quinne giggled again. Her own grandmother hadn't liked them on Christmas either, but she thought Augusta was funny. And she asked Magnus who he'd sold his hairbrush to. And then she saw Samuel and raised an eyebrow. "Ah, yes, one of those fascinating modern outfits. Blake wears them occasionally too. I never understand them," she said, as Samuel stopped in front of her, thinking it was all a joke at first, bowed low, kissed her hand, and said, "Bonsoir."

"Ah, of course, that explains it," she countered.

"French. Naturally. They used to wear satin knee breeches and brocade coats. So what can one expect from them now?"

"So do the British at court, Mother," Gwyneth reminded her, and Sybil stepped up next to Samuel, to introduce him to Augusta properly. "Mrs. Campbell, this is Samuel Saint Martin. He's Lili's son, Bettina's grandson." There was a long silent pause where even Samuel looked stunned, and Augusta more so.

"Which makes him . . . my great-great grandson . . ." she said with a startled expression. As far as she knew, Lili was still a child herself. It was a big leap for her to understand.

"And his daughter, Laure," Sybil introduced her as well, and she was wearing a proper black dress of Caro's, and her own high heels, as Augusta stared at Samuel and his daughter, struggling to assimilate what had happened.

"I saw them in the front hall today when they arrived," Angus added proudly.

"What were you doing there?" his sister asked him. He never left his room in the daytime, and wasn't supposed to.

"Lost my bagpipes for a minute . . . Phillips found them. All well. Pretty girl," he said, indicating Laure. Augusta glared at him and everyone laughed, which broke the tension.

"My brother has appalling manners where women are

concerned," she explained to Samuel. "And you're French, then. But Lili is American. She was born here." She was trying to sort it all out, and to Augusta, Lili still existed in the present. Gwyneth stepped in, from the other end of the table.

"She took French citizenship, Mother. Louis, Bettina's husband, adopted her in France. Do you remember?"

"Oh, yes . . . of course I do . . . nice of him, since that other one disappeared," she said, referring to Tony Salvatore.

"He died in the war, Mother," Gwyneth corrected her. And Sybil led Samuel to a seat next to her at the table. Phillips had set the right number of places. He always did now, and had again tonight, as though someone had told him. She wondered if Gwyneth had. Samuel was looking bewildered when he sat down. Sybil introduced him to Gwyneth and Bert, his great-grandparents, who looked alive and well and in good spirits, contrary to the sad end he knew they had come to. And then Sybil introduced him to each of the children, while Caro and Andy explained to Laure who the players were, and their relationship to her. And sitting near each other, her resemblance to Lucy was even more striking, and so was Samuel's to Bert.

"I'm not quite sure I understand," he said softly to Sybil, as everyone watched him and his daughter. The Butterfields had obviously felt sufficiently at ease to include him and Laure at dinner that night, and be visible. After all, he was one of them, and so was Laure. They were Butter-fields, whatever their name or nationality. "Have you hired actors to impersonate the family?" he asked her. How else could they all be there? What was remarkable was that they looked exactly like the photographs Sybil had shown him that afternoon. Blake felt almost sorry for him as he tried to absorb something that made no sense whatsoever and defied reason. Blake had been through it too, in the beginning, and he wasn't even related to them.

"They're not actors," Sybil said gently, as Gwyneth overheard her and smiled. "We thought that the first time too. The family is all here. In this house. They never left after"—she chose her words carefully for their sake— "after they entered another dimension. They all came back, except your mother. She never really had any ties to the house. She was too young when she left."

"Are you telling me," Samuel stared at Sybil intently, "that the entire family is here, all of them, still living in the house a hundred years later?" Sybil nodded assent, and Samuel stared at them one by one, thinking it must be a joke, but as he looked at them, he knew it wasn't. "That is unbelievable. It's not possible. Did you know it when you bought the house?"

"No, we didn't."

"Did they appear to you one by one?"

"No. We heard noises and walked into the dining room three days after we moved in, and everyone was here, just like you did tonight." And she'd seen them after the earth-quake the night before.

"It was quite shocking at first," Augusta said to him. "But we all got used to it, and they're very nice people and we love them. We wouldn't live without them now," she added warmly, which impressed Sybil and Blake, and touched them. "And you, dear boy, are related to us, so we had to have dinner with you. We wouldn't miss it. I hope you'll stay here with us." She was being unusually gra-cious, and Samuel was nearly speechless. His daughter was very quiet too. It really was like entering another dimension, and he had no idea how it worked or if they were now trapped there. Sybil could see a slight panic in his eyes.

"You can come and go as you wish. It's just an honor to be included in the Butterfields' lives. And it has worked very well for us." Except that Magnus was disappointed that Charlie was slowly growing up, but they still had fun together. Magnus would always be the age he died.

"Can others see you?" Samuel asked the group collect-ively, and they all shook their heads.

"Only the Gregorys and two of the children's friends, Max and Quinne," Bert explained. "We're very happy to have them with us. And we hope you and your daughter stay too, for as long as you like." Samuel let Phillips pour him several glasses of wine before he felt calm again.

"I'm sorry. I couldn't tell you on the phone, or you

would have thought I was mad or drunk when I called you," Sybil said, and he nodded. "But I wanted you to come and meet everyone and see the house. I didn't know then if they'd be willing to meet you or not. But even so, I thought it would be worth a trip to visit the house, and maybe you could write the family history."

"It certainly is worth the trip," he agreed. "And this is so much more . . . important . . . and exciting . . . and so moving. What an extraordinary experience," he said quietly, and smiled at Sybil. "Thank you for sharing this with me. I would never have known otherwise." He was sorry his mother wasn't there, but he understood why. She had always been so adamant, even with him, about not having any tie to the house in San Francisco, and no interest in it, not being there since she was a baby, not being American, and being French. Her emotional ties were to the Lambertins, her adoptive father's family, and not the Butterfields.

And then he wondered about something else and asked Sybil quietly, as his guide through their extraordinary world. He felt privileged to be there above all else, and felt a bond to them he never knew he had. Laure seemed to as well and loved her new friends. "What year are we in? I haven't been able to figure it out."

"It took me a while too. It's 1919 for them, exactly a hundred years behind us, to the day," which made sense from the clothes they were wearing and the events they discussed. It felt to him like asking about the time difference with another country where you were planning to travel. Only in this case it was measured in centuries, not hours. And if it was 1919 for them, he understood why his grandmother wasn't there. She was in France then.

For the rest of the evening, Samuel joined in the conversation, and Laure and the young people had fun together. Angus offered to play the bagpipes for them in celebration, and everyone said another time. Having Samuel and Laure there had energized them all, and after the Butterfields had retired for the night, as mysteriously and instantaneously as they always did once they left the dining room, Samuel sat with Sybil and Blake for a long time in the kitchen, talking about it and drinking wine. He had never had an experience like it before, and doubted he would again, away from this house.

"Thank God you bought it. Imagine if we'd never known," he said to his hosts. "And what do you do about the things you know and they don't? We've both read the book," he said, looking at Sybil. "If they're in 1919, they don't know what's coming in 1929 and after that. Have you warned them?"

Sybil shook her head. "Blake and I have talked about it a lot. It doesn't seem fair if we don't tell them, but wrong if we do. We can't change it for them. The war, the stock market crash, the accidents, the deaths. They all happened a hundred years ago. We can't rewrite history. We can only try to gentle it for them when it happens, and console them. But, oddly, they have much to teach us, so we don't make the same mistakes." He hadn't thought about that, and when he did, he realized she was right. In a way, it was a blessing for all of them. "And even when they die, they come back," she explained. "They're so tightly bound to one another and this house, they don't leave for long. It took Josiah about four months to come back. And when Augusta died of Spanish flu, she was back in a month. She's a strong soul." They all laughed, and Samuel went upstairs that night, shaking his head over the remarkable evening he'd had, and slept till noon the next day. He came downstairs and found Sybil in the kitchen. He had a terrible headache and a hangover.

"Did I dream all that last night?" he asked her. "How drunk was I?"

"No, you didn't, and you weren't drunk." She smiled at him. She had a slight hangover too, but he had drunk more wine. "Laure is out with my kids, by the way. And we're taking you out tonight." They wanted to show him and Laure a little of San Francisco, and she suspected that the Butterfields were worn out from the night before too. It cost them something to appear that strongly and be so connected to someone new. Gwyneth had come to see her that morning, and they had agreed to skip dinner that night. The next day was New Year's Eve, and they'd all be up late again.

Sybil made him a cup of strong coffee and scrambled eggs, and he felt better afterward. And Blake suggested they go out for a drive and look around.

"I feel like I'm in another world, or caught between two worlds," Samuel said to them and Blake nodded.

"You are, to some extent. Your old world is still here, just as ours is, but this other world that they're part of is open to you too. We don't know how it happened, but we're very glad it did."

Samuel thought about it for a minute, as he looked at the Golden Gate Bridge and smiled at them. "So am I. Thank you for finding me and getting me here," he said, as Sybil patted his hand, and they drove back to the house. He wasn't sure which world or dimension he was in, but he felt oddly at peace.

Chapter 19

After a very entertaining dinner with Samuel and Laure in Chinatown the night before, the Gregorys and all the young people planned to go all out on New Year's Eve.

Samuel had rented a set of tails with Blake's help. Caroline lent Laure another dress. Sybil had bought a new evening gown the week before, and everyone met in the dining room for a fabulous dinner with oysters, caviar, lobster, pheasant, baked Alaska for dessert, and a great deal of very fine champagne, which they continued drinking in the ballroom as they had on New Year's Eve for three years. Samuel was still trying to decipher what he was seeing, and asking Sybil for explanations constantly. She was still encouraging him to write a book, based on Bettina's but going further and in greater depth about all of the family members, their histories and the people they had touched in some way and those who had touched them, and what they had done in their lives. And the key that linked them was the house.

They all kissed and hugged at midnight, and danced for long hours afterward. Samuel asked Augusta to dance the first waltz with him, and won her heart forever. She told everyone proudly that he was her great-great-grandson from France, which she managed to make sound like a compliment, which was a first for her. And she wouldn't allow Uncle Angus to dance with Laure, so he danced with Sybil instead, and in a little while Blake cut in, to save her from Angus's lustful remarks.

The evening seemed exceptionally festive, and everyone was in a good mood. There was no war on, everyone was healthy, Blake was out of danger with his business and had moved on, and Sybil had finally finished her book, which was cause for celebration in itself.

Samuel thoroughly enjoyed the evening with them, and was already sad that they were going back to France in a few days, but he said he had to return to the Sorbonne to teach his final classes, give one more exam, and say goodbye to the office and colleagues he had enjoyed for so long.

"Why don't you come back when you finish?" Sybil suggested. His visit had been a great success, and his Butterfield relatives loved him and Laure.

He sat and talked to Augusta after he danced with her and found her stories fascinating. Her mind was totally clear, despite her great age, although her brother's wasn't. And then, feeling the inexorable pull that Sybil had hoped for, he smiled at her as Phillips poured more champagne.

"I'll do it. I'll come back in February to start."

"To start what?" Sybil asked him cautiously.

"The book you want me to write," he said with a broad smile. "That's why you asked me here, isn't it?"

"No, it isn't, but that's a wonderful bonus. I tried to find you because you deserved to know your family, and for them to know the next generation, and Lili's son, and now Laure. You're part of all this, and you always will be, just as they are."

"You're part of it too, or they wouldn't have let you in," he said knowingly.

"We're adopted, you're blood," she said, and he smiled as he watched everyone dancing in the ballroom. Sybil went to tell Gwyneth that Samuel was going to write the book about the family and the house, and he joined them a minute later.

"May I help you with it?" Gwyneth asked shyly. She was thrilled he was going to do it, and she knew Bert would be too. And it was Sybil who had convinced him.

"Of course," Samuel said generously, and he turned to Sybil. "Will you help with the research?"

"I'd be happy to," she answered. She had finished her own book at last. And the Butterfield book would be much more fun to write than her huge official tome about design, although she thought her publisher would be pleased with it. But Samuel would put his heart and soul into the book about the family, and Sybil and Gwyneth would help. It would be a joint effort. They were a community and a family, and provided each other strength, love, and consolation, which was why they had come together, Sybil was convinced.

Sybil thought about it as Samuel led Gwyneth onto the floor, to dance with his very beautiful great-grandmother.

She fully understood now, and had accepted, that she could not protect them from the future and their own history, although the Butterfields had reached far into the future and changed theirs. They couldn't alter life events, or avoid challenges and heartbreaks. Whatever the century, their children had to grow up, wars could not be stopped, and their loved ones would die one day, whether they knew when or not. What mattered was the love the two families shared with each other, which had been the greatest gift to all of them, in a hundred years, whether the phenomenon could be explained or not. It didn't matter, as long as they were together at Butterfield Mansion. The future would always be uncertain, and the past was what it was meant to be, which was perfect in a way.

Blake came to find Sybil a few minutes later, and they stood together as Bert raised a glass and wished them all an excellent New Year, full of health, prosperity, and joy.

"To 1920!" the elders of the family toasted in response.

"I hope it will be a wonderful year for us all," Sybil echoed with feeling.

"As I recall, it was." Augusta smiled at their family and friends, and sipped her champagne.

They danced in the ballroom as two new years began, a hundred years apart.

Danielle Steel

*Turn over for more information about
Danielle's upcoming books . . .*

BEAUCHAMP HALL

It's never too late to take back control of your life . . .

Winona Farmington can't help but feel that life is passing her by in her deadbeat Michigan town. She hates her job, and her boyfriend won't commit. But she escapes the dreariness of everyday life with her favourite TV show, *Beauchamp Hall*, an English period drama.

When she makes a shocking discovery, Winona knows it's time to make a change and travels to the picturesque English village that's home to the world of *Beauchamp Hall*, in pursuit of a new adventure . . .

Coming soon

PURE HEART. PURE STEEL.

FAIRYTALE

Charmed. Trapped. Magical.

Camille Lammenais has grown up in the beauty of the Napa Valley surrounded by acres of her family's vineyards. After graduating from Stanford, she returns to help manage her parents' chateau. But their fairytale ends suddenly with her mother's death. Her devastated father is easy prey for a mysterious, charming Frenchwoman visiting the valley. But Camille begins to see past the alluring looks, designer clothes, and elegant manners of the Countess . . .

Fairytale is an enchanting rendering of a much-loved classic, and a reminder that good prevails over evil in the end.

Available now in paperback

PURE HEART. PURE STEEL.